Dangerous Ground

Jeff McEntire

This book is a work of fiction. Names, characters, places, and incidents are products of the author's imagination or are used fictitiously. Any resemblance to actual events or locales or persons, living or dead, is entirely coincidental.

For Jen and Meredith,
the two wonderful women in my life.

1

Ben Tuttle made his way through the noisy, well-dressed crowd at the Stanton Civic Center, and ducked into the nearest men's room. Standing at the first available sink, he gazed at himself in the mirror and frowned at the dime-sized mustard stain on his tie, the first new one he'd bought in six months.

"Shit," he muttered, jerking a paper towel from the rickety aluminum holder and blotting gingerly at it. No wonder the woman at the buffet had made such a smart-assed comment.

The older man washing his hands at the sink to Ben's left glanced briefly at the tie and cringed. "Stain magnets. That's pretty much all the damn things are good for."

"You've got that right," Ben snorted.

"That looks like a bad one. Silk's a bitch, ain't it?" Another man waiting for the sink had leaned in for a better look. His own tie bore an eye-jarring collage of stock-cars and checkered flags. "You ought to try them stain-guard ties they sell down at Target. Them son-of-a-bitches are as tough as nails. Stuff beads up on 'em like Turtle Wax."

"Thanks," Ben sighed wearily. "I'll keep that in mind." In the mirror, he watched the insincere smile fade on his own, soon-to-be thirty, face and wondered how the evening could get any worse. Stepping quickly away before he became the centerpiece of restroom conversation, Ben ventured back into the lobby, casually scanning the faces for a glimpse of the sultry blond from the buffet line.

Her good-natured jab had been surprisingly refreshing amid the otherwise catatonically polite conversation. "A bib would be cheaper, and a whole lot easier to clean," she'd said, smiling coyly and pointing at his tie. They'd shared a laugh over it, but self-consciousness had soon won out, and he'd excused himself to go and try to repair the damage.

He finally spotted her standing by herself at one end of the cash-bar, sipping a drink and looking decidedly bored. Her shoulders were bare in a stunning, strapless gown and her short blond hair exposed earrings that sparkled against the supple curve of her neck, yet her manner was somehow casual and unpretentious. Suppressing a smile, he walked over to the bar, standing directly in her line of sight. As he ordered a drink, he untied the ruined tie and with a dramatic flourish, pulled it from his collar, balled it up, and dropped it on the tray of the attendant that was passing by.

A loud chuckle erupted from her end of the bar. "Now that's something you don't see every day."

He raised a glass in her direction and opened his collar with his other hand. "Ah, but wouldn't you like to?"

His short, lightly spiked hair and impish smile gave him a wonderfully charming, boyish quality, and he obviously had the personality to go with it. An irresistible combination as far as she was concerned.

She raised her glass in return and walked over to join him. "I'm Kate. Sorry about the bib thing, I don't always think before I speak. It's a terrible disorder, really. Had it since I was a little girl."

"Well here's to more of that too – blunt honesty. Ben Tuttle, pleased to meet you. You've made my evening, and the stuffed-shirts haven't even started speaking yet."

She gave a wry grin and took another sip of her drink. "Not a big fan of Everett Greason?"

Ben propped an elbow on the bar. "Ah, not really. I have to confess, I'm not much into the whole big-money, big-politics thing. I'm only here because the president of my firm has done business with the guy since sometime before the great depression, apparently. He brow-beat us into coming. You know, a show of community support and all that. How about you?"

"I can relate. My family pretty much dragged me here against my will. If you ask me, the man is full of himself." Ben realized that he was staring and quickly took another sip of his bourbon.

"Isn't he like, the Bill Gates of the funeral business?"

"Oh, that was just the first chapter," she said, rolling her eyes. "Once he started dumping his money into state politics, he never looked back. These days he pretty much acts like he sits at the right hand of the Father, I mean, he seems that way when they interview him on TV, anyway."

"You seem to know a bit about him," Ben said. "Are you sure you're not an admirer?"

"Ha!" she snorted. "Trust me, he's got all the

groupies that money can buy. He damn sure doesn't need me."

Across the lobby, unnoticed in a shadowed alcove, an old woman stood watching their conversation intently. A woolen shawl was draped over her hunched shoulders, and she leaned heavily on an aluminum cane, her breath hoarse and labored. In her free hand, she clutched a ragged envelope.

Soon, as if on cue, a steady stream of people began filing past them toward the main hall. Kate shrugged, drained the last of her drink, and put her glass on the bar. "I guess that's our queue." She smiled warmly at him and started to leave, but hesitated, turning as if she wanted to say something else. For a brief moment, Ben was hopeful that she'd suggest they go somewhere together and skip the speeches, but she just smiled again and headed toward the door instead. "Nice meeting you Ben," she called over her shoulder.

He was already kicking himself for not stopping her. "Nice meeting you too, Kate," he called lamely after her.

Ben was still watching her walk away when he felt a vice-like grip tighten on his arm. He jumped and turned with a start find the old woman standing next to him, her hand clutching his arm. Her withered face was drawn up in hard resolve, and as she leaned close, uncomfortably close, her luminous eyes bored intently into his.

"Give this to Katherine!" she croaked, as she clumsily stuffed a folded envelope into his coat pocket. He recoiled and tried to step back, but she held his arm in a death grip. "They don't know about it. They never found it, and they never found Jimmy Smoot's notes, but she can. She needs to know the truth!"

"What are you..." Ben stammered, prying her bony hand from his arm. But she was no longer looking at him, she was looking away, across the lobby. When Ben followed her gaze, he saw Kate standing in an open doorway, a questioning look on her face. But he could only stare as she turned and disappeared.

"You have to make sure that nobody sees this but Katherine," the woman coughed, and Ben realized that she meant Kate.

"I barely know her," he stammered, taking a small step back. "We just..."

"Please!" the woman implored. "I need to know she'll get it." The fear in her expression raised the hair on Ben's neck, and he felt an overwhelming urge to bolt, anything to be rid of her. Instead, he nodded vigorously. "Okay, sure, I'll give it to her. What did you say..."

The woman did not wait for him to finish but hobbled quickly off and down a side hallway.

"Jesus!" Ben whispered, running a hand through his short, black hair and looking at his watch. He heard the MC begin and jogged over to the last set of double doors just before the attendant closed them.

The ballroom was filled with people, seated in pre-assigned groups of eight at large, round tables. Each table was immaculately decorated with a fresh flower arrangement and grouping of candles, while the speakers, including Governor Michael Chase and Everett Greason, sat at a long row of tables behind the podium.

Mercifully, the table that Ben's boss had reserved

for them was on the far side of the room, so he was able to skirt the perimeter without garnering too much attention.

Ben's boss was another story, however, and made a point of looking at his watch as Ben sat down.

"Sorry," Ben mouthed silently, still reeling from his strange encounter in the lobby. He gently patted his jacket pocket, half hoping he'd imagined it, but the crumpled paper was still there.

Applause erupted as the speaker introduced Governor Chase, and it was then that Ben spotted Kate. She was sitting at the table directly in front of the podium, facing his table. Having apparently watched him sneak in, she was now smiling at him amid the clapping, even as the middle aged brunette next to her leaned over to say something.

Ben did a momentary double take, and his smile waned, as he studied the older woman's face. He was no media hound, but he'd watched enough news coverage of charity events, and unless his eyes were failing him, Kate was sharing a table with Jean Chase, the Governor's wife.

As the governor approached the podium, Ben leaned over to Marvin Metzer, a friend, and co-worker who was seated to his right.

"See that table, over there. Yeah, right in front of the podium. Any idea who those people are?"

Marvin squinted. "I only recognize a couple of them, other than the first lady. It's Greason's family. That guy with the bad toupee is Walter. He's the one who runs Werner-Greason funeral home."

"Yeah, but how about that cute blond?"

Paul gave a low whistle. "She's looking pretty good these days."

"Marvin, who *is* she?"

Ben's boss scowled in their direction as the governor cleared his throat into the microphone.

"I haven't seen her in years, but I'm pretty sure it's Katherine Greason, Everett Greason's granddaughter."

Ben let his head fall to his chest. "Unbelievable," he whispered. He'd stood there with her at the bar, practically stuffing his foot in his mouth and she'd let him do it. Hell, she'd practically egged him on. She's probably getting a major charge out of this, he thought, looking again at her table.

"Good evening everyone," the governor began, propping his hands on either side of the podium. "I'd like to begin tonight by saying that it's an honor to be here with all of you, to pay tribute to a man whose life has been a model of public service, to his community, to our great state, and more recently, to the U.S. House of Representatives."

"Go Everett!" someone shouted, and laughter erupted amid a smattering of applause.

As the governor continued with his lavish praise for the elder Greason, Ben looked at his watch; it said six-forty-two. He found his mind drifting back to the conversation he'd had with Kate at the bar. If she'd been telling the truth, then there was certainly no love lost between her and her grandfather. But what had the old woman meant about learning "the truth"? The truth about what?

More laughter erupted as the governor wound down his introduction and he realized that Kate was trying to catch his eye.

Silently she mouthed "sorry," and shrugged.

As Ben was mouthing "thanks," Kate's attention was drawn to the back of the room. Ben turned to see the woman who'd given him the message for Kate, standing at the back. She looked pale and shaky, and when an attendant approached her to offer his help, she waved him off.

"And so, without further delay," Governor Chase was saying, "I give you tonight's guest of honor, Mr. Everett Greason!"

Ben and Kate exchanged glances as the woman made her way slowly toward the front, amid the thunderous applause, threading between the tables and turning heads as she went.

Everett Greason walked slowly to the podium and held up a hand, nodding graciously. "Thank you! Thank you all!"

The old woman was nearing Kate's table as the applause began to die down and Kate watched her every move. Jean Chase noticed her as well, and all heads at the front tables began to turn.

"I have tried, over the years," Greason began, but his words faltered as the old woman stopped fifteen feet from the podium and raised her hand to get his attention. Ben strained to hear as she said something, but she was too far away. Security guards began moving forward from beside the front table, but Everett Greason held up a hand to stay them and smiled benevolently.

"Ah, I think the nice lady has a question. Go ahead, ma'am."

There was a murmur among the guests, and while Ben could see that she was speaking, he still could not hear her words. Within seconds, however, the expressions of those within earshot changed suddenly from polite smiles to bewilderment and anger, and with that, the old woman calmly produced a pistol from under her shawl and opened fire.

Screams erupted from all sides as a rapid series of shots rang out, sending a shower of wood chips flying from the podium. A stunned Greason yelled and went down and the room dissolved into utter chaos. Guests leaped from their chairs to flee or dived for cover. The noise of shattering glass and falling chairs mixed with a rising din of shouts and screams. Transfixed, Ben sunk to his knees and peered over the tabletop in time to see the woman turn the gun toward the governor, who was being shoved to the floor and shielded by security guards. They had weapons drawn, and more shots echoed through the room. Just before Ben was knocked over by a panicked co-worker, he watched the old woman drop to the floor, limp and lifeless.

All around him, people were clamoring to get out of the main hall, sprinting toward exits, tripping over each other and those who had fallen. More police were rushing in through side doors, weapons drawn, shouting commands, shoving their way through the frightened crowd toward the podium. Ben's heart pounded in his chest as he crawled clear of his table and ran for an exit. He turned at the last minute to look back, hoping to catch a glimpse of Kate, but she was nowhere to be seen among the jumbled mass of faces.

Outside, in the glare of streetlights, emergency vehicles were already arriving amid the chaos as officers attempted to move everyone away from the building and seal off the area. Ben was shaking as he hurried down the steps amid a torrent of people, some of whom were crying openly. Others were desperately trying to find family members or friends they'd become separated from, but all around him, the hushed chatter had begun. Many people were still unsure exactly what had happened, but others who'd seen, or claimed they'd seen, were eager to fill in the blanks. Two news crews, who had been prevented from covering the speeches live, had positioned themselves on the steps of the Civic Center and were already attempting to interview witnesses for a live report.

Unable to find his co-workers, Ben stood by himself in the grass, stunned and confused by what he'd just witnessed; barely able to get his mind around it. The same woman who had approached him only minutes before, a woman who could easily have been his grandmother, had tottered up to the VIP table on her cane and started shooting at everyone. It was the craziest damn thing he'd ever seen.

Now it made perfect sense why she was so desperate to get her message to Kate. "She knew she was about to die," he whispered to himself under the wail of a passing siren. "It was her last chance." Ben wondered what could have been so important to her that it was worth being shot down like that, so important that it was worth being forever remembered as the woman who tried to assassinate a governor. And why had she picked him to deliver her message?

He put his hand into his coat pocket and felt the crumpled envelope there, checking around him, as if someone might see – might know somehow that he'd been in contact with her. His stomach clenched into a knot at the very idea. Guilt by association – it happened all the time. People in the wrong place, with the wrong person, and in the wink of an eye they were accused.

As he stood shivering in the damp night air, watching police surround the stretcher that carried Everett Greason to a waiting ambulance, Ben felt the urge to run to the nearest officer and give up the envelope along with his story, to wash his hands of the incident and walk away – but something held him back.

He felt oddly conflicted, unable to shake the image of the old woman's face from his mind. She had seemed sick, feeble certainly, but her imploring eyes had been clear and lucid. Whatever else had been wrong with her, he was fairly certain that she wasn't crazy.

As the ambulance carrying Greason pulled out of the parking lot, Ben wrestled with his options, but always managed to arrive at the same conclusion. He knew what felt like the right thing to do, even though it flew in the face of reason; he wanted to keep his promise, to find Kate Greason and give her the message. He would be treading on dangerous ground, but it was too late to back out now. He was already involved, like-it-or-not.

Governor Mike Chase sat in the back seat of the black, armor-plated Yukon as it sped down Cherry Street, amid a column of Highway Patrol cruisers and Stanton police cars, all with lights flashing. His hair and clothes were disheveled, and he was angrier than Captain Burk had ever seen him.

"Jesus Christ, Charlie, what the fuck just happened back there? Can you tell me? Can someone fucking tell me?" He was shouting now as he wiped a spot of blood from his chin and spat. "Security my ass! I'm surrounded by armed guards, metal detectors, and God knows what else, and some crazy old bitch waltzes right up to the podium with a pistol and tries to kill us all? What is that?"

Captain Burk sat in the seat opposite the governor, listening in stony silence to his tirade. As a captain in the North Carolina Executive Protection Unit, an elite unit of the North Carolina Highway Patrol, it was his job to protect the governor and the First Family, his job to prevent nightmare scenarios like the one that had just unfolded. And while they'd likely saved the governor's life, Burk knew with grim certainty that the incident would ultimately be viewed as a security failure. He would, in all likelihood, lose his job over it.

"Governor, we're still sweeping the scene, but we believe the shooter was signed in through the metal detector with a medical waiver. She was wearing an ID bracelet indicating metal alloy pins in one of her hips. Without a pat-down, it's problematic for security." Burk cleared his throat. "She was apparently not patted down because she..."

"Because she what?" Chase demanded.

"Because she's outside the profile, sir."

"Well I guess somebody better damn well change the profile then," he growled, rubbing his temple.

Captain Burk pointed at the small laceration on the governor's chin. "Sorry about the rough take down, sir. Would you like for someone to look after that?"

"No, no, I'm fine. Did she hit Everett? How's he doing?"

Burk's shoulder mike crackled. "Base to Mobile

16

One, you're cleared for Hawthorn Memorial."

"Negative base, we're ten-nineteen, ETA fifty minutes," Burk responded, before answering the question. "We don't have details yet sir, but we believe that she hit Mr. Greason at least once. They're on their way to Hawthorn now."

"Shit. I should be over there."

"I've notified Mr. Crenshaw, sir. He'll be checking on Mr. Greason."

"Good. I want to be kept up to speed on his condition. That man has done more for me than..."

Captain Burk nodded. "Yes, sir."

According to the doctors who came to talk to his family nearly two hours later, Everett Greason was a lucky man. He'd tripped and fallen as he turned from the podium, and as a result, he'd been shielded by the solid block of oak. One of the bullets had lacerated his left arm, which required several stitches, and he had a few bumps and bruises from the fall, but otherwise, they said, he would be fine. Because of his age, they wanted to keep him overnight for observation, to be on the safe side.

Kate Greason's head was spinning as she stepped out of the crowded waiting room to get some air. She was barefooted; high-heeled shoes clutched loosely in one hand. Her eyes were still red, and she limped slightly from a twisted ankle. One hip throbbed as well, a result of falling over a chair during the panic at the civic center.

Everything that had happened in the last two hours had been a blur – everything since the shooting. Yet the scene itself was burned into her memory forever, playing over and over in her mind like a surreal film loop –

utter disbelief as she watched a feeble old woman, standing five feet away, amid beautiful flowers and jovial smiles, pull out a pistol and try to kill her grandfather. Kate had seen the woman only minutes before in the lobby, talking to the man from the bar. She'd been struck by how uncomfortable he'd looked in the woman's presence, but there had been no time to ask him about it.

She took a sip from the water fountain and leaned against the wall, wondering how long it would take Everett to parlay the incident into a public relations coup. "I guess now he'll be a martyr *and* a saint," she whispered.

When she looked up again, she was pleasantly surprised to see Ben Tuttle standing in the main lobby, talking to a receptionist. She wondered at first if he'd been hurt, but when she overheard her own name, she realized that he was looking for her. A faint smile crossed her lips as she noticed his gaping collar and the open space on his white shirt that the ill-fated tie had once occupied. She walked over, just as the portly woman was turning him away. "I'm sorry sir, but the waiting area for Mr. Greason is for family only. You'll need to have a seat over there."

"But you don't understand; it's important I..."

"What's important?" Kate said as she appeared beside him.

"Kate? God, I'm sorry about what happened. Are you okay?" Her eyes were tired, and she looked as though she'd been in a scuffle; her hair amiss and her gown ripped on one side, yet she still conveyed the same radiance that had drawn him to her at the ceremony.

She nodded. "Yeah, I guess, sort of. What are you doing here?"

"I'm sorry to barge in on you like this," Ben said,

stepping away from the counter. "I know everything's really crazy right now; it's just that I didn't know that he, Everett Greason was, well...anyway, how is he?"

"Yeah, he's my grandfather, she sighed. Lucky me." She held up her hand. "No, I shouldn't say that. I don't mean him any harm. I certainly don't want him shot, for God's sake. He and I just don't get along. We never have. Anyway, he had to get a few stitches, got a few bruises, but other than that, he's going to be fine. I'm sorry, I should have said something back there at the bar."

"Don't worry about it, it's not a big deal," Ben said, but he was nervous, checking around them for anyone who might overhear. "Listen, I need to tell you about the old woman."

Kate's eyes narrowed. "You two were together just before..."

"No, it's not like that," Ben interrupted. "I have no idea who she is. She just walked up to me and started talking."

"About what?" Kate cringed as she put a hand carefully over the bruise on her hip. "And don't worry, I believe you. It was pretty obvious you'd never laid eyes on her before."

Ben shook his head. "It was weird. She grabbed my arm like she was going to rip it off and stuffed an envelope in my pocket. She told me to give it to you, specifically to you. *Only* to you."

Kate seemed incredulous. "Why me?"

"I think she was trying to warn you about something," Ben said, lowering his voice. "She said the envelope was something they don't know about, whoever 'they' is, and that you deserved to know the truth. She mentioned someone named Smith or Smoot." He shrugged. "I have no idea what she was talking about, but she wasn't going to budge until I promised to give it to you." Ben reached for his pocket to retrieve the envelope but Kate put a hand on his arm.

"Wait. What if it isn't safe? What if she wanted to hurt all of us? She could have put anything in that envelope."

Ben put his hand down. "Look, you'll probably find this hard to believe, but she sounded sincere like she really wanted to help you. I can't explain it, but I believe her."

The hallway was becoming crowded now, and the steady stream of pages and announcements from the intercom above them was grating on Kate's already frayed nerves. She rubbed her eyes and looked at her watch. "Do you want to go somewhere where we can talk, maybe get some coffee? I hate hospitals."

Ben nodded, relieved at her suggestion. He hadn't been able to calm his nerves since the shooting, knowing that possession of the envelope likely constituted withholding evidence, a punishable crime in itself. He only hoped that he'd made the right choice.

"What about your grandfather?" Ben asked as they headed for the door.

"From what my father said, he's awake and alert, already talking on the Goddamn cell phone," Kate grunted.

Ben stopped her two feet short of the entrance and pointed toward the parking lot, even as the double doors slid open, and the cool autumn air hit them in the face. A couple of news teams stood chatting on the sidewalk just outside the entrance, cameras at the ready. Kate groaned and did a quick about-face, doubling back into the lobby.

"There's a side exit down that hall," Ben said, leading the way.

Kate sighed heavily. "Why do I get the feeling that this is going to be the longest night of my life?"

The collective tension in the small private waiting room had eased considerably when doctors brought the news of Everett Greason's condition and prognosis, yet the scene was still far from calm. Greason and Werner family members continued to arrive, overflowing the waiting room and crowding the hall. They talked animatedly among themselves or on cell phones, while two police officers and a state trooper interviewed those who'd witnessed the shooting. Two other officers flanked the door to Everett Greason's room, with instructions to allow no visitors except immediate family and, per a direct call from the governor, his advisor, Steve Crenshaw.

While standing only five feet, nine inches tall, Steve Crenshaw was an imposing man, built like a college wrestling champion, with a face that only his now deceased mother ever loved. Apart from being Governor Michael Chase's most influential political advisor, Crenshaw was arguably the governor's oldest friend. They'd grown up together in the tiny town of Rutherford, North Carolina and had gone on to be roommates and fraternity brothers at UNC Chapel Hill in the seventies.

While they'd both become involved in politics during their college years, it was Michael who'd taken what Crenshaw like to call the "high road." He, on the other hand, had become enamored with the forbidden fruit; the power that belongs to those who work behind the scenes, brokering deals and twisting arms in ways that fine, upstanding politicians never can. He took to the darker side of politics like a fish to water, quickly building a reputation for ruthlessly leveraging favors and hoarding political assets.

When Michael Chase made his move into state politics, Steve Crenshaw became his greatest weapon, efficiently and discreetly laying waste to the reputations of candidates who opposed them and spinning Chase's accomplishments into political gold. They both knew, however, that to achieve their ultimate goal they would need the support of Everett Greason, a philanthropist and key player in the state political machine.

An alliance had soon been formed, but with Greason holding the deep purse strings, it had been formed on his terms. The results had been spectacular, with a previously unknown Chase garnering two terms as Attorney General, and two years later, winning the Governor's mansion.

In the process, Crenshaw eventually came to see Everett Greason as the real source of power, and while he remained outwardly committed to Chase, there was little doubt in his mind who he would align himself with, should the two men ever part ways.

Everett Greason sat propped up on pillows in his bed, an IV tube dangling from one arm, while a combination EKG and blood pressure monitor beeped quietly beside him. He was talking to his secretary about rescheduling appointments when there was a knock on his door.

Steve Crenshaw stuck his head in the door. "Hey, do you know where a guy can get a trim and blow-job around here?"

Everett Greason grinned his crooked grin and hung up the phone. "Yeah, I've got a nurse that can set you right up. She's about fifteen. That's about your speed isn't it?"

Crenshaw walked in and closed the door behind him, his smile fading. He walked over and sat down in a chair beside the elder Greason's bed. "Everett, are you hanging in there? You look like shit."

Greason snorted. "I'll be alright as soon as I get out of this dump. How's Michael?"

"He's fine. I guess everybody got lucky today. What the hell happened out there?"

"It was the craziest damn thing," Greason mumbled. "That old bitch just took her time, walked right up in front of me. Pulled out a pistol and started blazing away like the Goddamn old west. I thought my ticket was punched, I'll tell you."

"Did she say anything?"

Greason grunted. "Yeah. Right before she pulls out the gun, she raises her hand, like she wants to ask me something, so I say 'I think the lady's got a question...'" Greason stopped and gave a series of wracking coughs before continuing. "So, she says, 'Do you believe in hell, Mr. Greason. My father's waiting there for you.' Now what kind of bullshit is that? *My father's waiting there for you.*" Greason paused. "Do they know who she is yet?"

Crenshaw pursed his lips. "I just got off the phone with Charlie Burk. They believe the woman's name is

Evelyn Bayer Greene. She's over in ICU."

Everett Greason's face drew up in a scowl of disbelief. "What did you say? What was that? Not the last name, the middle name."

"Bayer," Crenshaw replied. "Why, do you know her?"

Greason's jaw had clenched tightly shut, and he turned to look away, seemingly unable to speak for several long moments.

When he finally turned back, Steve Crenshaw felt an uncharacteristic pang of fear coursed through him. His friend's face was colder and more menacing than he'd ever seen it. "Steve, you and I have to talk. And it can't leave this room."

The crowd at Panera Bread had thinned as closing time approached, allowing Ben and Kate the luxury of a booth by the restaurant's stone fireplace. Kate was grateful for the extra warmth, having forgotten her jacket at the hospital.

"One decaf latté, no sugar," Ben said as he slid into the seat opposite her and pushed a cup slowly across the table.

"Thanks," she said, her eyes never leaving the paper in her hand.

The envelope that lay unfolded on the table in front of her was yellowed and worn, addressed in faded pencil to Margaret Bayer Greene, at an address on Waddell Street, in Stanton. It bore a single five cents stamp, and the postmark read January 1955. The letter inside had fared no better with time, having faded so much in places that the writing was barely legible.

"So?" Ben said, leaning forward and studying her face for any sign of a reaction. "What is it?"

The corners of Kate's mouth drew down in a slight frown, and she shook her head slowly. "I," she began and looked up. "I'm not sure, but it almost reads like a suicide note."

"What do you mean, almost?" Ben asked. He held out his hand. "Do you mind if I have a look?"

She hesitated, her eyes dipping down again toward the paper. She seemed almost ashamed. "I don't like this – what it says. This guy is claiming that my family is doing some awful thing, but he doesn't say what."

"Who wrote it?" Ben asked.

She put the letter in his outstretched hand and looked away, into the embers of the fire. "It's signed, 'Dad.'"

Ben held the letter up to the light and squinted, his eyes skimming the words:

> Margaret,
>
> My time here is short, so I must be brief. I have done things in the employ of Andrew Greason and Mitchell Werner for which there is no atonement except in the fires of Hell. My guilt led me finally to betray them, however, in a feeble hope that the world will learn who they really are and what a terrible deception they are perpetrating on the people of this town.
>
> But they have found me out, Margaret. By the time you read this, I will be

25

gone. God willing, Jimmy Smoot will
have time to get his story out before
he is discovered. He is the only one
who can answer the questions you will
have. Look for Jimmy Southern.
You may never forgive me for what
I've done, but know that I will always
love you.
Dad
HC44-165-32
HS51-418-7

Ben looked up and puffed out his cheeks. "I see what you mean. It's like the guy knew his time was up, but he doesn't say how or why."

"Or who," Kate added sullenly. "Is he saying that he's expecting to be killed? By one of my evil relatives, no doubt."

Sensing her unease, Ben gracefully changed direction. "Did you notice the numbers here at the bottom?" he asked, running his finger over them.

"Yeah, that's kind of strange too. He just dropped them there with no explanation."

Kate cocked her head to one side as she remembered something Ben had said at the hospital. "You told me that she mentioned someone named Smoot, I mean, the old woman, right?"

"Yeah, I think she did." Ben closed his eyes and tried to recall. "She said *they* never found this envelope and they never found..." Ben quickly scanned the letter again. "Here it is. She said they never found Jimmy Smoot's notes. This is who she was talking about."

"It sounds like Jimmy Smoot is, or was, a writer or a reporter. But who is Jimmy Southern?"

"It could be an alias. A high profile reporter couldn't afford to use his real name if he was working undercover on a big story." After a moment lost in thought, Ben pushed the letter back to Kate. "So, have you ever heard anything about a scandal? I mean, has anyone in your family ever talked about anything like that?"

Kate propped her elbow on the table and rested her head in her hand. "This is probably going to sound strange to you, but I don't know my family very well. When I said my grandfather and I don't get along, that was pretty much the understatement of the year. It's not just my grandfather, it's most of my family, at least the ones running the almighty Werner-Greason funeral home. Growing up there was like living in a minimum-security prison. The only person I get along with is my grandmother, and she's a career alcoholic." As if snapping out of a trance, she shook her head and looked at the ceiling. "Jesus, what am I doing? I'm sorry, I didn't mean to..."

Ben smiled and held up a hand. "It's okay, really. Families are a pain in the ass, but we've all got 'em. You don't *even* want to know about mine, trust me."

The worry lines eased, and her mouth broke into a tired grin. "Yeah," she nodded, letting her eyes meet his. "Actually, I do."

"Okay, well," Ben said, rubbing his hands together in anticipation. "That's at least a three beer conversation, so I guess we'll just have to go out, then, won't we?"

"We *are* out," she said, motioning to the restaurant around them. But as her eyes came to rest on the letter again, her smile faded. "What the hell are we supposed to do we do with this? I don't know what it means," she shrugged. "Besides, it looks like ancient history."

Ben picked up the envelope and looked at the name on it. "Maybe so, but if this is the same woman who brought the pistol to the party tonight, then I'd say ancient history just showed up on your doorstep."

2

Across town, just outside the Stanton city limits, in the private upstairs residence of the Werner-Greason Funeral Home, Edna Greason, Everett's wife of nearly fifty years, sat in her favorite armchair, a half-empty glass of vodka in one hand and a cigarette in the other. Her eyes were fixed on the TV, where channel seven was running continuous coverage of the shooting. There was no trace, however, of alarm or worry on her pale, gaunt face – only an oddly detached curiosity. She felt less than nothing for the man if that was possible.

Theirs had been a marriage of convenience, of necessity to hear Everett tell it. It had come at the beginning of the family's meteoric rise to prominence and became an early casualty of Everett's seemingly insatiable appetite for power and fame. Edna had turned to alcohol to cope, and her gradual downhill slide had gone unnoticed and unchecked, lost in the shadows of the spotlights that were constantly trained on her husband. As her behavior had grown increasingly erratic, however, she had begun embarrassing Everett at social functions. Rumors had begun circulating about the sad state of

Greason's young wife.

Everett's solution had been simple; he distanced himself from her, telling friends and associates that tragically, she'd taken ill and couldn't leave the house. Over time, he became less and less willing to speak of her, until people simply stopped asking. It was as though she had died, and by all indications, the rest of the family, including Walter, her son, wanted to keep it that way.

Edna took a slow drag on her cigarette and let the smoke seep out of her mouth as she watched the jerky, amateur video of the shooting, for what seemed like the hundredth time. She would have given a pretty penny for a blow-up of the stricken expression on Everett's face as he saw the pistol pointed at him. It was the only time in her life she'd seen him terrified.

Galena, the family's long-time maid walked in with an armload of folded laundry, just as Edna was fiddling with the remote, backing up and advancing to just the right spot.

"Ha! That's it," Edna announced, pointing to the TV. "That's the money shot right...*there*, don't you think?"

Galena turned from the linen closet and furrowed her brow in dismay. "Miss Edna, you are so *bad*!"

Edna raised her glass in a mock toast to herself. "It's a shitty job, but somebody has to do it."

Her cell phone rang at that moment, from somewhere in the bedroom. "Galley, would you mind?" Edna implored.

Galena disappeared into the bedroom and emerged moments later, holding the gold-plated phone at arm's length to read the minuscule type on the caller-ID.

"I think it's miss Kate."

Edna set her cigarette down and answered the call. "Katie? Hello? Are you alright?"

Kate stood next to Ben's Explorer in the parking lot of Panera Bread, where they'd closed the place moments earlier. "I'm fine Gram, I'm just a little shaken up, that's all."

"Are you at the hospital?"

"No, I ah, had to get some air. I met a friend over at Panera, and he's going to run me by to check on you." Kate flashed a grateful smile at Ben.

Edna muffled the phone with her robe and turned to Galena. "Pssst. She isn't even at the hospital. She's at a restaurant!" she giggled gleefully. "That's my girl."

"Gram?" Kate called into the silence.

Edna was back. "Oh, you know I'd love to see you sweetie, anytime. I'm just watching the big event on the tube. It's a shame really."

"Yeah, I couldn't believe it. I still can't."

"If that woman had just been a little better shot..."

"Jesus, Gram!"

"Joking, sorry. I was only joking. You know how I am."

"We'll be there in ten minutes. What's going on downstairs?"

Edna stretched and let herself slide down in the chair until her legs were draped over the ottoman. "By the oh-so-familiar strains of Nearer My God To Thee and a few of the other greatest hits, I'd say they had a couple of viewings. But it's what, nearly ten? I'm sure all rubber-neckers are gone by now, so come on over, and bring your

31

friend." She lowered her voice to a conspiratorial whisper. "Is he cute?"

"Bye Gram. I'll see you in a few."

Since Ben had moved to town six years earlier, he'd attended only one funeral at Werner-Greason; that of Gladys Mays his real-estate agent, a good-hearted woman who'd gone out of her way to find just the right house for him and his now ex-wife. Just after their divorce, Gladys had been on her way to meet Ben to discuss a smaller place; something with less square footage, when she'd been killed instantly in a head on collision with a seventeen-year-old on his way home from a party.

And in a cruelly ironic twist, it turned out that he hadn't needed Gladys's services after all. Against all predictions by his friends and his attorney, his ex packed her things and left town three days later; no dear-Ben letter, no forwarding address. He got to keep the house, while Gladys Mays got a permanent spot in the Werner-Greason cemetery.

A nagging sense of guilt had left Ben feeling compelled to attend the funeral, and it was then that he'd gotten his one and only look at the state's largest funeral home.

Now, even in near-darkness, he remembered the wide brick sign at the entrance and the rows of Bradford Pear trees along the winding quarter-mile driveway to the funeral home.

"I really appreciate this," Kate said. "I know it's out of your way. I just wanted to check on her. Gram's a mess, but I love her. She's always been there for me in her own way."

They drove over a rise and saw the house itself, an imposing three-story structure with a row of columns lining the front steps. The few lamp posts that dotted the gently sloping land beyond the house illuminated evenly spaced rows of headstones, spreading out in all directions.

"I'd forgotten how big this place is. Where do I park?"

"Just stay on the drive and pull around back. The private parking lot is back there." She studied the empty front lot and sighed. "I'm glad the services are over. I'm just not up for it."

"So, this is where you...live?" Ben asked falteringly, as he pulled into a much smaller lot and parked next to a trio of polished black hearses.

His question surprised Kate, and she realized that with everything that had happened that evening, she'd told him next to nothing about herself. "Oh, God no," she said. "I live in a condo over in Brentwood Arms. I just work here; office work, accounting, inventory – it's not permanent, it's just, it's a long story. You want to come in?"

Ben had always been unsettled by the idea that people lived in funeral homes. He'd been reassured on several occasions that the living quarters were physically separate from the areas where the dead were prepared, but he'd never quite been able to get around the stigma.

She put her hand on his arm and smiled. "Come on; they won't bite, at least not until you're on the slab."

Ben winced. "Thanks, I'll spend the rest of the evening trying to get *that* picture out of my head."

"Funeral parlor humor," Kate shrugged. "You grow up around all this and nothing bothers you, trust me."

The private residence extended into an entirely separate wing of the building and easily had as much floor-space as two spacious homes. Kate explained that it had originally been built to accommodate the families of both its founders, Andrew Greason and Mitchell Werner. What had started out as a teeming, two-family business, however, had gradually converted to a help-for-hire operation as more of the young-adult family members chose other professions. Now, most of the rooms were empty; except of course for the apartments occupied by Walter, her father, and by Everett and Edna.

"Wasn't this a little like living in a hotel?" Ben asked as they walked down the richly carpeted third-floor hallway.

"Yeah, did you see The Shining?" Kate whispered.

"That bad, huh?"

"You have no idea," she quipped.

Despite the humor, Ben had noticed a marked change in Kate's demeanor from the minute they walked through the back door. She was quieter, almost pensive as if she'd withdrawn into some unseen shell. He knew all too well how powerful old demons could be, and he couldn't help but wonder how many of them Kate must face every day in a place like this.

"This is it," Kate said as they approached a closed set of double doors. "I should apologize ahead of time. I don't know what shape she'll be in. Normally I wouldn't..."

"Stop worrying, okay?" Ben put a hand on her shoulder, and she felt herself warm to his touch.

Kate knocked softly and heard a loud, "It's open" from inside. They opened the door and saw Edna, all five feet three inches of her, standing in the middle of the room in her nightgown and slippers, holding up a framed black and white photo.

"Come in dear, oh, I'm so glad to see you!"

As if the glass in her hand were not a dead giveaway, she swayed as she hurried over to Kate and hugged her, the photo still clutched in one hand.

"Hi Gram," Kate said. "Are you holding up okay, all things considered?"

Ben was quietly shocked at the woman's haggard appearance. Her hair was disheveled, her sunken eyes ringed with dark circles, and her sallow skin was wrinkled and pale. Yet there was a surprising twinkle in her eye and a genuine mirth in her laugh. Something about it reminded him vaguely of Kate's laugh.

Edna waved a hand dramatically in front of her face. "Pooh, I'm fine. They called me and said that the old bastard is going to be up and around tomorrow, so what's the big deal, right? He'll live to wheel-and-deal another day." She held up the photo and squinted, weaving unsteadily until Kate took her by the arm. "I was just thinking that your uncle Pete looks remarkably like Frank Sinatra..." Only it came out more like "Shinatra." Her voice trailed off as she noticed Ben. "Oh, is this the *friend* you were telling me about?" She attempted a wink at Kate and took Ben's hand. "It is a pleasure to meet you, young man. I told Kate that she could do better than Roger, and I see that she has."

Kate rolled her eyes. "Gram, why don't you turn in now? You could use a good night's sleep. Where's

Galena?"

"Oh, she's off doing maid things, somewhere."

Ben waited while Kate walked her heavily inebriated grandmother into her room and closed the door. When she returned several minutes later, she looked flustered.

"I haven't seen her like that in a while. Usually, she keeps it more, I don't know, under control."

"It's no problem for me," Ben said. "But I'm dying to know who Roger is."

"Jesus, you can always count on the relatives, can't you?" Kate smirked.

As they drove back through town, on their way to the civic center to pick up Kate's car, the streets were almost deserted. Traffic lights, flashing yellow, reflected in the glass of darkened storefronts as they passed through Stanton's older downtown business district.

Kate felt more tired and sore than she could remember. "So what do we do about the letter?" she asked, turning to Ben, who also appeared to be losing steam.

He took a deep breath and let it out slowly. "That's partly up to you. But I'm afraid we're past the point of giving it to the police, even if we wanted to."

As Kate looked away out the window, she could still see the old woman in her mind, falling to the floor amid a hail of bullets, and as much as she tried, she couldn't get her mind around it. What in God's name would it take to make someone do something like that? And was it possible that her family was to blame? It seemed almost too abstract to imagine.

"I'm not sure I want to talk to the police, honestly," she said finally, breaking out of her thoughts. "Maybe it's wrong, but if there's even a chance that my great-grandfather and Everett were involved in something despicable, then I want to know what it was. I could decide then what to do about it." Kate shook her head in disgust. "Self-righteous bastards," she muttered.

Ben drummed his fingers on the steering wheel. "So, if that's what you want, then maybe we can figure out what this guy is talking about – in the letter. There's not much to go on, but we're already in this deep. I don't see that we stand to lose much by poking around a bit."

Kate shifted in her seat and pulled one knee up to her chest. "Are you sure about that? I wouldn't turn down the help, but I don't want to drag you any further into this than you already are. I have an ugly feeling that there's not going to be much of an upside."

Ben gave her a tired smile. "Maybe not, but I figure, I've already shown such amazingly poor judgment tonight, why not keep the streak alive?"

She laughed and took his hand in hers. "I'm starting to think Gram was right about you."

The parking lot of the civic center was still bustling with police activity and news crews, but all entrances and exits had been blocked, and officers were checking IDs on incoming and outgoing traffic. Ben sat in his car and waited until Kate had walked the fifty yards or so past the flashing barrier to hers, and as she turned and waved, he could still see the strip of paper he'd given her with his cell phone number. He looked down at the paper in his hand with her number written on it and wondered what in the hell he'd just gotten himself into.

The governor's voice sounded terse. "Steve, level with me here. Do we need to be concerned about this woman or her father's connection with Everett?"

Steve Crenshaw sat in his black, fully loaded Lexus, on a side street near the hospital, chewing compulsively on the inside of his left cheek. He'd broken the skin this time, and he was already tasting the faint copper taste of his own blood. "Mike, there's nothing there. Greason worked with her old man fifty fucking years ago, that doesn't mean shit. They were business associates, that's all, no dirt for anyone to find."

"So what's her Goddamn beef with Everett, or with me for that matter?"

"We've got the hospital administrator working with us on that right now. The woman has terminal leukemia, for Christ's sake. Her blood work up apparently reads like a Chinese menu of prescription meds, including a couple that are off the reservation. I've been in touch with the police chief here, and they're preparing a statement. It's going to say that she was in the advanced stages of inoperable cancer and was heavily medicated at the time of the incident. Basically Mike, she was stoned out of her mind. She most likely had no idea what she was doing."

Mike Chase was silent for a moment. "What about that gibberish she was spouting about..."

"There was a lot of confusion about that," Crenshaw interrupted. "So we clarified it for the press. She told Everett to go to hell, plain and simple. It's taken care of. Anyone says different, they just misheard. Besides, she's in critical condition. They don't expect her to pull out of it."

"Good. That's good. We need for this one to go away fast, Steve. This old woman was no middle-eastern fanatic. We can't afford to be blowing away little old ladies; I don't care what kind of meds they're on. Keep me posted if anything else develops, got it?"

"I'm on it."

Crenshaw ended the call, rolled down his window, and spit blood onto the sidewalk.

As the midnight shift at Hawthorne Memorial Hospital began their rounds, Margaret Bayer Greene lay unconscious in the intensive care unit, in a drug induced coma. During three and a half hours of emergency surgery, doctors had removed two bullets from her chest and had attempted to remove a third that was lodged in her skull, at the base of her brain. While the third bullet had somehow not severed her spinal cord, it proved too risky to remove, and surgeons elected to leave it there – at least temporarily.

In the waiting room just across the hall, the lead surgeon had informed her brother and sister in-law of Margaret's condition and explained to them that the chances of recovery were slim. It was, he said, a miracle that she was alive at all.

"So, you don't mean she's definitely going to... I mean, there's some chance?" Larry Bayer asked. A farmer by trade, Larry still wore a pair of bib-overalls and work boots. One cheek was lightly streaked with grease, and his eyes were red and swollen.

In the hall nearby, a young male nurse in green scrubs and tennis shoes was checking the medications on his cart, but seemed particularly interested in their conversation, glancing now and then at the police officer who stood outside the old woman's room. Over the top of the cart, he watched the doctor put a hand on Larry's shoulder.

"Yes, there is a chance," the doctor said. "In part, that will depend on your sister, and her will to live. The mind is a very powerful thing, Mr. Bayer. It's just too early to know, quite frankly."

The farmer put his arm around his wife. "Thank you very much. Can we see her now?"

"Not for another couple of hours, I'm afraid. We're still concerned about infection. It would probably be a good time to stretch your legs, maybe get something to drink downstairs. She's stable, but she won't be conscious for several more hours."

The nurse pulled up a clipboard and began busily jotting notes as the doctor passed behind him and continued on his rounds. He watched Mr. Bayer and his wife turn the corner toward the elevators, but waited until he heard the ding of the elevator bell before palming his cell phone and texting, "all clear" to a nameless number in his contact list. He turned off his phone and waited.

Officer Brent Pulaski rocked nervously back and forth on the balls of his feet, distractedly watching the dwindling flow of people passing by in the hall outside Margaret Green's room. He looked again at his watch and wondered when the call would come. He kept wanting to pinch himself. Making the state highway patrol was something he'd fantasized about for years, like all the other beat-cops, but this was even better. The man from the governor's office had said EPU, Executive Protection Unit – the most coveted jobs of all, the elite. Pulaski had no idea what he'd done to get noticed, but he wasn't about to look a gift-horse in the mouth. The man had only asked for a few minutes of his time to discuss the particulars of the transfer and to explain how they would be bypassing the standard approval process. And as fate would have it, the man was going to be there at the hospital on business. Pulaski couldn't believe his luck. Technically he would be away from his post, but the nurse was no more than twenty feet away, and it was only a few minutes.

Just then, his cell phone beeped, and he snatched it from the clip.

It was the call he'd been waiting for.

"Yes sir," he said, looking both ways down the hall. "I'll be right there."

The man in scrubs closed the door behind him and hurried to the old woman's bedside, where turned off the heart monitor and produced a hypodermic needle from the bag he was carrying. He carefully injected its contents into her IV line and watched her face. But there was no movement, no sign, and he felt a pang of regret that she'd been sleeping so deeply. Just once, he'd like to see the look in someone's eyes when it happened.

Larry Bayer's wife sat at a small corner table in the mostly empty hospital cafeteria while her husband fed another dollar bill into a vending machine. The paper cup dropped into place, and steaming water poured into it, and he was just reaching for what was sure to be a lousy cup of coffee when he heard his name over the hospital intercom.

Please report to the nearest nurse's station, it said.

His wife looked questioningly at him, but he held up a finger for her to wait. Turning the corner, he strode the twenty feet to the Ground Floor C nurse's station, where the shift supervisor handed him a phone. As he listened, his eyes began to brim with tears, and he covered his face. "Oh no," he whispered, and the cup slipped from his trembling hand.

In the shadows of the hospital loading dock, even as Larry Bayer hurried to the third floor to find out what had gone so horribly wrong, the young man hastily removed his green scrub suit to reveal street clothes underneath. He threw the scrubs and a small plastic bag in the dumpster, donned glasses and a ball cap, and walked quickly to a waiting car.

He climbed into the passenger seat and closed the door, slightly out of breath as he turned to the man in the driver's seat. "It's done," he said.

The driver, a tall, bald man in a suit, nodded stoically. "Good," he said. "Excellent." He reached into the black bag that sat between them, and in one swift motion, produced a long-barreled pistol and fired once, at point blank range. The young man flinched, and for the briefest second, his face was frozen in shocked disbelief. As he put his hand in the widening patch of red on his chest and gawked at the sight of his own blood, his face went slack, and his lifeless body pitched forward into the dashboard.

After the driver patiently wiped off his speedometer display with a handkerchief, he eased the black Lexus out of the service lot, onto Ridgeway Drive, and disappeared, unnoticed, into the night.

Ben Tuttle sat on the edge of his bed, his head cradled in one hand, miserably tired but unable to sleep. The events of the evening had only amplified in his mind during the restless hour or so he'd spent trying to make himself drift off, and he'd finally given up. The glowing numbers on his alarm clock read one forty-seven.

After splashing his face with cool water, Ben donned sweatpants and retrieved his laptop from its bag by the door. With no prospect of sleep, he already knew he'd be taking a sick day, and right now there was only one thing on his mind.

He'd scribbled the names Margaret Bayer Greene and Jimmy Smoot on a piece of paper, which he fished from his suit pants pocket and unfolded on the desk beside his laptop. As he stared at the blinking cursor in the Google search box, he paused, his fingers resting lightly on the keys. He didn't like the feeling in the pit of his stomach. It reminded him of the dread he always felt riding up that first big hill on a monster roller-coaster. He couldn't see what was coming; what awaited him on the other side. All he could see was track at the crest of the hill, disappearing into blue sky, and that made the anticipation so much worse.

Yet Ben knew he was hooked. Sometime during the most surreal evening of his life, he'd crossed over, or more likely been pulled over an almost imperceptible line. Perhaps because of the exhilaration that inevitably follows danger, or because of Kate's intoxicating personality, caution had lost out to curiosity, and he was hooked. Now there was only one direction to go – forward. He looked again at the names on the paper and began to type.

In the living room of her duplex, Kate Greason continued to pace, the letter in one hand and her cell phone in the other, wrestling with the urge to try Ben's number. It was a silly idea; he would be sound asleep. It was two thirty in the morning for Christ's sake, of course he'd be asleep. Still, what if wasn't? What if he was like her? They'd seemed to be alike in so many other ways.

Despite her physical exhaustion, her mind had conjured a relentless tide of disturbing images and conflicting ideas, and with each passing hour, more unanswered questions. She hadn't even bothered trying to sleep.

He was a stranger, for all intents and purposes, someone that fate had thrown into her path, yet she'd felt comfortable around him from the moment they'd met. And he was sexy, very sexy. Who was she kidding? She couldn't remember feeling more attracted to a stranger. But it was more even than that; he was the only other person who knew about their connection, however unintentional it might be, with the woman who'd tried so desperately to kill her grandfather.

Kate hadn't been able to let it go. The implications in the letter were too troubling, and Margaret Greene's suicidal act stood as indisputable evidence of her conviction. Whatever truth she was fighting to discover, she'd been willing to die for it.

Kate stared at the phone and considered an alternative. Texting would be the safest; even if his phone had an audible notification, it wouldn't be likely to wake him, not after a night like tonight. But on the off chance that he was awake...

She keyed in "Hi sorry - know it's late. R U awake?" and sent the message.

As she saw it go, Kate cringed. After getting off to a better-than-average start earlier in the evening, she was probably blowing it by acting like an impulsive teenager. She had just gone back to pacing, imagining how irritated he might get at being awakened, when her phone chirped.

"U 2? Why not surprised? Call me?"

"I'll be damned," Kate said quietly, smiling at the twitter of excitement she felt.

"I'm really sorry if I woke you," she said when she finally had him on the phone.

"No chance. I've been on the internet for the last hour trying to find out who these people are. I'm halfway through a pot of coffee already." He paused. "Care to join me?"

The idea sounded wonderful. "I'd love to," she said, without hesitation. "I'm going crazy here. I'm afraid I look like hell, though."

He chuckled. "Good, you'll fit right in."

Fifteen minutes later she pulled into the driveway at 118 Oakmont Street, a modest split level house with a small yard and lots of trees.

Ben came to the door wearing sweats, t-shirt, and a wry smile. "Come in; it's freezing out there." His deep shadow of stubble and uncombed hair gave him a rugged look that amused Kate.

"We're nuts aren't we?" Kate said as she stepped into the tiny foyer and the welcoming smell of freshly brewed coffee, and pulled off her fleece jacket. She had traded her nightshirt for jeans and a sweatshirt and hadn't bothered with makeup.

"Definitely," he replied, hanging her jacket on a hook by the door. "Come up, and I'll show you what I'm finding. There's more about this Smoot guy than I expected."

She followed him upstairs, glancing briefly at his family photos on the wall and wondering slightly if she was out of her mind. He'd moved his laptop to the kitchen table, along with a compact printer, and had already printed out numerous pages that lay in a loose pile. He poured her a cup, and she joined him at the table.

"Okay," he began, handing Kate a page near the top of the stack and pointing. "I got a few hits for James Smoot and couple for Jimmy, but the one that grabbed me was this. It's an editorial column from nineteen forty-seven, from the Denver Examiner, and the author is one, Jimmy Smoot. No guarantee he's our man, but it gets better." As Kate skimmed the content of the article, Ben rifled through more papers and pulled another one.

"An exposé about corporate collusion with Germany during the war." Kate murmured. "So he was a staff writer for the Denver Examiner?"

"No, not exactly. More like a freelancer. I found a few more columns in the same vein. A couple were for the examiner, but there's one from a newspaper in Boulder and even one from the Chronicle in San Francisco. The full articles aren't always there, but there's a teaser. He was apparently an investigative reporter type, into whistle-blower material, political scandal, that kind of thing. This one is nailing a Colorado senator to the wall for using taxpayer money for private vacations and gifts to contributors."

"This is good stuff," Kate said. "But it would put our guy west of the Mississippi, wouldn't it? Why would he be in North Carolina, or better yet, in a place the size of Stanton?"

Ben gave her a final printout. "I don't know, but something brought him here. Look at this."

It was an article from the Denver Examiner, dated July 16, 1955, and entitled "Search For Missing Denver Man Continues."

"There must have been at least one more about him before this, but I couldn't find it," Ben said.

Kate skimmed the page as Ben went for more coffee. "They had proof that he came here," she said, beginning to read aloud. "When Union Pacific records confirmed that Smoot had purchased rail fare to Charlotte, North Carolina, the focus of the investigation shifted to the east coast, where local authorities pledged their full support. Yesterday, however, after a month-long investigation, a frustrated Sergeant Mack Stamey of the Charlotte Police Department questioned whether Denver authorities had thoroughly checked their leads, citing a total lack of evidence that Smoot ever arrived in the city at all. With no apparent evidence of foul play in Charlotte or in Smoot's home town of Denver, Sergeant Stamey accused his midwestern counterparts of sending his men on a 'wild goose chase.'"

She read more in silence, as Ben joined her again at the table, rubbing his tired eyes with his fingertips.

At last, she looked up. "They go on to talk about his sister in Georgia. She's the one who first reported him missing. They hadn't seen each other for years, and he calls her out of the blue and says he's going to be in North Carolina – wouldn't say why."

"Yeah, they were supposed to meet in Columbia, South Carolina just after the fourth of July holiday, but he never showed," Ben added. "And according to everything I've found, that's the last anyone ever heard from Jimmy Smoot."

Kate was quiet as she mulled over a question forming in her mind. "So I guess we should assume from Margaret's letter that Jimmy Smoot was writing something about my great grandfathers?"

"*Grandfathers*? Why the plural?"

"Oh, I guess I left that part out. On top of being major-league dysfunctional, my family tree is actually a kudzu vine," she smirked. "Mitchell Werner and Andrew Greason were the original founders of the business. Everett is the son of Andrew, and my grandmother, Edna, the one you met earlier, is Mitchell's daughter."

"Her maiden name is Werner?"

Kate nodded. "That's when we went from a tree to a vine, I'm afraid. Edna Werner married Everett Greason, God only knows why, and changed her name. The two families merged at that point, and everyone in the generations that followed on that branch is literally a Werner-Greason. So Mitchell and Andrew are *both* my great grandfathers."

"And Smoot supposedly dropped everything and came all the way out here to write about them?" Ben asked.

The idea made Kate shiver. Jimmy Smoot was obviously not some hack writing editorial chaff; he'd been a serious author who'd gained the respect of several national newspapers by exposing big-league corruption. And his work seemed very thorough, always citing sources; public records, internal documents, and reluctant witnesses he'd somehow managed to coax statements from. His was the kind of research that took time; months, or even years to complete.

Reluctantly, Kate moved to the laptop and typed her own last name in the search box, along with the name Smoot, afraid of what might come back. "Nothing," she said, exhaling sharply.

"I know. I already tried – sorry."

"There's nothing to be sorry for. I already told you, I want to know." Kate inched her chair closer to the keyboard and sat very still, her eyes staring blankly at the keys. She typed the names Smoot, Southern, and Greason. "Let's try this," she whispered and pressed the Enter key.

Near the top of the results list was an entry from the Charlotte Observer archives, from August of 1955, entitled "Sheriff Denies NC Man Is Missing Denver Reporter."

"Bingo," Kate murmured. "Listen to this. 'According to Sheriff Orland Houser of Stanton, North Carolina, the sightings by a local woman of missing Denver reporter James Smoot are now believed to be a hoax. Melanie Cheek, a waitress at Duke's Diner, yesterday retracted earlier statements that she had, on two occasions, seen a man in the diner who matched the physical description of Smoot. Cheek had reported the sightings to the police after she saw Smoot's picture in the paper, and repeated the claim to Observer reporter Leanne Wilkes in a July 25th interview. Cheek recalled that, on both occasions, the man was with three other men who she knew to be employed by Werner-Greason funeral home. The man, when asked, reportedly claimed to be Jimmy Southern.

When questioned by police about the incident, Werner-Greason co-founder, and owner Andrew Greason...'" Kate stopped. "Shit! That's all they have online. The rest of it's on file, whatever that means."

Ben leaned over her shoulder and looked at the screen. "Great. I've never understood that. Why go to the trouble to post half the article? Disk space is cheap." He shrugged. "They'll have it in the library."

Only when Kate leaned back in the chair and closed her eyes did she notice how uncomfortably exhausted her body was, nerves tingling and heart beating just faster than normal. It was a feeling she hated, but her mind was far from calm. Even now, she doubted that sleep would come.

Ben too had felt himself sliding into the surreal, altered state that accompanies sleep deprivation. He put a hand on Kate's shoulder. "Why don't we take a break, maybe see what they're saying on the news."

Kate nodded. "Good idea, I'm going a little buggy, I'm afraid."

The living room was dark except for the light from the TV. She sat close to him on the couch and instinctively, he put his arm around her. She smiled and leaned her head onto his chest.

A police officer stood in front of a bank of microphones, answering questions from the press. The caption underneath read "Stanton Police Chief, Willard Hughes."

Someone asked if they had determined a motive

for the shooting.

"No, not at this time," replied Hughes. "But we will be looking closely at Mrs. Greene's state of mind. We have confirmed that she was in the advanced stages terminal lymphoma, an aggressive form of cancer, and as such, may have been taking any of several strong, possibly experimental medications. We will be trying to ascertain which drugs, if any, were present in her system, and what effect they may have had on her behavior."

"Will an autopsy be performed?" a young woman in a suit called out.

Kate and Ben exchanged confused glances. "I thought she survived," Ben said.

"That's what they were saying on TV just before midnight. I wonder what happened."

Chief Hughes was responding to the question. "Yes, an autopsy has been ordered, and will most likely be performed in the next twenty-four hours. We will make those findings available as soon as we get them from the County Coroner's office."

Ben grunted. "I guess she didn't make it."

Kate looked up at him, her eyes tired and worried. "It may sound crazy, but I'd been hoping that we'd get the chance to talk to her again, maybe get her to explain all of this. I think she would have."

Her head settled back onto his shoulder, and as the voices on the TV droned on, blending into an almost soothing white noise, their eyes grew heavy at last. Exhaustion finally won out, and they both slept.

3

From his hospital bed, Everett Greason stared out the window as the darkness receded and light began to spread across the eastern sky, but he did not notice the sunrise, nor take any joy in it. As he waited impatiently for the doctor to come and release him, his mind was elsewhere, mulling over the conversation he'd just had with Steve Crenshaw. He hoped that Steve was right; hoped that this was the end of it.

The media had behaved predictably, snatching the breadcrumbs they'd thrown and running with them. Discussions were already gravitating toward the serious side effects of experimental cancer medications and how few recipients of these drugs were properly supervised. Others were debating the failure in the security protocol that led to the incident at the civic center. No matter, he thought. Let them yap about whatever they liked, as long as it wasn't him; as long as nobody went digging in the past and started asking the wrong questions.

Greason's jaw went tight as he thought again about Dan Bayer, the old woman's father, and once, a very long time ago, his most trusted associate. He remembered with vivid clarity the bitterness he'd felt when he learned what Bayer had betrayed him, the all-consuming rage that had taken hold of him. It was the only time he had ever lost control and acted impulsively, and his sloppiness had nearly cost him and his family everything.

Asphyxiation had been listed as the cause of Bayer's death; asphyxiation from the rope he'd reportedly used to hang himself from the banister in his foyer. That had been good enough for Sheriff Hauser, and in turn, it had been good enough for the press. By the time the coroner's report disappeared, nobody had bothered reading it closely enough to see the references to the anomaly; the fact that the bruising from the rope on Bayer's neck was more consistent with tissue that was already dead. At the time, it had been much easier for Hauser to excuse a missing report than to explain an anomaly.

Still, Crenshaw had better be right, Greason thought, flexing his good hand into a tight fist. He couldn't afford for people to start believing that this was anything other than the tragic consequence of one old woman's dementia; none of them could.

At seven thirty a nurse came into his room and brought yet another flower arrangement, assuring him that the doctor would be by shortly to discharge him. As she was leaving, his cell phone rang. He recognized the number immediately by the Washington area code.

"Everett, it's Paul. I heard about what happened; you're one lucky son-of-a-bitch." Paul Richards was the congressional representative for North Carolina's eleventh district and another of his oldest friends. But Richards' voice did not have the jovial ring that he'd grown accustomed to over the years; this time it had a hard edge to it.

"Paul, I was wondering when you'd call. How are things on the hill?"

"Better than they are there apparently. It seems I'm spending a lot of my time lately watching reruns of you getting shot at."

Greason grunted. "Not so flattering, are they?"

When Richards spoke again, his voice barely above a whisper, all semblance of cordiality was gone. "Everett, what are we talking about here? I don't like the smell of this, one damn bit."

"That makes two of us," Greason replied. "But so far, the only thing anyone is talking about down here is what we've told them to talk about. As for Bayer's daughter, she died last night; succumbed to her injuries."

"I saw that."

Greason winced as he shifted in his bed. "Whatever she knew, or more likely guessed, died with her. She never regained consciousness after Mike's boys got through with her. They did a number on her."

"That's all well and good Everett, but how the hell could she have known anything in the first place?"

"I haven't figured that out," Greason said. "But I've got Crenshaw on it. The police chief here is a good friend of mine; Willard Hughes. Crenshaw tells me he's going to play ball with us on this one. If they find anything, we'll know about it first."

"We'd better," Richards said. "Keep me posted."

It was not a request.

For a frightening moment when Kate opened her eyes, she was completely disoriented. Her neck was painfully stiff, and she was alone in a room that she didn't recognize, curled up on a strange sofa. Mercifully, the sensation passed as she recalled the night before, and Ben. It was Wednesday morning. She'd driven over here in the middle of the night. After spending hours at the computer, she'd curled up next to him and watched TV until they'd drifted off together. With the memory, the room seemed suddenly warm and inviting. It was his room, his personal space. There was something sensual about waking up there, on his couch.

Kate stood up on weak legs and crossed the room. Ben was not there, nor was he in the kitchen. She called down the hall, and when there was no answer, she walked to the end, where his bedroom door stood open. She could hear the shower running and, over the sound of the running water, she heard him humming softly. Kate smiled and tiptoed to the bathroom door, which was also cracked.

Before she could talk herself out of it, she slipped off her jeans and pulled her sweatshirt over her head, letting her clothes fall at her feet. With a shiver of anticipation, she unclasped her bra and let her panties fall to the floor. Instinctively, she covered herself with one hand as she eased into the soothing heat of the bathroom, amid the billowing wisps of steam, and walked to the shower.

Ben was rinsing the soap from his hair when he heard the shower curtain rustle. He turned to see Kate, naked, climbing in beside him, and couldn't keep his mouth from falling open.

"Mind if I join you?" she smiled, taking in the

sight of his muscular body as he gazed longingly at hers.

With only a smile, Ben reached out, pulled her gently under the hot water with him, and kissed her, slowly at first, then, with the urgency that they both felt as their bodies pressed tightly against each other.

They made love under the steaming water, more passionately than either of them could remember, and much later, when they stepped out, they were trembling with exhaustion. They dried off in silence, stopping frequently to kiss, and lay down together on his bed in the pale light of early morning. For the second time that day, Ben and Kate slept.

At eight thirty, as Everett Greason was being assisted out the front door of Hawthorn Memorial amid a tightly knit pack of reporters, Lieutenant Terry Wallace sat in the darkened security room of the Stanton Civic Center with its security director, Ed Meeker, reviewing tapes of the shooting from three different cameras. Wallace had already pulled extra duty to cover the previous night's gala, and when everything went to hell, he, like nearly everyone else in the department, had his shift extended – until further notice. He was going on eighteen hours straight, and the strain was beginning to show.

"Jesus, Ed," he snapped, standing up and wiping his face with a handkerchief. "Can't you get some air going for Christ's sake? It feels like a blast furnace in here."

"Sorry Lieutenant," the man shrugged, with a faintly amused smile. "This is as good as it gets, I'm afraid."

Wallace grumbled something under his breath and opened the door to the hallway, flooding the room with light and cooler air. Sweat had soaked through his shirt, forming dark patches under his arms and down the center of his back, and the steady trickle had left the waistband of his underwear soaked.

They'd watched the shooting from at least four different angles, in slow motion, fast motion, and with endless freeze frames that showed important details of the action. The monotonous process had eventually stripped the scene of all fascination for Wallace and reduced it to an almost mechanical series of motions.

He leaned against the door frame and breathed in the cooler air, privately convinced that he was wasting his time. They all knew what had happened by now; it was pretty straightforward. The old woman parked her car at the event, tucked a pistol into an elastic band around her thigh, near the hip that had the metal pin in it, and went inside. She set off the metal detector, as she knew she would, but produced a MedID bracelet to confirm that metal had been permanently embedded in her body. The good natured security guard had politely asked her to sign a form, wished her a pleasant evening, and waved her past. She'd waited in the lobby with all the other guests until the opportune moment, and made her play, pistol now concealed beneath a folded shawl on one arm.

"We've still got the lobby-cams," Meeker called behind him from the monitors.

Wallace sighed. "Fine, let's run them and wrap this up."

On the tape, Margaret Bayer Greene moved very slowly, compared to the other guests. At Wallace's urging, they'd sped the playback up sixty percent, and it hadn't even mattered. After making one trip to the ladies room, undoubtedly to remove the pistol from its hiding place, she stayed rooted to one spot, in the shadows of an alcove on the wall opposite the main hall. The other guests, meanwhile, moved in jerky fits and starts, grouping and ungrouping, mingling, zipping back and forth across the frame, milling around the buffet line in a comical sort of dance. Through it all, probably fifteen minutes in real time, the old woman stood, practically motionless.

Wallace was just reaching for the dial to increase the speed yet again when Ed Meeker stopped him.

"Whoa, did you see that?"

When Wallace looked up, the woman was moving slowly out of the frame. "See what? Yeah, she's headed into the main hall."

"No, before that." He stopped the tape and rewound it in fast motion.

Wallace saw it this time; backward, and just a flash, but he saw it. His eyes narrowed, and he moved closer to the monitor, hoping that he'd been mistaken.

She was back in the alcove now, standing patiently. Meeker stopped the tape and played it at normal speed. "Here," he said. "Watch this."

The woman moved suddenly, surprisingly quickly from the shadows, and approached a man just past the end of the buffet line. His back was to the camera, but she stood very close to him and began speaking, leaning even closer, with one hand on his arm.

Wallace tensed, the stifling heat around him suddenly forgotten. He couldn't believe what he was seeing.

"Stop!" he snapped and pointed to the screen. "Back up, just a little. Right there! Now play it slow."

It was unmistakable. The woman reached into the man's suit coat and put something in the inside pocket.

"I'll be damned," Wallace muttered.

"She definitely gave him something. Look at that."

He played the motion again and froze just before her hand disappeared inside the jacket. The image quality was mediocre, and as Meeker zoomed in, it blurred into a grainy soup, but a distinct patch of white was visible at the top of her closed fist.

"What is that?"

"Paper, maybe," Meeker said, as they both squinted. "Could be anything. Might even be a reflection off of something metal. It's too far away to tell."

"Can you enhance it?"

"No, we're already down to pixels. Maybe someone with the right equipment could get you another ten percent, but you're still not going to get detail."

Wallace continued to stare at the frozen image. "Well whatever it is," he said softly, wiping the sweat from his upper lip. "One thing's for sure. We've got ourselves another player, and that makes it a whole new ballgame."

The tape from the civic center created a major stir at the Stanton police station. Wallace and a half-dozen other officers, including Captain McGinnis, his superior, and Chief Hughes, sat around a conference room table, all focused on the TV that had been wheeled in on a cart.

Everyone in the room knew that Chief Hughes was mad, but it was Captain McGinnis who spoke first. "So, let me see if I've got this. We now have our shooter passing something off to a second suspect, presumably a white male, who never faces the camera, and who we can't follow after the exchange because some Goddamn genius put up a hooray for Everett Greason banner in the lobby and blocked half the security camera's field of vision. Is that about the size of it?"

Wallace nodded. "Yes sir, that's about it."

"Perfect," McGinnis growled.

"Who's working the guest list?" Chief Hughes asked.

"Pearl, Rogers, Kowalski, and Murdock," replied a heavyset sergeant at the end of the table.

Hughes drummed on the table with his fingers and scowled. "Gentlemen, I don't have to tell you that this changes the equation – exponentially. Our jobs just got a hell of a lot more complicated. McGinnis, throw everyone we've got at that guest list ASAP and focus on what they saw in the lobby, *before* the shooting. If we have to re-interview some of them, so be it. I want to know who this guy is."

"What about the press?" McGinnis asked.

Hughes was already shaking his head. "No, absolutely not. The news hasn't even hinted that anyone else was involved. So our man here thinks that we don't know about him, and I want to keep it that way. I'm flagging this one as need-to-know, even in the department."

Those around the table exchanged glances. It was a rare step, one that he'd only ever taken twice in his eight years as head of the department. He got up and walked to the TV, which displayed a grainy still image of the new suspect's back as he stood beside Mrs. Greene. "Leland, what could the video forensics rats tell from this?"

A young sergeant to his left cleared his throat and

leaned forward. "Just guessing sir, but probably height, weight, shoe size, make of the suit, that kind of thing. And depending on how much profile they can see, they might even pin something down on facial structure."

"Well, that's a hell of a lot more than we've got right now," sighed Hughes.

Wallace spoke up. "Sir, the event was invitation only, reserved seating. We've already got the seating chart, and if all the camera clocks were in sync, we should be able to get a fairly accurate list of people who were still out of their seats when this conversation happened. It may not give us much, but it'll narrow the field."

"Good. Very good." Hughes looked at his watch. "I've got a meeting downtown, but I want to know about anything that bubbles up on this, and I do mean anything. I'm talking twice dailies and anything in between. Is that clear?"

Outside, as the Chief walked to his car, he pulled a business card from his wallet and looked at the official North Carolina state seal that graced the front. Beneath it, in gold letters, was the caption, "The Office of the Governor." The politeness of the man who'd given it to him late last night had been dangerously transparent. He was to be kept apprised of all developments in the case, no matter how trivial. The governor would be personally grateful, he'd said, for Hughes' cooperation, and his discretion. But there was no mistaking the threat beneath his words.

Hughes had thought it very strange at the time, given that the case appeared to be open-and-shut. But now he understood, and he didn't like it. The man who'd given him the card knew something. He knew there was more to this than everyone believed. But how could he know? The question continued to gnaw at him as he climbed into his car, turned over the business card, and dialed the number on the back.

"Mr. Crenshaw, Chief Hughes, Stanton PD," Hughes began softly. "Something's come up."

Kate found the orange juice in Ben's refrigerator and poured a glass for both of them. She wore a long sleeved, button-down shirt she'd borrowed from his closet and smiled as she set the glass down on the table beside him. "Don't think that I go around doing things like this."

Ben sat beside her in boxers and t-shirt, munching a bagel and reading something on the laptop. "Like what?" he smirked.

"Well, you know, like...this."

"That's not what I heard," he grinned.

She slapped at his arm.

"In fact," he continued, "I happen to know that you get guys all the time like this. You know, set up the whole emergency, crisis, shooting-type, ploy-thing, and just reel them in. I'll have to admit; it's pretty effective."

"Jesus, you're as bad as Gram!" she laughed. "What time does the library open?"

"Unfortunately, it's been open for hours. What did you tell them at work?"

"After last night, they didn't even expect me. Walter said they'd already brought in the part-time woman to fill in."

"Walter, you mean, your dad?"

"I prefer Walter, always have," she sighed, getting

up and heading for the doorway. "I'm going to get dressed. We take longer, remember?"

The Stanton library was a modern, well-equipped facility that had been completely renovated and up fitted, thanks, in part, to a large donation from Everett Greason. It had been one of many community development projects that he'd spearheaded over the years, and now, like several other buildings in the state bore his name.

While the library was in the process of scanning periodicals and making them available online, the back editions were still stored on microfiche, in the basement, along with the older audio-visual materials. Ben and Kate found the Charlotte Observer listing they were looking for in the index, and with the help of the clerk, a student with bottle-red hair and a diamond stud on the side of one nostril, located the box of microfiche and loaded a reader.

They pulled two chairs up to the large back-lit screen and soon they were scrolling through the fabulous fifties, both of them skimming while Ben operated the controls. They past stories from the Korean War, Senator Joe McCarthy's campaign against communist sympathizers, the testing of the world's first hydrogen bomb on a small atoll in the Pacific, and the first ascent to the top of Mount Everest, by Sir Edmund Hillary.

The variety pages they saw were peppered with names like Marylyn Monroe, James Dean, and Elvis Presley. Black and white televisions were advertised, along with a new show called I Love Lucy. They even came upon an article about a man named Ray Kroc, who had opened a series of popular hamburger stands with two brothers named McDonald.

"Jesus, this seems like a long time ago," Ben mumbled. "Stanton couldn't have been much more than a scratch in the dirt back then."

Kate shook her head. "I don't know. There were apparently enough people here to keep a new funeral business booming."

Finally, they scrolled into August of 1955.

"Okay, now we're talking," Kate whispered. "That's it, stop there."

They found the article on the third page and, too eager to wait for a print-out, read it together on the screen.

"So the waitress, the Cheek woman, dropped her claim," Ben said. "And Andrew denied any connection."

"He admitted that someone named Jimmy Southern worked there, but look at that." She read from the text. "Greason reportedly told authorities that James Southern worked briefly for Werner-Greason, as a laborer on the cemetery grounds crew, but that he had recently resigned, citing an illness in the family. According to Greason, temporary workers are not required to complete the standard job application, and as a result, he was unable to provide authorities with any background information on Southern."

Ben snorted. "How convenient. The two of them just happen to go missing at almost exactly the same time."

"And according to this, Sheriff Hauser quietly closed the investigation the next day."

"No offense Kate, but how come nobody called bullshit?"

Kate was still reading. "Apparently they did. There's an editorial about it on the next page, and they're not pulling any punches."

As he read, Ben whistled. "You're not kidding. They basically call Andrew a liar and accuse Hauser of covering the whole thing up."

"But there was nothing they could do about it, apparently. With no trace of Smoot or Southern and no photos for comparison, their hands were tied."

"And Hauser was the law," Ben said. "In that day and time, nobody would have been willing to square off with him over something they couldn't prove."

Kate looked up. "Doesn't my letter prove it?"

"Close, but no cigar," Ben replied. "First of all, even if the guy who wrote it said outright that Smoot and Southern were the same person, which he doesn't, then it would still just be someone's opinion. There's no real proof there."

She leaned back in her chair and crossed her arms. "I just wish I knew what he was working on when he disappeared."

"Well, whatever it was, it never saw the light of day. We'd have found something by now." Ben cast a sideways glance at her. "What about Everett? How much would he know about this?"

Kate huffed. "Believe me, if it happened at Werner-Greason, Everett knows about it. For that matter, he could have been involved. He's old enough, God knows."

"Maybe that's why the old woman did it," Ben said. "I mean, she could have gone after Andrew while he was still alive but she didn't."

Kate frowned. "What do you mean? He *is* still alive."

"Andrew Greason is still living?" Ben was

incredulous.

"If you can call it that. He's wasting away in an elite, private-care facility just outside of Asheville. He's been there for over a decade; barely knows anyone anymore. Everett doesn't even go and see his own father. How's that for compassion?"

"I'm beginning to see what you mean," Ben said.

"As for the Jimmy Smoot thing, I wouldn't dare approach him with that. He already thinks I'm a traitor for bailing out on the family business and running off with Roger. This would send him over the edge."

"Roger again," Ben nodded. "So where is this Roger dude now?"

"Well, funny you ask. He's standing right over there."

Before Ben could catch himself, he'd whirled around to look.

Kate was already laughing.

"Watch it. Payback is hell," he warned.

Someone shushed them from across the room, and Kate dropped her voice to a whisper.

"Actually, he moved to Maryland and went into real estate."

"Good thing for him," Ben grinned. "I thought for a minute I was going to have to whip his ass."

Kate smiled her irresistible smile, leaned over, and gave him a long, lingering kiss.

When they parted, she grew serious again, remembering why they were there. "So, what now? What do we have left to go on?"

Ben laced his fingers together under his chin. "We don't know anything yet about Margaret Bayer Greene's father. He said that he worked for Andrew and Mitchell. Maybe there's something there, but if his job was as bad as he says it was, I doubt we'd find anything in the papers."

"I've got my laptop," Kate offered. "They've got Wi-Fi here. Let's set up in a cube upstairs and see if there's anything out there."

They'd printed the Observer article and started to collect their things when Ben took Kate's arm. "Wait a second. Can I see that letter again?"

She dug it out of the side pocket of her purse and handed it to him. He opened it and looked again at the two numbers on the bottom of the page, beneath the closing. "We haven't done anything with these either," he said, holding up the paper.

"So let's split up. I'll find a study carol, and you use one of the library PCs. Maybe between us, we'll get lucky."

HC44-165-32
HS51-418-7

The numbers weren't a standard format that Ben was familiar with, and he was surprised when a search on one of them yielded dozens of hits. None were exact matches, but they had similar alpha-numeric components. Most were references to aerial photography, surveys done by the Army Corp of Engineers, the Department of Transportation, or the USDA.

The librarian at the reference desk pulled his glasses down to the end of his nose and studied the piece of paper Ben had given him. "We do have most of the aerial surveys from these agencies; satellite imagery, that sort of thing. Particularly those of North Carolina. It's all on film or fiche downstairs."

Ben thanked the man and turned to leave.

"We have the actual photos for some of them stored in the back down there," he called. "But they're just loose in boxes I'm afraid. The lady's name is Janet. She'll be glad to help you."

Ben debated going to find Kate, but he didn't know yet whether he was on the right track. He decided to wait until he had something, then he'd surprise her.

Janet, a middle aged wisp-of-a-woman, with gray hair and lips that seemed permanently pursed, was the supervisor – the red haired girl's boss. She retrieved a binder that contained a chronological listing of the aerial surveys of the state, since the first one in 1934. Indented beneath each header, Ben saw a range of numbers that roughly resembled his, presumably showing map grids and associated ranges of individual photographs.

He looked first for HC44-165-32, skimming the entries from newest to oldest, beginning with a USDA Vegetation series from 1962. When he reached a 1948 DOT survey, Ben felt a chill of anticipation; the first four characters of the sequence matched his.

The eighth row down contained the range he was looking for; HC44-150-70 through HC44-190-18. "Yes," he whispered, tapping the book with his finger. He started off with the binder to find Kate but Janet, who'd been watching him from her stool, snapped her fingers. "Excuse me! I'm sorry, but that binder can't leave this area."

"Oh," Ben frowned. "Well, would you be able to pull the roll that has this survey on it? I'll be right back. I have to go and get my...my friend." He'd almost said "girlfriend," but caught himself. Kind of scary, he thought.

But the librarian was shaking her head. "Unfortunately, I can't hold reference material while you..."

"Fine," Ben snapped. "Thanks. I'll wait here. Thanks for your help."

Luckily, his cell phone had reception, and he was able to call Kate. "Hey, how's the scavenger hunt?"

"I've found something here," she said. "Where are you?"

"I'm back down in the dungeon, and I've got a bead on one of these numbers, probably both of them, but I can't leave," he grumbled, lowering his voice and turning away. "The gate-keeper won't hold any of this stuff if I leave."

"Librarians, you've got to love them, don't you? Stay put, and I'll be down in a few. I've got to copy this URL because I can't print anything. The woman's father, the one who wrote the letter was Dan Bayer. And I was right. The letter is a suicide note."

"No shit? The guy killed himself?"

"*Hanged* himself, according to the article. And nobody could even figure out why. I'll explain when I get there."

"Jeeze, that's harsh," Ben mumbled.

"What did you find?" Kate asked.

"I got a hit on one of the numbers. I think they're reference numbers for early aerial photos of North Carolina. The first one is from some Department of Transportation survey from 1948."

"Photos of what, in particular?"

"No idea. Maybe I'll know by the time you get

here if Janet doesn't revoke my library privileges."

Kate chuckled. "Just charm her. I'll be right there."

Ben was staring at one of the readers when Kate trotted down the steps and walked over with her bag.

"So what have you got?" she asked, setting her things down beside him and running a hand through his hair.

"Stanton," he grinned. "And I was right too. This place was barely big enough even to *be* a town."

At first glance, the black and white photo appeared to be one of farmland, trees, and pastures, with a few thin ribbons of road winding through the landscape. From above, nothing was recognizable at first, but as she leaned closer, she realized what she was seeing. "Oh my God, that's the courthouse," she said, pointing to a small cluster of buildings at the center of the picture. "And that's the boxy three story building beside it, the one where Everett's office is today. I can't believe it. There's almost nothing here."

"Look at Marshall Street! It's practically a cattle trail. Once you get out of this area, there's nothing on it but houses."

"That's so weird," Kate said. "Now it's miles of fast-food and strip shopping centers. I can't imagine what that must have been like."

Eventually, they picked out a few familiar buildings, including the original Stanton Elementary School, which had long since been rebuilt, and even a much smaller version of the library itself.

"So why would Dan Bayer have wanted Margaret

to see this?" Kate asked, still engrossed in the image.

"Oh, this isn't the one from the letter. I haven't gotten that far yet. I got sidetracked – never made it off of center-city here."

Ben looked again at the number on his paper and began scrolling slowly through images, checking the index numbers in the upper left-hand corners carefully as he went.

Kate helped him look, and a dozen frames later she grabbed his shoulder just as he spotted the number himself. "That's it," he said.

After a moment, Kate put her hand to her mouth. "Whoa, that's my house! I mean, it's the funeral home. I'd recognize the curve in that driveway anywhere. There's the pond, and that's where the new cemetery is now." She was pointing animatedly at the lower left area of the screen.

From the aerial perspective, Ben was having a hard time picking out anything he remembered from the Werner-Greason home or grounds.

"Can you zoom this thing in?"

"Yeah, hang on." Ben fumbled with a knob and the area on the screen expanded until they could almost pick out individual trees. When he navigated back to the Werner-Greason estate, paved roads were clearly visible, along with two parking lots and several side buildings.

"It's all there," Kate said. "I always thought they started out small and added some of this stuff later, but everything is there; the guest house, the garden, the maintenance shed. That's Lark Hill, what they called the original cemetery, the old one up in the corner. They added to it for ten years or more before they opened the new section; this area here. It's all covered in headstones now. Look, that's a hearse. It's fuzzy, but I can tell by the shape."

Ben looked questioningly at Kate. "This is a blast from the past, but what are we supposed to be looking for?"

She shrugged and knelt down beside him. "I don't know. Is there anything else in the frame? All I see is farms and trees."

Ben pulled the perspective back to show the image at seventy-five percent.

"What's that?" Kate asked, pointing to a wide tract of forest North of the estate. A short, straight line appeared among the trees.

"It could be part of a road."

"I don't know. It's perfectly straight. Most roads don't look like that. It looks more like..."

"An airstrip?" Ben finished. "It's the only other thing that would look like that, but I don't see any houses within a mile of it, other than yours. I don't even see a road that connects it to anything."

"I never heard anything about an airstrip being back there. Course, I don't even know who's property that is," Kate replied.

"It's not your family's?"

"No, I'll show you. Go back to Lark Hill for a minute."

When Ben brought the funeral home and grounds back into focus, she studied the image carefully, steering the viewer over the razor thin pathways that crisscrossed among grave markers in the old cemetery. "See that pathway right there? It ends at an iron gate that borders the woods. You wouldn't be able to tell from the photo, but there's a No Trespassing sign on it, always has been, and Everett used to warn us about the land owners. He said they were as mean as snakes. He supposedly butted heads with them over that land. Years earlier, they had promised to sell it to Andrew but backed out, and when Everett tried to negotiate, they weren't even willing to talk."

"You never heard any planes taking off or landing when you were growing up?" Ben asked.

Kate shook her head but seemed suddenly mesmerized by the black and white patches on the screen, her eyes darting quickly from one side to the other. After a moment, she hung her head and closed her eyes.

Ben was at a loss. "Uh, are you okay?"

"I've seen this before," she said softly. "This view of the graveyard, I remember seeing it somewhere before. It's killing me because I can't remember where."

Ben's pulse quickened. "Recently?"

"No, definitely not. Like, a long time ago, maybe even when I was a kid. It just won't come to me."

"So, why is this photo so important? Is there something about the airstrip?"

"Your guess is as good as mine," Kate sighed. "Have you found the other photo?"

"No, but I've got the page it's on. It's an Army Corp of Engineers survey from 1941. While I'm loading it, tell me about the suicide guy, Dan Bayer."

Kate sat down and propped one foot up on the rung of Ben's chair.

"Okay, according to the article, Margaret Bayer Greene's father, Dan Bayer, was a pretty heavy hitter in Stanton during the forties and fifties. He was a prominent accountant, but he also practiced law off and on, mostly during the forties. He eventually gave it up for full-time accounting and was well liked and well respected. Everything was going great for the guy right up to the time he hanged himself."

Ben stopped loading the reader and frowned. "That's screwed up. The article didn't mention either of your grandfathers or Werner-Greason at all?"

"Nope. The only possible link might be the Community Development Board. He was a member, and so was Andrew. I looked it up. It was a group of local businessmen who were working to get economic growth jump-started in Stanton. But there was nothing about him working with or for Andrew or Mitchell directly. If there was anything going on, it was strictly under the table."

"What reason did the article give for his suicide?"

"They didn't. Margaret was thirty at the time and was apparently devastated. When they interviewed her, she said she had no idea why he'd done it, and without a note, the police would only say that his motive was unclear."

There was a click as Ben closed the housing on the fiche reader. He started to say something but just grunted instead.

"What is it?" Kate asked.

"It wasn't like that in the letter," Ben began, frustration creeping into his voice. "A normal suicide note would be talking about regrets, misery, whatever. This guy is talking about being in *danger*. He says Andrew and Mitchell found out that he betrayed them and now he'll be dead soon. Isn't he as much as saying that they're going to whack him?"

"It just seems like something out of a movie,

that's all. Everett's an asshole, granted, but there's a lot of assholes out there who don't go around 'whacking' people."

"True," Ben mused. "But if Dan Bayer was right, these guys had a lot more to lose than most people. Whatever they were supposedly hiding..."

Kate was getting the same anxious look he'd seen on her face in the restaurant. "Let's just see what's on the other photograph," she said. "All the speculating in the world isn't going to give us any real answers."

The second set of images, from 1941, showed an even more sparse incarnation of Stanton. Many of the structures in the small downtown were absent, along with dozens of houses and other miscellaneous buildings on the outskirts of town.

"Werner-Greason didn't even open until forty-four," Kate remarked. "These would have been taken before they even came to Stanton."

Eager to see what the property looked like before the funeral home, Kate urged Ben to move on. But when he did, they found only a blank spot in the row, and the words "Image Missing" where the photo should have been. Ben swore under his breath.

"That's too much for coincidence," Kate whispered, looking around them as if someone might be watching.

Ben silently nodded his agreement.

"Does that mean the image was never there, to begin with?" Kate asked. "Or was it just left out when the rest of these were put on microfiche?"

"There's only one way to know. We need to see if they have the originals here. The guy upstairs said they keep some of them in boxes in the back. I guess I'll go and talk to my buddy at the desk."

Fortunately, Janet was nowhere in sight, having apparently left on an errand. The red-haired girl behind the counter meanwhile, seemed clueless and disinterested. "I don't have any idea," she yawned. "Poke around back there all you want, just don't take anything or Janet will be ragging on my ass for an hour."

They thanked her and ducked through the doorway, into a large, dimly lit room that was crowded with rows of tall shelves. Boxes of all sizes were stacked here on the shelves, almost to the ceiling.

Kate squinted at the handwritten label on the box nearest her. "What are our chances in all of this? Maybe we should wait for Janet."

"No way. She wouldn't have let us back here under threat of torture. I'm hoping Red doesn't tell her. Maybe by the time she figures it out, we'll have what we need."

Fortunately, the boxes were well labeled, and even under dim light, it didn't take them long to find the aerial survey collections.

"You know, back then, they literally pieced these squares together like self-stick linoleum tiles to make a mosaic of a particular county," Ben said, holding up one of the photos. "It must have been a huge pain in the ass without computers."

Kate had disappeared around the next row. "They didn't know what they were missing," she called. "Hey! I've got it!" She read off the leading characters as Ben hurried to find her.

"That's the one," he said.

The photos were in sequence, and halfway through the box they reached the pane ending in six, but the number on the next photo ended in eight. Theirs was missing.

"Damn, the original is gone too," Kate groaned.

They rifled forward and backward in the box, hoping that it had been misfiled, but all the others were there, in sequential order. On the last pass, Kate suddenly grabbed Ben's hand as they flipped open a space between six and eight. Her hand darted into the v-shaped gap, and she pulled out a tattered index card that had been wedged near the bottom of the box, like a placeholder.

Before Kate even had time to read the writing on it, her cell phone rang, blaring a piece from Vivaldi's Four Seasons into the silent room. She groped for the phone, dropping the index card in the process, and as they both grabbed for it, they knocked heads and winced in pain.

At that moment, they heard the door to the room swing open with a bang, and a voice that could only be Janet's, called out "Who is that? Who's in here? Come out now! This room is off limits to anyone other than library staff!"

Through gritted teeth, Kate looked at her phone. "It's Gram," she hissed, turning the phone off. "I'll call her back."

Ben had retrieved the card with one hand while he massaged his head with the other. "Are you okay?" he whispered.

"I said, this room is off limits!" the Janet voice croaked.

"Sorry!" Ben called weakly. "We'll be right there."

He helped Kate up, and they walked around the corner to find Janet glaring at them from the doorway. "I'm going to have to insist that you respect our policies here. This is not a..."

"Give it a rest," Kate growled. "Your handy helper out there gave us permission to be here, for your information, so maybe you should take it up with her."

Janet recoiled and let them pass. "I wasn't aware," she stammered, her tone softening considerably. "It isn't policy. She's new. I'm sorry for the misunderstanding. Is there something I can help you with back there?"

"No," Ben replied, his mouth drawn into a feeble smile. "We're fine."

They took their things and headed upstairs, leaving a pensive Janet chewing nervously on her lip.

"She's probably worried we'll complain," Kate snorted, with a last look back. "And why are you looking at me like that?" She poked Ben in the ribs.

"Like what?" he grinned.

"You're smirking."

"No, I'm just impressed, that's all," he said. "I didn't know you had such a dark side."

Her eyes narrowed. "Well consider yourself warned."

Outside, the early afternoon sun had warmed the air to a comfortable temperature, and they sat down on the end of a rock wall at the top of the steps.

"What did the card say?" Ben asked, pulling it from his pocket.

"You tell me. I didn't have time to read it before we cracked heads."

The card was blank on both sides, except for a phone number, written in tiny letters one corner. No area code, just a seven digit number.

"So this means what?" Ben asked, throwing his hands up. "Did the library put that there?"

"It doesn't look like something the library would do," Kate said, taking the card.

"Well, this much we know; somebody went to a lot of trouble to make sure that nobody ever saw that photo. Why would the person who took the tile leave a card with a phone number?"

"It's a local number. Why don't we just call it and see what happens? We can say we have the wrong number and hang up."

Ben considered the idea, but he wanted to err on the side of caution. "We should use a public phone. Everyone has caller ID, and with the media fiasco that's going on right now over the shooting, the last thing we need to do is draw any attention our way. That could be a disaster."

They found a phone booth at a gas station on the corner of the next block and Kate volunteered to do the honors. She dropped some change into the slot and dialed the number, and Ben was standing close enough to hear the click as someone answered the call.

"Hello?"

After a fleeting moment of confusion, Kate's eyes grew wide, and she clapped a hand over her mouth as if to keep herself from speaking.

"Hello?" the voice said a second time.

Kate hung the phone up without a word and stepped away. "Shit," she whimpered. "Holy shit."

"What?" Ben pleaded, taking her arm. "What's wrong?"

Her eyes had begun to tear, and her voice trembled. "That was Leanne Parks! I'd know her voice anywhere. I've known her practically my entire life." Tears spilled down Kate's cheeks as she hurried down the sidewalk, leaving Ben agape behind her. "This is all true isn't it?" she cried, throwing her arms up in frustration. "It's not just some bullshit somebody made up. He *is* involved."

Ben hurried to catch up to her. "Talk to me, Kate. What's wrong? Who is Leanne Parks?"

She stopped and turned to face him, her voice hardening. "She's Everett's secretary, okay? That number rang straight through to his goddamn office!"

4

On the third story of the Stanton Courthouse
Annex, in the corner office, Leanne Parks continued to
stare at her phone. She didn't know why, but she felt
strangely alarmed.

There had been many occasions during her tenure
as Mr. Greason's secretary when she'd seen or heard things
that had made her uncomfortable; snippets of a heated
argument with someone he would not identify, a cryptic
email, hastily drafted and urgently sent, a package or letter
that he insisted on opening himself, in private. But she
knew better than to ask. Above all else, Mr. Greason
valued loyalty and discretion in his employees, and he'd
compensated her well enough over the years to be able to
expect both. Yet, this was different. It gave her pause.

She'd always known about the seventh phone line,
since the day he hired her. He'd made no attempt to
explain it to her, simply instructed her. She was never to
use it, under any circumstance. When it rang, if it rang, she
was to take the caller's name and number, and tell the
caller that someone would return the call within the hour.
She was then to deliver the caller's information to Mr.

Greason immediately, wherever he was. He'd told her these things twenty-two years ago.

She'd worried about the mysterious phone line for the first few days, then, occasionally over the next few weeks, but it never rang. Within six months, she'd practically forgotten about it.

Three minutes ago, line seven had rung for the first time in twenty-two years, and Leanne nearly forgot what she was supposed to do. She hadn't been prepared. None-the-less, she'd at least managed a couple of feeble hellos. She was at once relieved, yet strangely unnerved, that the first and only caller on line seven had hung up before she could play her part.

So Leanne did the only thing she could think to do; she copied the phone number from the caller-ID, paged Mr. Greason at home, and began answering the other calls that were holding.

The cold, lifeless body of Vincent Forest Calhoun lay naked on the second of three stainless steel tables in the Werner-Greason preparation room, tubes protruding from the carotid and femoral arteries. Walter Greason stood nearby, trying to focus on the jaw suture he was preparing, as Pavarotti's golden tenor voice played softly in the background, but even his favorite music did not calm him. He slammed the suture hook and wire down on the rolling cart and kicked it, sending it careening away from him, until it crashed into the wall. The clatter was nearly deafening, but he didn't care, and Vincent Calhoun certainly wouldn't.

The door swung open, and Everett walked in, a stern look on his aging face as he took in the scene.

"Damn it, Walter, have you lost your mind? That kind of thing isn't making all of this any easier."

There was a cold look in Walter's eyes, as he turned to face his father. "Well, it's good to see that you're taking time out from interviews and press conferences to grace us with your presence."

"This is national press," Everett growled. "If we can contain this thing, we'll get more mileage out of it than..."

"And what if we can't contain it Everett?" Walter snapped, slamming his palm down on the preparation table beside him and sending a shudder through the body that lay on it. "What then? Go ahead, tell me! Only this time skip the bullshit. All I ever heard from you from the time I was twelve was how this thing with Bayer and Smoot was a closed chapter. All the loose ends were tied up, you said. And you were just so goddamn sure about it, weren't you?"

Everett leaned heavily on the work table nearest him and shuffled a step closer to his son. "Walter, we can't afford hysterics right now. I'm as concerned as you are, but if that bitch had any real proof, she'd have been shouting it from every street corner the day her old man died. And I'll swear this to you, if anyone comes at us with anything short of proof, we're going to watch them choke on it."

Walter looked at the cadaver beside him, but his mind was somewhere else.

Everett continued. "Our people are all over this, but in the meantime, it's critical that everything here be business as usual. You can manage that, can't you? Bachman is going to lay low until further notice, just as a precaution."

"What about the shipment from Vienna?" Walter asked, still gazing at his charge. "It's already been paid for."

Everett grunted. "I'd trust Gunter, but they won't ship it to him – it's policy; no third party. We'll have to pick it up, I'm afraid. It's just a chance we'll have to take."

Walter sighed heavily and walked to the corner of the room to retrieve his cart, which had spilled some of its contents on the floor. Everett turned to leave, but his son's voice stopped him in the doorway.

"Say what you like, but it's no coincidence that somebody's nosing around down at the library, and you know it."

"Let them," Everett said, without turning fully around. "There's nothing to find."

By mid-afternoon, Ben and Kate had settled on a patio table at Starbuck's, but they'd ended up in decidedly disparate conversations on their cell phones. Ben was patiently trying for the third time to talk an untrained co-worker through the process of rebooting one of their production servers, and Kate had taken the opportunity to call her Gram.

"I just think all the sympathy has made him even more unbearable," Edna lamented. "And we've still got family hanging around. It's just been so much commotion. You should stop by, you know. Carla and Dean are leaving to go back to Knoxville this evening, and you haven't seen them in years."

"I know Gram, since I hurt Carla's feelings over the Christmas duck napkin holder things."

Edna snickered. "That was a hoot; I'll have to admit. You just came right out and said it. The look on her face was worth a million bucks."

Kate was stalling, and she knew it. She screwed up her courage and tried to relax. "Gram, I was just curious, do you know what year Andrew and Mitchell build the house?"

"Why yes, I do, as a matter of fact. They started in the summer of 1945, just after the end of the war, and finished a year and a half later."

"What about the property? Do you know who used to own it before we did?"

There was silence on the other end, and Kate winced, wondering if she'd overstepped.

"You know, it's funny," Edna said, her voice sounding dreamy. "I should remember that, but I don't. The name Holt comes to mind, or maybe Harding. Oh hell, sweetie, you know my memory is like a goddamn sieve. Why would you possibly want to know about that?"

As Ben leaned forward and pinched the bridge of his nose, Kate could tell that he was having a hard time maintaining his professional tone. "Just check the network connection on the back of the box, then. If all the web services are running, then it has to be a hardware problem, okay?"

"Oh, sorry Gram," Kate said. "I'm a little bit distracted. I ah, just saw some old pictures of Stanton in a display downtown and it made me think about how long our place has been there, that's all."

To Kate's surprise, her grandmother's voice changed, sounding uncharacteristically steady and sincere. "Are you sure, there's nothing else on your mind, honey?

You know you can tell me if there is."

Kate felt a knot rising in her throat as if she were a little girl again. It was as if her Gram could see right through her. She wanted desperately to tell her Gram everything that had happened, but she didn't dare. As much as Kate loved her grandmother, she knew that her drinking would make secrecy nearly impossible, and there was too much to lose.

"Thanks, Gram. I know I can. It's nothing, I was just curious, that's all."

"Kate, please be careful," Edna said evenly. "Your father and Everett are, well, very private people. This family has been through a lot, some of it way before your time, and they're not likely to understand your curiosity, not just right now. All I'm saying is, sometimes it's best to leave the past in the past."

Ben had just ended his call and was sipping his now lukewarm coffee as he watched her with great interest.

"I know Gram," Kate was saying. "I understand. There's nothing to worry about. I wouldn't bring it up to either of them, believe me. Okay, you too. I love you."

Kate ended the call and sighed. "What is it about that woman? Just when I think she's fried her brain completely, she surprises me."

"What did she say?" Ben asked.

"She warned me about bringing up the past to either of them. She reminded me how sensitive they are about it. But it wasn't so much what she said as how she said it, like the fog in her brain lifted completely for a minute. She talked to me like she was the soberest person on the planet."

"You don't think she knows about all this, do you?"

Kate shook her head. "I don't think so. I was really close to her growing up. My mother passed away when I was nine, from a rare form of cancer. Gram practically raised me. I think she would have told me, maybe not when I was a kid, but later."

"I'm sorry about your mom. That must have been hard."

Kate shrugged. "You get a pretty tough skin when that happens. You have to. But thanks."

"What was it you were asking her?"

"I wanted to know about when the house was built. I thought about it when we were in the library. If I'm right, then that earlier picture would have been taken several years before my family even bought the land."

Ben leaned forward and crossed his arms on the table. "So what would have been there, and why would Everett want to hide it?"

"Who knows? If it was like the rest of the county, it would have been nothing, just woods or fields. The old cemetery would have been there; it dates back to the mid eighteen hundreds, but other than that, I don't have any idea." She reached for her cup but stopped. "Oh, and there was one other thing; she thinks they bought the land from somebody named Holt or Harding."

"You think that if we can't find the actual photo, then..."

She was nodding. "At least we might be able to talk to somebody who knows what was there. It's better than nothing."

Kate opened her mouth to say something, but

Ben looked up, just as she felt a tap on her shoulder. A woman and her husband were standing just behind them.

"I'm sorry to bother you," the woman said. "Are you Katherine Greason?"

Kate grew tense, wondering what she was in for, but managed a polite smile. "Yes, I am."

"We just wanted to tell you how sorry we are about what happened yesterday. We thank the good Lord that he's alright." The man was nodding sympathetically.

"Thank you very much," Kate said.

"Tom's father passed last September," the woman continued. "Your folks looked after everything for us. They did him up real nice, didn't they Tom?" Her husband nodded again. "They treated us just like we were family. I was telling Tom just the other day..."

As the woman continued her monologue, Ben watched, half amused, as Kate's smile turn to stunned disbelief. Thinking quickly, he eased his cell phone under the lip of the table and discretely dialed Kate's number.

The Four Seasons promptly began emanating from her pocketbook and Kate grabbed for it. As she did, Ben cleared his throat and managed a wink.

"I'm sorry. Could you excuse me?" Kate sighed. "I'm expecting an important call. Thank you, though." Seeming slightly disappointed, the couple shuffled off as Kate retrieved her phone.

"Oh, hi. Yes," Kate said, her voice trailing off into a grin as she watched them go. Ben was chuckling.

"That was smooth," she conceded. "I owe you one. I guess I should have seen that coming. My face is all over the news, unfortunately. I guess we should go, before a crowd forms, huh?"

Later that night, over a hastily prepared dinner at Kate's place, they formed a plan of sorts. Ben's firm was located downtown, closest to the county courthouse, allowing him relatively easy access to county real estate records dating back to the incorporation of Stanton in the early nineteen twenties. He would find out what he could about early ownership of both the Greason estate property and the adjoining forest tract, where the old airstrip was presumably still located.

Kate's day-job, on the other hand, placed her squarely at ground zero; in the private residence of Werner-Greason Funeral Home, easily the most likely source of information, but clearly the most dangerous. While she had direct access to both Walter's and Everett's private offices, as well as a file room with years of historical records, her day-to-day responsibilities did not give her a legitimate reason to be in any of these places.

That's where Mort-Man came in. It was the nickname Kate had coined for the high-end mortuary management system they'd installed two years earlier. Mort-man hosted the all important Werner-Greason master-calendar, the undisputed key to running a successful operation, and the one place where she could see where everyone would be, every minute of the day.

She would use it to look for a window of opportunity when both Walter and Everett were safely offsite and the other staff were preoccupied with services. Then, and only then, would she discretely go looking. Ben was reluctant at first to agree, arguing over dessert that it would be too risky, but Kate insisted she could take the heat if she got caught. She was, after all, family.

At eight-forty five Thursday morning, Lieutenant Wallace turned off Tryon Boulevard, into the parking lot of Digital Edge Technologies, the Charlotte imaging firm they'd hired to analyze the civic center security tape. He'd begun the drive in a foul mood, angry at having been ordered by Hughes to courier the tape personally. It wasn't the kind of duty someone of his rank ever pulled. Yet now, as he studied the logo by the door, he found that he was very curious; about the work they did here, but more so about the man on the tape.

He'd spent the last day and a half thinking about it, and something was bothering him. In his considerable experience, the twenty-second hand-off on the tape didn't look the way it should have, the way he would have expected it to. There seemed to be a physical tension between the Greene woman and the man in the picture that he wouldn't normally associate with complicity. It was only slightly discernable on the poor quality image, but it was there, none-the-less, and it gave him a sinking feeling in his gut that he couldn't explain, at least, not yet. Of course, the so-called experts at Digital Edge probably wouldn't even notice.

At noon, Chief Willard Hughes and the county coroner appeared in front of Hawthorne Memorial Hospital and gave a brief statement to the press regarding the results of Margaret Bayer Greene's autopsy. According to the coroner, she had died at approximately twelve forty A.M. on Wednesday morning, from complications resulting from multiple gunshot wounds. As to the question of medications, they had found several potent prescription drugs in her system, along with trace amounts of Dedrafexaline; Dedra-fi for short, a high-risk, experimental antidepressant that had been pulled from medical trials two years earlier.

The drug had performed spectacularly at first, but within six months, several subjects began exhibiting extreme side-effects, some bordering on clinical schizophrenia. Chief Hughes said that they were still trying to determine where and how she obtained it.

"Was the drug responsible for her state of mind at the time of the shooting?" a blond reporter near the front shouted.

The coroner stepped to the microphone, but Hughes covered it with his hand, raising his voice so he would be heard. "I'll let Dr. Forest respond to that, but we aren't taking questions today. We'll provide an opportunity for questions at a later time."

"When?" someone else shouted.

"At a later time," Chief Hughes repeated. He nodded to the coroner and removed his hand from the mike.

"Dedrafexaline is a monoamine oxidase inhibitor," the coroner began. "It modifies the production of certain enzymes within the brain. This class of medications is particularly sensitive to drug-drug interaction and has been shown to worsen the patient's depressive tendencies if improperly used. In Mrs. Greene's case, there were several medications present which may have caused an adverse reaction, including one for hypertension. So, while I cannot give a definitive answer to your question, there is little doubt that drug interactions played a part in her state of mind."

Hughes ended the press conference at that point, amid more shouted questions, and the local stations went back to their regular programming.

"I thought that went well," Steve Crenshaw said through the smoke of his cigarette, as he leaned back and crossed his legs.

Across the desk, Hughes sat watching him with an odd mix of respect and disdain. He'd returned to his locked office to find Crenshaw waiting for him; a calculated move, clearly designed to intimidate. Typically, he allowed no one else in his office while he was out, not even the secretary. "Maybe, for you," Hughes replied. "But I'm going to take some heat for it. This is too big to keep a lid on for long, and you know it. Half the people on the force know we're looking at a second suspect and these guys are being grilled about the case every day by God knows who. Somebody will slip, they always do. Maybe tomorrow, maybe next week, but it'll happen, and once the cat is out of the bag, I won't be able to blow them off like I did today."

"Of course you won't," Crenshaw conceded smoothly. "We're not expecting you to. We just want to know what you know, the minute you know it. And, if it's necessary for security reasons, we may ask for twenty-four hours lead time before you go public with your findings, that's all. How are the interviews going?"

"At last count, we've got two hundred and sixty-eight people on that list, and a good twenty percent of them aren't local; out of state in some cases. Jesus, we've even got a couple from Europe. Even with a first pass phone screening, we'll be lucky to hit most of them by the end of next week."

"You'd think at least one or two of them would have been paying attention."

Hughes grunted. "Yeah, you'd think so, but you might be surprised. I wouldn't hold my breath." His pager went off, but he ignored it, continuing to study his enigmatic guest. "I don't suppose it would do me any good to ask what dog the governor has in this particular hunt."

Crenshaw flashed his greasy smile again as he picked up his coat and stood to leave. "The governor just wants to see justice done, as always." But as he passed, he stopped and put a hand on the corner of Hughes' desk. "You know Willard; this thing has turned up the heat on Michael to get his Crime Taskforce in place. He's counting on finding someone strong from the local level to head it up, and just between you and me, your name is at the top of the list. I don't think it would be very hard to keep it there."

Ben suffered the usual re-entry burns from being out of work for a day. He spent the morning catching up with unanswered emails and phone calls, barely made a staff meeting at ten, and interviewed a painfully unprepared job applicant at eleven. By the time he finally ducked out and headed down to the courthouse, he already felt frustrated and burned out. What he found in the Mercer County real estate records only made things worse.

He reached Kate in the Werner-Greason office, where she was working on inventory planning for the upcoming year. The funeral business purchased early, based partly on projections from previous years and population growth in the area, and partly on the availability and pricing of supplies. It was normally a hectic process, one which Walter and Everett took particular interest in. Orders were often large and mistakes costly.

Kate seemed on edge at first but softened at the sound of his voice. She apologized for not being in a position to talk and asked if Ben could come by after work. "I can give you the cemetery portion of the dime tour," she said softly. "It'll give us some fresh air and get me the hell out of here."

Ben wanted badly to spill what he'd found, or at least give her the condensed version, but he held himself back. He knew she wouldn't like it, and he didn't want to put her in a bad position, especially with her family close by.

Instead, he made the drive across town at five thirty and arrived at Werner-Greason just as a funeral service was wrapping up. Cars streamed past him as he drove up the long, winding drive, and a dozen or so people clustered on the front steps. A young man looked up as Ben's car passed and Ben felt a pang of guilt, as though he were an unwelcome spectator at the scene of an accident – and like an accident, he was quietly relieved it was someone else and not him.

Kate was waiting around back, on the steps of the private entrance, but the moment he stepped out of the car, she knew that something was wrong. Even as her heart sank, she mustered a smile and kissed him. "I'm glad you came over."

"Me too," Ben said. "I just wish I had better news." He glanced nervously around the parking lot. "Is there somewhere we can talk?"

She nodded, taking his hand and leading him

across the parking lot, through a gap in the hedge row. Shadows enveloped them as they traversed a short passage, reminiscent of a hedge maze, before emerging into one of the most beautiful gardens Ben had ever seen. Grass-covered pathways wove among artfully landscaped beds bordered in stone and filled with roses and an assortment of other flowers he did not recognize. The babbling of water from the fountain in a small fish pond filled the air around them, and an ornately carved white gazebo with a cedar shingled roof stood on the far end, ringed with beds of more beautiful flowers. Songbirds perched on a cast iron weathervane that rose from the roof's peak.

Ben gaped. "This is amazing!"

Kate made a sweeping gesture with one hand. "It's Gram's masterpiece," she said. "The men in the family made all the decisions about everything else here, and they didn't want it, but Gram put her foot down. She wanted to make a beautiful place where people could come and shut out the world, just sit and think. She always said it was for the families of the deceased, but I think she needed it as much as they did." Kate sighed. "God knows I came here a lot growing up. It was my private oasis." She squeezed Ben's hand. "So tell me what you found."

He exhaled deeply. "Okay, here goes. For starters, they own it all. Your family owns everything within a mile of this place, in any direction, including the property with the airstrip."

Kate's brow wrinkled in dismay. "They own it? Since when?"

"Since the original land purchase, back in 1944. Andrew bought it, and now Everett's name is on the deeds."

"Are you sure?"

He shrugged. "It's right there in black and white."

Kate's disbelief turned to anger as she tried to assimilate what she was hearing. "So he just lied to us," she growled, taking several steps down the path and whirling back around. "Why am I not surprised? That son-of-a-bitch just made it all up to scare us so we'd stay off the property."

Ben cleared his throat. "That's not all. It gets better, or worse, I guess, depending on how you look at it."

"Of course it does. Fine. Let's hear it."

"You remember how you said they started out small and bought the property in pieces as the business grew?"

"Yeah?"

"That wasn't true either. Between them, Andrew and Mitchell bought all of it from three different people, over the course of one week. Nearly two thousand acres at one shot."

Kate was beginning to feel a little light headed. "Jesus, do you know how much that would have cost, even back then?"

"Yeah. I do. It's right there on the deeds of sale; it adds up to just under half a million dollars. And if that isn't scary enough, get this; it was paid in cash – *cash*!"

Kate stared into the greenish water of the pond and shook her head. "Poor struggling entrepreneurs my ass," she murmured. "Half a million dollars in 1944? Today that would be worth what, several million?"

"Easily, and that doesn't even count the start-up cost for the business itself," Ben said. "And whatever they paid to build all of this."

"They were rich weren't they?" she smirked.
"Filthy rich from day one. They just didn't want anyone to
know, not even their own family."

Ben nodded. "It definitely looks that way."

Kate sat down on a bench beside the water and
began fidgeting with her hands, studying them as if she
were trying to figure something out. Finally, she chuckled
darkly. "All I can think about is how much this reminds
me of the first time I ever saw a dead body."

"How do you mean?" Ben asked, sitting down
beside her.

"I was six or seven, I think. The basement was off
limits, especially the preparation room. I didn't know what
went on in there, but there was this smell. It was weird,
awful, like nothing I'd ever smelled before, and it came
from the door to that room. I kept sneaking back down
there, trying to get the nerve to open the door just a crack,
just enough to see what was making that smell. I was
terrified of what I would see, but I couldn't stay away, no
matter how much I tried."

"So what happened?" Ben asked, already knowing
what the answer would be.

"I finally did it," she sighed. "Unlucky for me, it
was a bad one, a young couple who'd been in a car crash.
God, it took Gram like, a week to calm me down. I never
really got over that."

"Jesus, that's harsh," Ben said. "But I guess I see
what you mean. This is already smelling pretty bad."

She put her hand on his knee and patted it lightly.
"Only this time, there's something a whole lot uglier
behind this door, isn't there? I can feel it. But we're going

to open it anyway."

He knew Kate was right, and briefly, he wondered again if they were doing the right thing. There was a chance, however slim, that she wouldn't be able to cope with the truth, even if they found out what it was. And if she, like most people, harbored an innate instinct to protect her family, she might be turned by it in the face of extreme pressure. If that happened, she would turn against him as well. Any chance to kindle the spark between them would surely die in the process, and they would part ways, possibly even as enemies.

But he knew that Kate would never be able to drop it; they'd already come too far for that. His only hope was that she would be strong enough to stay the course. It was a risk he would have to take.

"I think you're right," he conceded. "I'd say there's a good chance it will get worse, maybe a lot worse," he said. "We have to be very, very careful if we keep going with this."

Kate shook her head. "There's no ifs. We can be as careful as you want, but we have to keep going. Ignorant bliss is one thing, but knowing half the picture is pure torture."

But put his arm around her. "So, how about that tour you promised me? You can show me the gate and the No Trespassing sign you were telling me about. We can take bets on what we'll find when we sneak over the fence and go exploring."

"Be serious," Kate scolded. "It's nothing to joke about."

"Who's joking," he said. And when their eyes met, she realized he wasn't.

A long paved drive separated the Werner-Greason Funeral Home from what Kate referred to as the new cemetery, which spread out across twenty-three acres of gently sloping land on the eastern side of the house. The cemetery was, like most others in the modern day, uniform in all respects; nearly treeless, it was divided by uniform driveways into uniform subsections which were filled with uniformly spaced rows of uniformly sized headstones that lay almost flush with the ground. And like so many other modern cemeteries, for all its uniformity, it had no character whatsoever.

The same could not be said of the old cemetery. Nestled into a tiny, very hilly, uneven corner of the property, it was, in every respect, a classic graveyard. Here, under the shade of two hundred-year-old oaks, narrow, sometimes steep, pathways wound among a sea of headstones of all shapes and sizes.

Tall obelisks and statues were scattered among shorter, vertical markers in random fashion while other gravestones were grouped by family name and surrounded by black, wrought iron fencing. In the farthest corner, at the base of a particularly steep, horseshoe shaped hill, stood an imposing row of mismatched, if ornately carved mausoleum facades. Their double iron doors had long ago succumbed to the elements and now wore a heavy coat of rust, along with newer chains and locks to keep out the curious.

Atop this oddly shaped hill was the oldest of the family plots, dating back, according to Kate, to the early 1800's, and accessible, like those plots on tops of the other hills, by way of steep concrete steps.

With only the resident hosts of birds and squirrels for company, the peace here was nearly total, and Ben understood why Kate found it so appealing. "They don't make them like this anymore do they?" he said, running his hand across the top of a nearby stone.

"It's a shame, really," Kate said. "There's so much atmosphere here; the place is dripping with character. I'm probably weird, but cemeteries never bothered me. They just seem so serene, the good ones anyway. But hey, the times are a-changing, right? It's always about the money. The little square cookie-cutter stones are half the price, you know, and cheaper to maintain; more profit for the funeral vultures. So while the owners get richer, cemeteries get more boring, and the hapless customers are paying as much as they ever did. Don't you just love the circle of life?"

"Ah, when you put it that way, yeah," he grinned.

As they walked hand-in-hand past the row of mausoleums and around the end of the hill, Ben saw the iron fence and the gate that marked the supposed edge of the property. It was adorned with a locked chain and still bore the faded No Trespassing sign that had served Everett so well in keeping the children out of these woods.

They peered through the iron poles of the fence into the woods beyond.

"You didn't say anything about a road," Ben said, pointing to the forest floor. "It comes right to the gate."

"I wouldn't exactly call it a road. It's more of a path, really," Kate frowned.

Ben was looking over his shoulder, in the direction of the funeral home, but the trees obscured his view. "They can't see us very well at all up here can they?"

"Why? What are you thinking?" Kate asked, slightly alarmed at the eager tone in his voice. "You're not wanting to..."

Ben had taken a couple of steps along the fence and was studying the cross-bars at the middle and top of it as if measuring. "We can get over this," he said.

"Ben no! The grounds people drive all over the property in those little green yard-carts. If someone comes, we'll be screwed."

But Ben had already thrown one foot up to the middle cross-bar and was pulling himself up and over. Kate looked frantically around them, but there was no one in sight. "You're crazy!"

He swung his other leg over the top and dropped nimbly to the ground on the other side. "There, no big deal. You're next." He put his hands through the fence and laced his fingers together, offering her a step.

"Jesus," she muttered, casting another wary glance over her shoulder before stepping into his hands. "You're lucky I'm wearing jeans and tennis shoes."

They found the wooded road in surprisingly good condition, stopping several times to examine what appeared to be a recently cut sapling or a tire tread mark in the dirt.

"Someone's maintaining this," Ben said. "Do you ever see anyone back here?"

Kate shook her head. "I've never seen anyone set foot in here, not even Carl, our groundskeeper. That's one of the reasons I believed that bullshit line about the crazy neighbors. I figured if the men in my family weren't willing to risk it, I sure as hell wasn't."

"Never underestimate the power of propaganda," Ben mused, scuffing his shoe in the dirt.

"Propaganda, lies, it all amounts to the same thing," Kate muttered as she pushed a branch away from her face. "So who did own this property before my snake-in-the-grass ancestors bought it?"

"This section and the land the cemeteries and the house are on all belonged to a guy named Wayne Holt. The land farther east belonged to a widow named Reaves, Bonnie or Betsy, I think. And the land west of the house belonged to some other guy. But the aerial photo we saw is almost all the Holt property."

"And of course, he's probably been dead for years, right?"

"He popped up, or I should say, his family popped up on the census data in the western North Carolina mountains, in Bryson City. And yes, he died in 1997. But he has a son, Eddie Holt, who still lives there. If my math is any good, the guy would be old enough to remember this place."

"Well that's something," Kate replied.

"So, what are you doing Saturday?" Ben grunted as he stepped over a fallen log. "Feel like a road trip?"

"I don't see that we have much choice. Without that picture, he's our only shot."

"And it's a long one," Ben added heavily. "We don't even know what we're looking for."

As the woods began to thin, the road straightened, and they saw blue sky ahead. Ben stopped suddenly. "What the hell is that?"

Through a gap in the trees, Kate saw what he was

pointing at. It resembled a paved road, running perpendicular to the one they were on, but it was much wider than an average two-lane road, and its surface was not black, but rather a mottled patchwork of earthen colors. They hurried down the last straightaway for a better look and cautiously emerged into an enormous clearing, beside what could only be an airstrip. Cutting a vast and unnatural looking swath through the forest, the raised runway was twenty-five yards wide, straight as a ruler, and so long they could barely see the end of it.

A heavy netted fabric, painted in greens and browns, covered the entire length of the paved surface. "This is camo netting!" Ben exclaimed, squatting down and running a hand across it. "Acres of it! They use it in the military to cover equipment in the field. It's practically invisible from the air. I've even heard of pot growers using it to hide their crops."

Over Kate's objections, he grabbed an edge of the fabric and pulled, walking several steps backward, toward the center of the runway and exposing the pavement beneath. "Look at that!" he said, dropping the edge of the netting. "This is all wrong."

They'd agreed that the airstrip from the photo if it still existed at all, would have been abandoned decades earlier, and would no doubt be in a complete state of disrepair. But the surface he'd exposed was not timeworn and broken at all. It was a smooth, deep black, with bright white lines and arrows. "It's even got low-profile runway lights, for God's sake," he said. "Somebody ran power all the way out here."

"How is this possible?" Kate demanded. "Nobody uses an airstrip for fifty years, and it looks like it was painted yesterday?"

"Kate, are you sure you don't remember hearing planes coming or going – any time at all?"

"Look, we're not that far from the house. I mean, I know I'm a little distracted sometimes, but I'm not stunned. Those things are really loud when they take off." Kate looked anxiously around them. "Are *you* sure that this property is in Everett's name? What if you made a mistake?"

Ben shook his head and started pacing. "No, there's no mistake. The survey drawings were there, plain as day. The spot we're on isn't even close to the border. This tract goes on in that direction for another hundred acres, and the name on the deed was Everett R. Greason."

"Okay then," Kate said. "I've got an idea. We're both in decent shape. Let's each take a side, jog it. There has to be another road coming in from somewhere else. Whoever's using this place sure as hell isn't driving in and out through our cemetery."

Ben agreed, and they broke into a slow jog, scanning the tree line on opposite sides of the runway, but several minutes later when they reached the far end, they'd found no sign of a road or path of any kind.

"What the hell is going on here?" Kate panted, leaning over and putting her hands on her knees. "This is totally screwed up."

The sun had begun to fall low in the sky, and long shadows were beginning to creep across the airstrip, giving the camouflage-colored tarmac an even more unsettling, almost sinister look.

"I don't know, but I'm ready to get out of here. It's getting late, and we don't want to get caught out here after dark. We got what we came for," Ben said, still a little out of breath.

"Yeah, but it raises a hell of a lot more questions than it answers," Kate grumbled as they started back down the runway. "Someone goes to the trouble and cost of keeping up a first-class, private airstrip that they never use – *for fifty years*? Why would someone do that?"

Ben wiped his forehead with the back of his hand. "Only one reason I can think of; contingency. If you're not using a place like this to traffic something illegal, then you're keeping it for peace of mind. You want to know that you can fly someone or something out undetected, on a moment's notice."

"Good theory, but there's only one problem. Look around; no planes, no hangar."

"That's all high maintenance stuff compared to a strip of asphalt. If they want to keep this hidden, then they'd have to keep the planes somewhere else, probably close by." Ben noticed that Kate seemed far away. "What is it? Did I say something?"

She shook her head. "No, it's just me. I was just thinking that Everett always seemed like an asshole to me growing up, and most of the time my dad wasn't much better. I was always intimidated by them, but I can't ever remember being afraid – until now."

5

The shadows along the wooded road were deeper now, as Ben and Kate made their way back toward the cemetery, trying to pick up the pace before darkness overtook them. As they came within sight of the gate, Kate grabbed Ben's arm without warning, and pulled him low to the ground, throwing a finger over her lips for quiet. She pointed toward the gate.

Through a curtain of branches, Ben saw two men huddled together beside a four-wheeled, electric yard cart, just on the other side of the fence, examining something one of the men held in his hand.

"Shit!" Kate hissed. "That's Walter and Carl, the grounds-keeper."

"What are they looking at?" Ben whispered.

Kate's breath caught in her chest as she squinted at the object in her father's hand. She grabbed her purse and began rifling through it. "Damn it! It's not here. Oh, no," she groaned.

"What?" Ben implored.

"I think that's my cell phone. It's not in my purse! I must have dropped it when we climbed the fence. We're busted."

"Wait!" Ben urged. "Just wait. They may not come in here looking. If they do, we'll leave the road and hide in the woods, okay?"

She nodded, but he could feel her trembling next to him. His own heart raced as they waited for what seemed an eternity, unable to hear anything except muffled voices. Finally, the men climbed into the cart and drove silently away, taking the phone with them.

"Come on," Kate urged. "We have to move. They'll go looking for me. They know I'm still around because my car's still in the lot. For that matter, so is yours, and they've never even met you."

They jogged the rest of the way to the fence and, after checking that the coast was clear, scrambled back over. "This is terrible timing," she continued, as they hurried through the old cemetery, past the horseshoe hill and the now fully shaded row of mausoleums. "Since the shooting, everyone's been acting paranoid. I mean way worse than usual; a lot of private meetings and closed-door conference calls. They're definitely on edge. This is just going to throw up a big red flag. I'm so sorry."

"It's not your fault," Ben said. "Shit happens. They can't prove we were in there anyway." But he wasn't so sure. The stakes in their search seemed to be getting higher by the hour, and with each new discovery, he became less certain that Kate's family connection would afford them any leniency, should they get caught. These people were obviously hiding something dangerous, something that he now believed they would do nearly anything to protect.

Kate took Ben on a shortcut, behind a tall row of cypress trees that adjoined the old cemetery, bypassing the newer section altogether. From there, a narrow path led through the edge of the woods and came out on a sidewalk, to the rear of the garden they'd stopped in earlier.

Across the valley, at the top of the cemetery, two yard-carts were parked, their drivers silhouetted in the setting sun as they sat and watched.

"Unbelievable," Kate said, pulling Ben through the hedge and into the garden. "Carl's got a couple of yard-apes posted as sentries. I don't like this at all."

"What do we need to do?"

"Get you out of here, for starters. I'll have a lot easier time talking my way out of this if I don't have to factor you into the story. No offense. We can catch up later. I need to tell you a couple of things I found on the calendar."

He kissed her briefly before they headed back out to the parking lot behind the house, where an automatic timer had already turned the porch lights on. Kate walked Ben to his car, and he was just opening the door when a voice called from the open bay of a garage. "There you are."

Kate flinched and turned to face her father, who emerged from the shadows, still holding her phone in his hand. "I've been looking for you. I found your phone up in Lark Hill." He smiled coolly, but his tone made it clear that he expected an explanation."

"Thank God," Kate stammered. "I was afraid I'd lost it. Ah, Walter, this is Ben Tuttle, a friend of mine. Ben, this is my father, Walter Greason."

Ben started to extend his hand, but Kate's father made no move to return the gesture. Instead, his eyes remained fixed on his daughter. "Doing a little exploring this evening, were you?" he asked.

"This is Ben's first time here. I was giving him the dime tour, and I must have dropped it. We stopped back by the garden to talk, and I just forgot about it. I'm really glad you found it." She held out her hand for the phone, but her father made no move.

"You know," he said, still smiling. "You should be more careful around the property lines. Someone over there may think you're trespassing. I'd hate to see you or your friend get shot."

Ben swallowed hard, unnerved by the hard edge in man's voice.

Kate chuckled feebly. "You're always so dramatic. I'm sure they're not that bad. Anyway, I know to stay off the neighbors' land. You've only warned me a thousand times."

Finally, he handed her the phone and turned to go back inside. "We need to go over those orders before you leave tonight. I think you used an outdated vendor list. We're not using Westmoreland Casket for the oak line anymore, and several of the other items need corrections." As if his meaning wasn't clear enough, he glanced at his watch before walking away.

"I'll be there in a few minutes," Kate said, more impatiently than she meant to. But Walter did not reply as he disappeared into recesses of the garage, leaving them both glaring behind him.

Though each of them burned with indignation at her father's brazen rudeness, Ben could only guess at the deep sense of shame that gripped Kate. Even as she seemed to wither from the inside out, neither of them spoke what was on their minds, certain that the ogre-of-a-man was still watching them.

Instead, in what was surely an open display of her contempt for Walter, she stepped into Ben, wrapped her arms dramatically around his waist, and kissed him deeply, letting her tongue play between his lips. Unsure at first what to make of her theatrics, he hesitated briefly before succumbing to her teasing and kissing her with abandon. Screw the old man if he doesn't like it, Ben thought.

And from his vantage point in the shadows, Walter Greason most certainly did not.

On Friday morning, just after roll-call, Lieutenant Wallace called officers Pearl and Rogers into his office for a progress report on their interviews in the civic center shooting. Their results were more disappointing than even he expected.

"No one?" Wallace barked. "How far down the list are you?"

"We've taken statements from everyone through McMurray, sir," Pearl offered, shuffling the papers in front of him. "That's one-thirty-two out of two-sixty-eight."

"You've got to be shitting me! No one in a hundred and thirty people can ID this guy? For Christ's sake, he and the Greene woman weren't hiding in a coat closet! They were standing in the middle of the God-damned lobby!"

"Yes sir, that's a fact," Rogers nodded solemnly. "Approximately half that number claim they remember seeing the old woman in the lobby, but only nineteen of them saw her talking to anyone."

Officer Pearl cleared his throat. "Of that group, eight stated they got a good enough look to give us a description, but quite frankly sir, they're all over the board. We didn't even get a unanimous on white male, dark hair. One of them claims she saw a young white female with short blond hair; the other saw a black man."

Wallace closed his eyes and gripped the bridge of his nose tightly with two fingers, but said nothing.

"As it stands now," Rogers concluded. "None of them are willing to pick the guy out of a lineup. They won't even agree to sit down with the sketch guy. Sorry, sir, we're still hoping to get lucky."

"Damn it, you better put luck on the back burner and start digging." Wallace snapped. "Do you know how much shit is going to be flying around here if the press gets wind of this and we're still running around with our dicks in our hands?"

But even as Wallace was angrily dismissing the two officers, Chief Hughes found himself sidestepping the question when confronted by a news team outside the station. The press, it seemed, had already gotten word of a possible second suspect.

"We have no evidence to support that," he replied, with a wave of his hand. "As I've said, our investigation is continuing, and it would be premature to speculate on our findings before it's concluded."

"Chief," a man shouted. "It's rumored that..."

Hughes cut the man off. "If I took the time to speak to every rumor and theory that's flying around out there right now, I wouldn't have any left over to do my job, and I'm not sure the taxpayers would appreciate that.

Now if you'll excuse me, I've got work to do."

Four blocks from the Stanton police station, in his third story office, Everett Greason opened his desk drawer and retrieved the small bottle of pink pills he kept there. He'd forgotten exactly what they were and frankly, he didn't care. His doctor had prescribed them years earlier for anxiety, and they'd always worked wonders – at least until now.

All week he'd watched stories about himself, now the benevolent community father, now the driven, self-motivated entrepreneur, now the elder statesman; whose life was nearly tragically cut short by a senseless act of violence. It should, by all accounts, have been his finest hour. Even Mike Chase said so. The governor was, after all, enjoying his resurgence as a result of the fiasco.

But rather than basking in the glow of a sympathetic media and riding the wave of community support to even greater political gain, Everett Greason was becoming sullen and withdrawn. Each day, he had been less able to focus on anything except the growing threat, unseen by those around him, yet conceivably more dangerous than any he'd faced in half a century. And each day his resolve grew to stamp out the threat, in whatever form it revealed itself, no matter what the cost, human or otherwise. After fifty-five years, there was far, far too much at stake.

Kate drove to Ben's house that evening, after a tense working session with her father. She'd managed somehow to keep her demeanor calm, despite the storm of questions that raged in her mind; despite the gnawing fear that her father was not what he pretended to be. And while he hadn't questioned her openly again about the cell phone incident, his manner had been noticeably more guarded. He'd dropped a well-placed comment or two about loyalty and a family's right to privacy, and several times, from the corner of her eye, she'd noticed him watching her, studying her with a fixed gaze as if trying to make up his mind about something. The effect had made her skin crawl, but she'd pretended not to notice.

Ben was cooking pasta when Kate arrived with her overnight bag. He'd already printed out satellite photos of the Werner-Greason property, including several detail shots of the airstrip site, both sections of the cemetery, and the house and outbuildings. If Eddie Holt's memory needed jogging, they would have to suffice.

He'd also managed to find a FAA listing for private airstrips in the area. There was no mention of one within ten miles of the Greason property.

"Wouldn't they all have to be registered?" Kate asked as she pulled a loaf of French bread from his tightly packed freezer.

"The legitimate ones would. But if this one is designed for one-time use, then they wouldn't give a rat's ass about a FAA fine. Whoever, or whatever would be long gone by then."

Kate knew she should be hungry, but her appetite had always dwindled in times of stress, and now, she barely touched her food, choosing to sip her wine instead. "So what did you tell Eddie Holt?" she asked.

"The truth," Ben shrugged and finished chewing. "More or less. I told him we were doing some research on the history of the Werner-Greason property and we couldn't find anything from that period. I said we just wanted to talk to someone who remembered the place."

"And he agreed?"

"Not at first. He thought we were related to the Greasons."

Kate stared. "*Hello.* We are. One of us, anyway."

Ben patted his mouth with his napkin. "Ah, not for our visit with Eddie tomorrow, I'm afraid. I had to think up something fast. You'll be playing Kate Tuttle, my wife."

Kate's face flushed before she had time to check herself. "Ben, you didn't say anything about that. What if he figures it out?"

"He won't. Just throw in a few 'dears' and a couple of 'honeys' and he'll never know the difference."

"Aren't you the sexist? Why didn't he want to talk to anyone from my family?" Kate smirked.

"He didn't say. Maybe he will tomorrow."

Ben glanced skeptically at Kate's nearly untouched dinner. "Not so hungry?"

She reached across the table and took his hand. "It's not the food, and it's definitely not the chef. I just can't get all of this off my mind. It's wearing me out. And speaking of that; what time do we need to leave in the morning?"

"My alarm's set for six," Ben said.

Kate rolled her eyes. "Great."

They awoke the next morning to a heavy gray sky and began their trip in a steady rain, heading west on Interstate 40, into the Blue Ridge Mountains, toward

Asheville, Fontana Lake, and ultimately the small rail town of Bryson City. Their moods were introspective, each of them mulling over the events of the last few days, and both of them anxious about meeting Eddie Holt.

Ben tried several times to lighten the conversation by talking about his college years at Appalachian State, or his childhood antics in Boone, but Kate seemed far away. Quietly, he began to worry.

A small part of him, the part that was falling hard for her, had begun to hope that Wayne Holt's son would remember nothing, that their meeting would be fruitless. At least she would have no new reason to be afraid. That part of him secretly wished that all of this would go away, for her sake, for *their* sake. What did it matter, after all, if Everett Greason was a crook? They were all crooks in some way, weren't they?

But clinging to wishes was pointless. In his gut, he knew that they couldn't walk away, no matter what the outcome; no matter what the cost. And everything they'd found so far told him the cost would be high.

The Whistle-Stop Diner sat by the tracks in Bryson City's historic downtown, flanked by shops teeming with tourists. Saturday was the busiest day of the week for the Great Smokey Mountain Railroad, Bryson City's most popular attraction. The restored 1895 steam locomotive carried passengers in open-sided cars on a scenic ride through the southern tip of the Smokey Mountains, past Fontana Lake and the Nantahala River.

From their booth by the window of the diner, Kate and Ben were transfixed by the arrival of the morning train, and were busy watching its passengers depart, when someone spoke. "Excuse me, Ben Tuttle?"

They turned to see a burly man in blue coveralls and work boots standing beside their table; his hands thrust deep into his pockets. His hair was disheveled and old grease stains marked his bare forearms. The man appeared cautious, even skeptical of Ben and Kate.

Ben stood up. "Yes, Eddie Holt?"

"That's me."

"Good to see you. Glad you could come. This is Kate, my wife."

Kate's stomach gave a small lurch, and she feigned a gracious smile.

Eddie sat down opposite them in the booth, looking decidedly uncomfortable, and turned his gaze to the train outside.

"We appreciate your time," Ben began. "As I said on the phone..."

"Before we get started," Eddie interrupted, catching them both off guard. "I need your word that that Greason fellow didn't put you up to this."

"No," Kate said. "Not at all. We're just interested in the history of the place, Stanton I mean. That's all."

"Absolutely," Ben agreed.

Eddie nodded. "Alright then."

Ben could tell that their lunch guest was a no-bullshit kind of guy, so he wasted no time in getting to the point. "We were looking back to the later nineteen thirties and early forties in Stanton. Specifically, in the area where the Greasons set up their business. We know that Andrew Greason bought the land from your father in 1944, but we can't find any photos of that area from the early years before your father sold it." Ben shrugged. "We know you were pretty young, but we're hoping you can tell us what would have been there around that time."

The waitress appeared at their table and Ben insisted that everything be on one check.

Eddie thanked him and scratched the deep stubble on his chin, before responding. "Well, you're right. I wasn't more than a little kid then, but I reckon I still remember the place pretty well. My daddy had a good spread down there. He farmed some of it; grazed horses up in them hills by the highway, seventeen I guess it was."

"Did your family live there, on that property?" Ben asked.

"We lived just west of there, on route twelve. My daddy used to carry us on the back of the pickup down there to feed the horses, and we'd go work the hay a couple of times a year. That's about it."

Ben pulled the aerial photos from a manila folder in his bag and slid one across the table. It was the widest shot, showing all of the cleared property and some of the forest. "I printed this off the internet so we could show you the piece of property we're most interested in."

Eddie studied it carefully for a moment. "So what's all this stuff?" he asked.

"It's the Werner-Greason funeral home," Kate chimed in. "I know it's hard to recognize from directly overhead."

"I wouldn't know," Eddie grunted. "I ain't been there since we left, my daddy neither." He gave a low whistle. "That's a whopper of a graveyard they put in."

"They just added all this new section here to the old one that was already on the hill," Kate explained.

Eddie frowned. "What old one?"

Kate pointed to a small area in the photo. "Here," she said. "These little dots are the old headstones and markers, and these are the paved paths."

"Why are you calling it old?" he asked.

"It's nearly two hundred years old," Ben said. "Some of the markers there are from the early eighteen hundreds."

Eddie held up a hand. "Whoa, now. Back up a minute. I'm not sure we're talking about the same piece of land. There wasn't any graveyard on *our* land."

"Yes, but this is where the horses were," Kate corrected. "Not where you lived."

"I know what piece of property I'm looking at," Eddie said, a note of impatience creeping into his voice. "This here's highway seventeen, and this is the pond where we used to go fishing. And right here, where you say this graveyard is, was, whatever, that's where our horse barn used to be. I went there a hundred times, lady. We played all over them fields, and I know damn-well there wasn't no graveyard there."

Ben felt a strange, sick feeling wash over him like he was falling in a dream, only this was no dream. He and Kate exchanged a worried glance but tried to mask their concern.

Suddenly, Kate laughed and tore the aerial photo in two, then quartered it as she turned to Ben. "Sweetie I told you this stuff off the internet was trash. Somebody doctored this up. That has to be it; probably just trying to send suckers like us on a wild goose chase." Her laugh seemed genuine, but Eddie wasn't buying it.

He was looking hard at Ben now as if he suspected he was somehow being duped. "You've been to this place, haven't you? You told me how old some them stones are, remember?"

Kate held her breath and watched Ben's face, wondering how he could possibly maneuver out of this one. But he didn't try.

"Look, Eddie," he sighed. "We're just trying to figure this thing out. I'm sure you're telling us the truth, but we *have* been there. Kate grew..."

"I grew up near there," Kate said, cutting Ben off and nudging him with her knee. "My family knew the Greasons and I went there a few times when I was a little girl, to that cemetery I mean." She shrugged.

But Eddie's frown only grew deeper. "Look, I smell some kind of bullshit here, no offense ma'am, and I don't much like it," he said, sliding out of the booth and standing to leave. "I don't remember meeting those folks, but my daddy never had too much good to say about 'em. If this is what you're telling' me it is, then I'd say you need to be talking' straight to the horse, not to me. I've got a drive shaft needs fixing', so I'll be on my way. Good luck with whatever it is you folks are doing."

He started to walk away, but Kate put a hand on his arm. "I'm sorry," she said. "Could I just ask you one more thing, please?"

Eddie did not answer, but stopped and waited.

"Why did you or your father never go back there if that's where you grew up?"

He turned to her and snorted with contempt. "Cause that was part of the deal, lady. Old man Greason offered my daddy way more than that land was worth. To this day I still don't know how much. But my daddy had to agree to pick up his whole family and move 'em out here, two hundred miles away. But that wasn't the worst of it; he had to agree to never come back, not him, not any of us. Never. Now what kind of a man does something like that? He looked between Kate and Ben one last time and walked away. "Ya'll have a good day."

6

Autumn had come to the mountains, and as the last remnants of the rain cleared, a crystal blue sky framed patches of rich, golden yellows and fiery reds breaking out in the landscape all around them. But Kate and Ben weren't watching the scenery. Since they'd left Bryson City, still reeling from their conversation with Eddie Holt, they'd been engaged in a heated debate about his claims.

More agitated than ever, Kate had begun drumming on the armrest with her fingertips, stopping between comments to chew on the side of a fingernail. "I don't know how he could be wrong either," she finally snapped. "But he is. For one thing, not all of the graves up there are older than 1945, remember? The dates more or less radiate out from oldest to newest; in the order, they added graves. There must be hundreds of stones with dates later than forty-five."

"Fine," Ben said. "Maybe those are legit. But that doesn't change anything. The whole section we walked through to get to that fence was old; those mausoleums, the stones, everything. I don't remember a single date over there newer than 1900. That's the part we should be

121

worried about."

"Ben, you don't seriously believe this guy, do you?"

He raised his eyebrows and shrugged. "I don't know what to believe, honestly. The guy has no reason to lie. And I don't think he was confused about the property; the road and the lake are unmistakable landmarks."

"So you think Andrew and Mitchell conjured a cemetery out of thin air? Just went down to Cemeteries-R-Us, and picked one out? That's what you're suggesting. Honestly, Ben, I grew up there, running around in that place, doing séances with my friends at Halloween, studying there on a blanket in high school." She shook her head. "Christ, I even made out with Tim Nash under that huge oak tree after one of our dances."

Ben frowned. "You made out in a graveyard?"

"That's not the point," she huffed. "Everything about it is really old. You saw those gravestones yourself. They've got that black mold stuff on them, and they're worn down and chipped. It takes a long time for granite to wear down like that."

"Look, I don't know what they did, or how they did it, but I think that's why they took that aerial photo out of the collection. We kept thinking there had to be something important in it, but maybe that's the point; there's nothing in it but fields and a barn. Maybe that photo is so damned important because it proves the old part of the graveyard wasn't there at all. It fits doesn't it? Why else would they want Holt and his family to practically leave the state and never come back? Can you think of another good reason? Cause at this point, I'd welcome another suggestion."

She threw her hands up in the air. "Fine! Let's suspend reality for a minute, for the sake of argument, and say you're right. You're not, but we'll pretend you are. Why exactly would they fake a cemetery?"

Ben felt himself becoming irritated. "Damn it, Kate; you read the letter. It says that Andrew and Mitchell were deceiving the people of Stanton, right? I don't know why that's what we're trying to figure out."

When he turned to look at her, she'd fallen silent. Her expression told him that the truth had been there all along. She'd only been arguing with him because the idea was so surreal, so wildly improbable, it had shaken her to her core. What he saw in her eyes at that moment was more than fear, it was helplessness. She was watching the very foundation of her world beginning to crack, and she was powerless to stop it.

He reached across the center console and took her hand. "I'm sorry. I don't mean to be impatient. I know this is hard."

"Do you?" Kate asked, her emotion beginning to show. "This isn't hard. It's completely fucked up." She turned and looked out the window, but did not let go of his hand.

They rode in silence for several minutes before she wiped her eyes and turned to him again. "How could we prove it?"

"What?" Ben asked, caught off guard by her question.

"If Lark Hill is fake, how could we prove it?"

"I was just thinking about that. You said something back there about granite taking a long time to age. Do you know if there are different types of granite, different grades?"

She nodded. "Definitely. I heard a lot about that growing up. There've been some pretty big scandals in the funeral business over sub-standard granite being sold at premium prices and..." She stopped mid-sentence and chewed on her lower lip. "The families sued because, after ten years, the stones looked like they were a hundred years old."

"Exactly," Ben said excitedly. "So you get a bunch of sub-par stones, carve old dates in them, maybe sandblast them a little..."

"And within a few years," Kate finished, "you've got a reasonable facsimile of a two hundred-year-old graveyard."

"What sized piece of granite would a stone-mason need to be able to tell the grade?"

"Not much at all, maybe just a good sized chip," Kate replied. "And the grounds crew would never notice. So many of the gravestones out there are already chipped, you could probably find a piece on the ground."

Her face darkened suddenly, and she wrinkled her brow.

"What?" Ben asked. "What is it?"

"If the pre-1945 headstones really are fake, what about the graves?"

"Jesus," Ben said. "Good question."

"I mean, is there anyone buried there at all?"

Ben turned a worried eye in her direction. "If those headstones are bogus, then I sure as hell hope not."

That night, as TV news reports continued to follow the continuing investigation into the attempted assassinations of the governor and Everett Greason, Ben learned that there were rumors of a second suspect. The reporter referred to a possible accomplice; specifically, a young white male.

Even as an officer told reporters that he could "neither confirm nor deny" those rumors, Ben felt a queasy chill come over him, and his heart began to race. When Kate tried to reassure him, he only became agitated.

"I knew this was going to happen," he said, jumping up and pacing the room. "I'm screwed if they figure out who I am. We both are because if they find me, they're going to find you. Kate, we could be arrested and charged."

"Charged with what, talking to an old woman?"

"Withholding evidence! The letter, remember? If they know about me, then they know she gave me the envelope."

"But they don't know. You heard it yourself. Ben, if they had any hard information, they'd have picked you up in a heartbeat."

Ben was still pacing, rubbing the back of his neck with one hand, and he didn't respond.

"Look, I dragged you into this," Kate said, taking him by the arm. "This is my problem; it's not yours. If you want to go to them and give them the letter I'll understand, believe me. Maybe that's what we should have done in the first place, I just..."

"No. We're not taking this to anyone, at least not yet," Ben said at last. "The only way out of this is to finish it. All we've got right now are pieces that don't add up to anything. If we cash in now, it's for nothing. We have to risk staying in the game long enough to find out what's going on, so we'll have enough proof to make it all..."

"Stick," she finished darkly, knowing what he was thinking, even if he didn't want to say it.

"Worthwhile, I was going to say. If we bail now, you may never know what they're hiding. I'm not sure either of us could live with that."

"So, what do you want to do?"

Ben walked to the window and looked out at the night. "I want to hurry," he said.

Sunday morning presented a perfect window of opportunity for them to inspect Lark Hill. According to Kate, no one on the grounds crew at Werner-Greason would be working that day, and Walter and Everett would be attending church services, along with Carl Lentz, the head grounds keeper. Church was to them, she explained quite sarcastically, an exercise in public relations, a covert sales opportunity not to be missed. As a result, their attendance was unwavering.

Sunday also traditionally brought the heaviest traffic into the cemetery. It was the day most people chose to visit the grave of loved ones or walk the pathways that crisscrossed the gently sloping valley. Some of them even wandered into Lark Hill, drawn by curiosity or perhaps a need for the type of comfort only such places can provide.

The extra people would help camouflage Ben and Kate's presence there. With tensions in the family already running higher than normal, Kate knew they couldn't afford another confrontation.

This time, however, their visit to the old graveyard was different. As they walked among its ancient trees, crusty weathered stones, and iron fences, they looked around them with skepticism and doubt. Still, the authenticity of the place seemed absolute, and they soon found themselves struggling with the theories they'd so readily put forth the day before. Kate, in particular, wore a faint grimace as she inspected stone after stone, sometimes running her foot over a patch of grass or stopping to stamp her foot as if she half expected the ground beneath them to be hollow. She felt betrayed, visibly repulsed by the idea that her lifelong familiarity with what amounted to an old friend, had all been a lie.

Ben nodded politely to a woman passing by with her little girl and waved Kate over when they were out of earshot. "I'm having a hard time with this," he confessed.

"You think *you* are?" Kate snorted. "Look at all this! I don't see anything phony about any of it. How could they have done all this?"

"I know," Ben said, pulling out the pad and pen he had in his pocket and handing to Kate. "Let's just stick with the plan. We'll do our due-diligence, and then we'll know, right?"

She took the pad and pen, and they walked together to the steep horseshoe hill, where the oldest graves were.

"I'll take the mausoleums," Kate offered.

"I'll get those inside the fence, up top," Ben countered. "And pick up any loose pieces you find. We'll need them."

Kate kept a close watch on the time as they copied down names and dates of death, signaling Ben on two occasions when other visitors approached. They'd agreed it would be best not to let anyone see what they were doing,

127

for fear of arousing curiosity or even suspicion.

Everett had often bragged over the years that there was nothing that went on at Werner-Greason that he didn't know about. Kate had always considered it an exaggeration, and now more than ever, she hoped she was right.

Beside the mausoleum facades, she found several large chips of granite, the largest of which was nearly the size of her palm. Ben found a piece as well, at the base of a gravestone that had been chipped by a falling tree limb. When they'd each copied several dozen names, they met again in the curve of the horseshoe to compare notes.

"How far back do yours go?" he asked.

"1833 is my earliest," she replied, skimming the list. "Avery Youngblood. How about you?"

"The ones in that fenced in area up there have got to be the oldest. I could barely read some of them. I've got 1804, 1807, and possibly 1802. There are families up there, even a few markers for kids. And the inscriptions, they're all different, different style, different look." Ben shook his head. "If this is a con-job, it's major league, that's all I can say."

When they had made their way back to the parking lot, Ben agreed to wait in the car for Kate while she ran inside to get something from the office. She ducked in the back door of the residence and made a b-line for the office, where she copied contact information for three stone-works businesses in the area, one in Stanton, and two farther out in the county. She was hurrying back down the hall, hoping to sneak out without being seen, when she nearly ran into her grandmother, who was emerging from the kitchen with a freshly poured scotch in her hand.

Edna squawked and pulled her drink out of harm's way, sloshing several drops onto the carpet in the process. "Oh, Katie! You scared me to death. I wasn't expecting you today."

"Hi Gram," Kate said. "Sorry! I didn't mean to scare you."

"Give me a hug!" Edna interrupted, squeezing Kate with her available arm. "You picked a perfect time for a visit! They're all down at Jesus hour buying votes and digging up stiffs. It'll just be us girls."

Kate winced. "I'm sorry Gram, I didn't come for a visit. I just stopped to get something. There's someone waiting for me in the car."

"Oh, I see," she grinned. "Is it that cute turtle-boy?"

"Gram, it's Tuttle, Ben Tuttle," Kate scolded as she looked nervously at her watch.

"Oops, didn't mean for that to slip out. Turtle, Tuttle. Tuttle, Turtle. It helps me remember things." She took a sip of her drink and patted Kate's arm. "I hope he's nice to you. Is he?"

"Yes Gram. He's very nice to me. Listen, I hate to run, but I..."

"That's fine, dear; you run on." Edna kissed her cheek and Kate started into the kitchen.

"Let's plan on dinner Tuesday, alright?" Edna called after her. "The boys will be away all day in New York to pick somebody up. I mean, pick up *some body*," she chuckled. "Okay?"

"Sure Gram, I'll try," Kate called back,

remembering the calendar entry she'd seen in Mort-man for Tuesday. The whole day had been blocked in for both Everett and Walter, with no event description other than, NY. On her way to the car, it occurred to her that dinner would be the perfect cover for an evening in the residence. Snooping in the offices during the day would be risky with staff still on the clock, but during the evening, with the staff gone for the day and Edna sequestered in her apartment, she would have unfettered access. Yes, she thought, as Ben smiled at her from the driver's seat, I'll definitely be coming for dinner.

Reed Stone Works was located on the north side of town, in an industrial section that housed a scrap-metal reclamation plant and a tire warehouse. The modest facility produced a variety of stone products for construction and landscaping, as well as granite monuments and grave markers for regional funeral homes. Kate arrived promptly when they opened for business on Monday morning.

She'd chosen them specifically because they weren't a prime vendor for her family's business, and as a result, there was less chance she'd be recognized. Walter kept their contact information in the office and used them under exceptional circumstances, but the bulk of Werner-Greason's work had always been contracted to Beckley, a much larger company whose founder had a long-standing friendship with Everett.

The receptionist in Reed's small, shoddy looking office, asked Kate to follow her out to the yard, to talk to someone named Chad. They walked through a half-acre dirt lot, crowded with stacks of uncut stone slabs and loose piles of rocks, before spotting Chad. He was rough-looking, balding man with a wide gap between his front teeth that showed every time he smiled. He wore orange earplugs to drown out the deafening whine of stone saws that filled the dusty air around them and only removed them when he'd motioned Kate inside one of the buildings.

Over the ringing in her ears, Kate introduced herself as Cindy Johnson and showed him the chips they'd gathered from Lark Hill. He pursed his lips and inspected each one in turn before speaking. "Miss Johnson, is it? This is some shitty stone, pardon my French, but it is. Where did you get this?"

Kate was prepared for his question. "My brother is having problems with a contractor from out of town. I think they used this granite for one of the projects and I agreed to bring it down here for you to look at."

The man scowled. "Well I won't ask you who he's dealing with, but if he's already paid for the job, he got screwed. I'm not even sure this *is* granite. We like to use a dark-grade Barre or Georgia, sometimes a medium, but in contracting you want durability." Seeing the blank look on Kate's face, he explained. "It comes in dark, medium, and light grade, depending on how dense it is." He shook his head and spat. "Hell, even light-grade granite would be harder than this, and we almost never use light. We wouldn't go anywhere near something like this."

"So if they did use it, what would happen?" Kate asked, already knowing what his answer would be, but somehow wanting to hear him say it.

"Well, stone decays, over time – any kind of stone. But if it's high-grade, that can take thousands of years. On the flip-side, if you use shitty product, like this, you can see it starting to decay in thirty or forty years, which is overnight in the stone business." Chad handed the samples back to her. "I think if I were you, I'd tell my brother to go find himself a good attorney."

Chad escorted Kate back to the office and stood at the window, watching her as she walked to her car. "She looked awfully familiar to me," he said to the short, rotund woman behind the desk. "I've seen her face somewhere. Lately, I mean."

"I thought the same thing when she walked in here," the woman said. "I think it was on TV. Maybe she's a movie star." She turned back to her romance novel. "You'll be kicking yourself one day for not getting her autograph."

Unable to focus on anything now but the ever-deepening mystery that surrounded Kate's family, Ben had negotiated with his boss for the rest of the week off. There would be hell to pay when he returned, but he didn't care. His best chance to clear himself, should the police pick him up for questioning, was to have hard evidence of Margaret Greene's real motive. Even devoting his full attention to the search might not be enough. They were running out of time, and he knew it.

Ben was already on a first-name basis with several of the clerks at the Hall of Records, and one of them, a young brunette, helped him locate the listings of deaths in Mercer County, dating as far back as 1845. The earlier records had been destroyed in a fire, she said, but those that remained were complete. They should have contained entries for everyone on Ben's list who had died after the mid-1800's. Should have, but didn't.

There was no record of Louise Carter, who, according to her headstone, had died in 1866, "Beloved Wife and Mother", or Harold Waterman, dead in 1853 from influenza. He could not find Eugene Dawes, who supposedly died in 1878, or Ben and Sheila Vincent, mother and father who died that same year, or seven-year-old William Aster, who had "Gone With The Lord" in 1895. Ben's pulse quickened as made his way down the list. One by one he searched the files and one by one, he found nothing. Not a single name they'd collected was here.

He stopped by the front desk and thanked the clerks before stepping outside and taking a few deep breaths of fresh air. He'd already talked to Kate about her visit to the stone works, and now he struggled to get his mind around the implications.

Eddie Holt's assertions had been completely correct. The cemetery that Kate called Lark Hill was not there when Eddie grew up, nor was it there in 1941 when the Army Corp of Engineers did their aerial survey of the state. It was in fact, a fabrication, like an unimaginably detailed Hollywood set; the monuments, the mausoleums, the elaborate carvings and inscriptions, the rusted iron fences, the walkways, even the slightly raised mounds of earth; all of it; constructed sometime between 1944 and 1945. "Old cemetery my ass," Ben muttered under his breath, as he remembered the aerial photo from 1945. "The damned paint was probably still wet when that was taken."

"Isn't this enough to tell someone?" Kate

implored, as they made their way down a secluded section of the greenway in Harmon Park. "There has to be a law against what they did. It's twisted at the very least."

"You asked me the other day why anyone would want to fake a two hundred-year-old cemetery. I keep thinking about it, trying to come up with something, but every new idea sounds crazier than the one before."

"Try me," Kate said, looking away into the woods that bordered the path. "We passed crazy a week ago."

"Okay, well, the best case scenario I can think of is that they needed credibility in the funeral business when they first started out. As in, customers are more comfortable with someone who's already established. Lark Hill would have established them practically overnight, voila, instant credibility."

"That's reaching," Kate said, shaking her head. "I can see doing something like that on a much smaller scale, but that's way, way over the top just to make a good impression. Next?"

"They're using the graves to hide something. The names are bogus because there's something besides bodies in them. The last place anyone would look is in a buried coffin."

Kate had considered this herself but had dismissed it as absurd. Hearing Ben say it out loud made it seem less so. "That's more like it," she said. "Only there's a problem with that."

"Yeah?"

"If you bury something in a grave, maybe in a coffin, then you either leave it there forever or you dig it up. I can only remember twice in all the years I've spent here that I've seen them dig up a grave. Once was to move a body to another location at the request of a family, the other was when the court ordered a woman's body exhumed as part of an investigation. There are dozens of graves up there; if they were even using half of them to store something, they'd have dug *something* else up in fifty years."

"Is it possible they could have done it at night, or some time when no one was around?"

Kate shook her head. "No, it's a big deal to dig up a grave. Even with the backhoe, the ground is scarred for weeks. You couldn't hide that."

Ben frowned and glanced tentatively at Kate. "Okay, then what about bodies?"

Kate grimaced. "What about them?"

"What if there are graves up there, but instead of the people whose names are on the stones, there are bodies they were paid to dispose of. I told you it would sound crazy, but think about it. Nobody would ever know. A court isn't going to order anyone to dig them up because the names don't even belong to real people."

"Jesus, Ben," Kate frowned. "You weren't kidding."

"So you think it's out in left field."

She threw her hands up. "I don't know what to think. But I'd probably say no to that too. They own a crematorium for Christ's sake. If you bury a body, coffin or no, you always run the risk of someone digging it up. You're just preserving evidence that could convict you. If you cremate the body, problem solved. No mess, no evidence. Besides, everybody knows the last thing you ever do with murder victims is bury them in your back yard." Kate stopped suddenly and put her face in her hands.

"God, I can't believe I'm having this conversation, about my own family! Do you know how screwed up that is? And I'm going to be the loser here; I can feel it – whatever they did. My life will be trashed." She crossed her arms and walked a few steps ahead.

At first, Ben didn't know what to say. She was right, and he couldn't deny it. If her family were involved in a criminal cover-up, she would likely be harassed and questioned, possibly even accused. And more importantly, she wouldn't be able to look anyone she knew in the eye if the truth came out; her shame would be too great. Her innocence might keep her out of jail, but she would be left with nothing. He walked up behind her and wrapped his arms around her waist. "I'm sorry," he said. "You don't deserve this. It isn't fair."

Kate kicked at a pine cone on the path. "Fair, ha. Whoever thought that word up should be shot."

Everett and Walter were already gone when she arrived at work in the office on Tuesday. According to Edna, they'd left late the previous afternoon in a hearse, which meant they were going to pick up a body. Most of their business was local, but on occasion, for one reason or another, an out-of-state request came in. It didn't particularly matter to Walter. If they were willing to pay the exorbitant price for out-of-state pickup, he was more than willing to fill out the paperwork and make the drive.

What struck Kate as more than a little odd, however, was that Everett had gone along. It was a task he'd begun delegating around the time she was born, and now, only went on rare occasions when a close friend had died, and the family specifically requested that he handle the remains. Walter ran everything, including transport. No, she thought, this had to be something else, something far more important.

On her way in, she spoke to several of the half-dozen other people who made up the small staff. They'd come in a half-hour earlier and were already busy, some cleaning and preparing chapels for the day's services while others worked downstairs with the deceased in Walter's absence, making last minute adjustments to clothing and hair, touching up makeup, and buffing caskets to mirror-sheen perfection.

Before getting settled for the morning, Kate promptly logged into her computer and double checked that there had been no last minute change of plans on the calendar. Her eyes were tired, and she felt shaky from the night before. Her awkwardly aborted attempt at love making with Ben seemed a pathetic testament to how distracted she'd become. And she'd barely slept, despite the extended massage Ben had given her to take the edge off.

After hanging her coat up, Kate headed upstairs and found her grandmother in front of the TV, flipping channels with the remote.

"I can't stand television anymore," Edna lamented. "You know some of the shows these days even give people seizures. That's what I read on the internet, anyway."

Kate kissed her cheek. "Don't believe everything you read on the internet, Gram. Listen, I'm nearly out of Everett's business cards downstairs. Do you know if Everett has some more in his office?"

"I wouldn't know about that. You'll just have to

look and see." Edna stopped flipping when she reached The Morning Show. "Do you think this new girl is better than Deena Hanks? I don't think either of them can hold a candle to Jane Simmons," she continued before Kate could reply. "It's just hideous the way those no-account bastards treated her after so many years."

"I've got work to do; I'm headed back down. Are we still on for dinner tonight?" Kate asked on her way out.

"Oh yes! Kevin is going to whip us up something healthy. Some vegetarian thing he's trying. Come by later, and we'll talk."

The offices in the northeast corner, on the top floor of the residence, had been designed in the beginning by Andrew and Mitchell to provide a nearly unobstructed view of the cemetery and grounds. An adjoining doorway allowed the two rooms to serve as a kind of management suite, a command center of sorts, from which they ran all aspects of the business. In later years, Everett and Walter would occupy the same spaces, but only briefly, as Everett's burgeoning political career increasingly demanded his presence elsewhere. Eventually, when the town council allocated an office for him the courthouse annex building, his old office would remain vacant and dark for days at a time.

Lately, however, that had not been the case. So much so that even Kate had noticed. Her grandfather seemed to be spending more time at the funeral home than she could ever remember, randomly pacing the halls, hovering near doorways, as if listening for something that he couldn't hear. All in all, Kate had never seen him this way. It only added fuel to the fire that burned steadily now, in the back of her mind.

When she came to the corner, Kate looked to her left, down the length of the adjoining hallway, but there was no sign of movement. Behind her, the door to her Gram's suite was still closed. She tried the knob on Everett's office door and felt her pulse quicken as it turned in her hand.

Clinging to the hope that her thin cover story about business cards would suffice, she stepped inside. Her visits here had been few and far between over the years and they'd always been brief, but the room had a magical quality to it that she'd never forgotten. It was richly furnished, like many offices from its era, with a dark mahogany desk and credenza, wall-to-wall book cases, leather arm chairs, brass lamps and ashtrays, original oil paintings, and even Persian rugs, garnered well before the trading of such items was declared illegal. But it was the nature of its furnishings that set it apart from other offices, even the exceptional ones.

Everett's love for the funeral business was surpassed by only one thing; his passion for antiques and fine art. This was the only place, in or out of the house, where he allowed that passion to manifest itself. Here, it was unbridled.

According to family gossip, nearly everything was extremely valuable. But more than that, each piece had a story. The desk was irreplaceable; hand-carved in Italy by a master craftsman during the First World War as a wedding present for his only daughter. Sadly, German soldiers in a passing convoy killed the young girl mere days before the ceremony and, unable to bear his grief, the poor carver laid down on the desk and shot himself. A suspiciously dark swirl in the wood grain was rumored to be a stain from the man's blood.

The paintings were original oils by Vermeer and Haals, from their early years, while the small sculpture on a pedestal in the corner bore the name Rodin. The matching pair of ornately jeweled lamps with gold embroidered shades belonged to a Rabbi in Poland, who bartered them for glass windows when those in his synagogue were smashed. Even the ashtray, a classic deco design, hand-carved in black onyx, had a remarkable, if decidedly dark, history; it had supposedly belonged to Adolf Eichmann, a lieutenant colonel under Hitler, during the years of Jewish deportation to Ghettos and concentration camps.

Kate felt as though she'd broken into a museum as she tiptoed around the desk, looking at stacks of papers, scanning the credenza for something – anything. "What the hell am I supposed to be looking for?" she whispered to herself.

She considered the desk drawers but wasn't sure how long her nerve would hold up, or how far she was willing to push it. After another anxious minute of fruitless searching, however, she returned to the drawers and tried the top one. It too was unlocked, and here, among the paper clips, sticky pads, and other assorted supplies, she found a manila folder labeled Bachman, on top of a stack of loose papers and magazines. Kate smirked as she spotted a box of Everett's business cards on the opposite side of the drawer.

Inside the Bachman folder, she found a single color photo of a chair. She turned it to get a better look and was astounded. On closer inspection, it looked more like a throne than a chair; it's surfaces were inlaid with intricately designed patterns of precious stones and gold; its seat a padded red velvet and its legs plated in burnished gold leaf. She'd never seen anything like it.

"Having any luck?"

Kate jumped and let out a screech as she whirled around to find her grandmother's head peering in the still-cracked door. The photo slipped from her hand and landed in the drawer.

"Shit!" Kate gasped, clutching the top of the desk to steady herself. "You nearly gave me a heart attack!"

Edna seemed pleased with herself. "Payback is a bitch, they say. I'm only kidding dear; I'm sorry. Did you find the cards?"

Kate pushed the photo back into its folder with a trembling hand and held up the box of cards. "Just found them," she managed. From the corner of her eye, she saw Edna's gaze fall briefly on the manila folder and she braced herself for a comment, but it didn't come.

"Good," Edna said instead. "It's a wonder you can find anything in this mausoleum of an office." But there was something odd in her grandmother's voice; something put-on and insincere. It made the hair on Kate's arms stiffen.

By the time she returned to the main office downstairs, a flurry of phone calls was coming in about the first service of the day, a funeral for ninety-one year old Carlene Roeper. The local paper had misprinted the time of the service two days earlier, and while most of the resulting chaos had subsided, Kate was still hearing from angry Roeper family members and confused florists trying, to schedule deliveries. Kate's curiosity about the photo she'd found in Everett's office was quickly eclipsed by the demands of the morning, and she didn't have time to revisit the matter until lunchtime.

Ben stopped by for what was fast becoming their daily lunch routine; a walk to Lark Hill. Besides being the most private spot on the property, it now seemed the most fitting place to confer. They'd vowed to scrutinize every inch of the place until they found a chink in its seemingly flawless design. This way, they could look and talk at the same time.

"It was an amazing chair," Kate said, after relaying the scant results of her search to Ben. "But I don't know what to make of it. There was only the name on the folder."

"Bachman," Ben mused. "Maybe it's some antique he's lusting after."

"This was no average antique," Kate said. "It was the kind of thing they lock up behind bulletproof glass in the Museum of History. You should have seen it. It probably had a million dollars' worth of gemstones in it. If those were diamonds, forget it, all the way to the moon." She shook her head and knelt down beside a headstone and tried to wiggle it. "Everett's wealthy, no doubt, but he's not packing that kind of money."

Ben sat on another stone and watched her. "What's your plan for later, after dinner?"

"By the time Gram and I finish dinner, everyone will be gone," Kate replied, standing and dusting off her hands. "Carl will have everything closed up, and he'll be in his apartment in the guest-house. Gram is always sauced by seven or eight, and she'll be glued to her chair. I'll have the place to myself; just me and the stiffs. I'm going exploring again, only this time, hopefully, sans heart failure. Between Everett's office and the file room, there's got to be something there."

"Where's the file room?"

"In the basement, across from the preparation room."

"Great," Ben quipped, as they turned back toward the house. "When are Walter and Everett coming back?"

"Later tonight from what Carl said. Up and back, that's a hell of a lot of driving for a day and a half."

"Especially in a hearse," Ben said. "How are you going to know when they get here? You can't afford to get caught in the act."

Kate cleared her throat. "Well, actually that's where you come in."

7

At eight thirty, just after dark, Ben pulled his Land Rover off the main road, into the parking lot of a long-deserted gas station, and killed the lights. Most of the windows in the small, crumbling building were missing, and uneven patches of concrete covered the area where pumps once stood. A lone street light bathed much of the small lot in an eerie glow, but he chose a spot in the shadows, on the far side of the structure. From his vantage point, Ben could just see the entrance to Werner-Greason, through some trees in a bend of the two-lane road.

Kate's plan had been to position him in just such a place, away from the road, but with a clear line of sight. By her estimate, if he called her as soon as he spotted the hearse, she'd have just enough time to straighten up whatever she'd gotten into and clear out before Walter and Everett showed up.

It had sounded simple enough at the time, and Ben had readily agreed, but as always, there had been a catch. She didn't have accurate information on their return time, so he could be waiting in a cold car, in the dark, for hours. And there was no room for error; one unfortunate

144

distraction, a wandering eye, an innocent turn of the head at the wrong moment, and they would drive past him, unnoticed. If that happened, it would all be over very quickly. "Good thing there's no pressure," Ben sighed as he looked again at his watch.

Kate's dinner with her grandmother had been pleasant, yet somewhat disappointing. She'd hoped to steer the conversation toward the early years of Werner-Greason, on the off chance that her Gram would reveal something, anything that might help them. Kate was sure that Edna harbored important memories, but the past had always been a closed book for her, one which she opened under the rarest of circumstances.

But her grandmother had launched into a rambling monologue about the pitfalls of marriage before Kate could get a word in edgewise. As the meal progressed and Edna helped herself to more wine, Kate was treated to a litany of Everett's shortcomings as a husband and father, and Edna became brasher with each new accusation. Kate listened politely through dessert, and while she agreed with much of what she heard, she was glad when her grandmother excused herself and went to get ready for bed.

She'd called Ben and given him the go-ahead to come over, before heading back downstairs to make a final pass. Carl Lentz, the groundskeeper and interim manager in Walter's absence, was a very early riser and as such, was usually in bed by nine. From the kitchen window, she had a clear view of the guest house and saw a light in the window of his upstairs apartment. Once he had settled in for the night, Carl never came back over unless her father called him.

As Kate walked quickly through the lobby, peering into each chapel, in turn, she recalled the old fear she'd had as a child. Each time she'd seen one of the coffins at the far end of one of these darkened rooms, her mind had conjured the image of a corpse sitting up and turning to look at her. Children have mad imaginations, Kate thought, as she hurried back upstairs, looking nervously over her shoulder.

She found her grandfather's office unchanged, with one disturbing exception; the manila folder in his top desk drawer was gone. For a moment, Kate wondered if she'd taken it out, but her memory was clear. The folder had been there. "She took it," Kate whispered in disbelief, staring at the door. Something about the idea alarmed her. It had never even occurred to Kate that her grandmother, for her seeming hatred of Everett, could be complicit in his dealings. "No way," she said softly, shaking her head. There had to be another explanation.

The name on the folder was still fresh in her mind, and under the B's in Everett's Rolodex, she found what she was hoping for; a business card. Not surprisingly, Gunter Bachman was a dealer of antiques and fine art. What gave Kate pause was the address in the lower left corner; 31st Street, New York.

Her mind raced to make a connection. And as disturbing as it was, it made perfect, twisted sense. No wonder Everett went along, she thought. What if they're not going up there to pick up a body at all? What if the hearse is just a cover?

But when she remembered the chair in the photo, her knees felt weak. If the chair was real, authentic, it could easily have been worth millions of dollars. No street dealer of antiques would be handling something like that. Suddenly, she felt silly for letting her imagination run amok. The idea was ludicrous. Still, it seemed a bizarre coincidence.

Half an hour later, having turned up nothing that related specifically to Lark Hill or the period in question, Kate crept out and headed for the basement. The file room was the only other place she could imagine finding documents dating back that far, yet even there, she knew it would be a long shot. If Everett and Walter had been fooling everyone, they hadn't done it by being careless. There would be nothing obvious. She would have to look for invoices, payments to vendors, requests for speciality contractors, anything that might point to the real reasons for what they'd done.

When Kate reached the bottom of the basements steps, she instinctively reached for the light switch but stopped herself at the last second. Even though the tiny ground-level windows here were glazed, Lentz would see the light, should he happen to look out. It was not a chance she could afford to take. Instead, she crept through the semi-dark, her heart pounding in her chest, feeling for the corners she knew all too well until she came to the wall opposite the preparation room. She ran her hand along its surface until she felt the recess of the file room door.

Fumbling at first with her key, she managed to get it into the door and heard a click as it opened. The narrow, windowless file room was pitch black, but here she dared turn on a light before closing the door behind her. She faced two rows of filing cabinets, on opposite walls, with a center aisle between them for easy access. Above the cabinets, shelves had been installed to handle oversized items such as blueprint rolls and survey maps.

Kate rubbed her hands together in anticipation. "Okay," she said. "I know you're in here somewhere. Come to mama."

By nine forty-five, Ben was beginning to feel like a caged animal; claustrophobic and on-edge. Twice he'd gotten out, once to stretch briefly, and once to relieve himself behind the battered dumpster in the back corner of the lot.

He tried to keep the car warm by starting it every few minutes and running the heater full-blast, but he'd begun to shiver in spite of this strategy. And with nothing to do but think, his curiosity about Kate's progress had begun eating away at him. He didn't dare call her to ask, however; her job would be difficult enough without a false alarm.

As the evening wore on, traffic on the two-lane road in front of him had dwindled to one car or so every few minutes. Out of sheer boredom, he'd started counting them. He'd just mumbled "thirteen" when he caught a glimpse of movement in his rear-view mirror. Before he even had time to react, a blinding blue strobe light flashed in his eyes and lit up the entire parking lot.

"Shit!" Ben growled, looking frantically around him as he strained to think of some excuse he could give the officer, but his mind drew a blank. He felt sick at his own carelessness. He'd been so busy patting himself on the back for his choice of reconnaissance spots that it hadn't even occurred to him that it might also be the hardest to explain, should the police see him there. Hell, he hadn't even thought about the police.

An even brighter, white spot-light flooded his car as a man's voice boomed over a speaker. "Mercer county sheriff's office. Put your hands where I can see them and remain in your car. I will come to you."

"Shit," Ben said again, raising his hands to head-level, like someone who was being robbed at gunpoint. He heard a car door open and shut behind him, and the beam of a flashlight danced across his dashboard and into the passenger's seat, but he kept his eyes caged to the front.

A sudden rapping on the window made him flinch. The officer was motioning with one hand. Ben used his left hand to lower the driver's window.

"I need to see your license and registration," the man said.

"Officer I was just," Ben began.

"Driver's license and registration," the officer said, more forcefully this time.

"Yes sir, no problem," Ben stammered, groping for his wallet. He handed his license to the officer, and as he was reaching for the glove box, where he kept the registration, he saw a pair of headlights approaching on the road, coming from the opposite direction. To his horror, they slowed and turned into the entrance to Werner-Greason. Against the reflection from the spotlight, he saw the unmistakable silhouette of a hearse.

Kate's arms began to ache, and small beads of sweat formed on her forehead as she moved from drawer to drawer, leafing through reams of tightly packed folders. Several times she froze and listened, startled by a faint creak or a thump. She knew it was the house, making noises she'd heard a thousand times before, but each time her nerves became more frayed.

Near the back, in one of the top file drawers, she found a folder labeled "Maintenance Log." It contained pages of entries for maintenance and repair work done on the house from the early 1960's to around seventy-five. Behind the log pages, were original invoices for many of the jobs and services listed there; one for installation of track lighting in the chapels and outer lobby, another for a burglar-alarm system in the guest-house in May of 1972, and still another for low-profile sprinklers for the west lawn.

Kate was ready to move on to the next folder, convinced that this one, like all the others, contained nothing she could use when a single sheet caught her eye. It was a receipt from 1965, from a company called Fire Resources Inc., for Halon-1301 – lots of it. Kate knew little about fire protection systems, but she'd been in several banks and computer rooms that were equipped with Halon and had seen the warnings posted on the walls.

The gas, when sprayed into a confined area during a fire, would pull all the oxygen from the room, smothering the fire nearly instantly, along with anyone trapped inside. For this reason, all Halon equipped rooms featured a bright red shut-off button, prominently displayed on an inside wall.

Kate pulled the page from the folder and held it up to the light, wondering if there was any other use for Halon. There had to be; there was no fire system in the house, and certainly not one in any of the lesser buildings. It seemed a small thing, a minor inconsistency, but it bothered her. She was folding the paper to put it in her pocketbook, when she heard a much louder noise, from just outside the file room door.

In a panic, Kate ran to the door and turned off the lights, nearly tripping over a cardboard box she'd left in the aisle. Someone had unlocked the deadbolt on the basement door, and they were wrestling with the lock on the door knob. As she quietly closed the file room door, bright light flooded the basement. Kate ducked low to the floor and clenched her eyes shut. Damn it, where was Ben?

She heard muffled voices now, and she stood and peered out the tiny window in the door, careful to remain in the shadows. Everett and Walter were propping open the double doors to the basement, preparing to wheel in what would normally be a casket on a gurney. As they stepped outside and walked up the delivery ramp, Kate shoved the folded paper in her pocketbook and checked her cell phone. There were no missed calls.

"Damn," she hissed, worried now that something had happened to Ben. He wouldn't have abandoned her unless something had gone very wrong. Whatever the case, she was trapped. They would know she was here somewhere; her car was still in the parking lot. She had to find a way out before one of them went looking for her.

As she peered again out the window, Kate saw them return from the parking lot, but they were not pushing a casket. They came through the doors wheeling a large crate, strapped to a dolly. While the wooden crate was easily large enough to hold a refrigerator, it clearly contained something much lighter, as they were able to maneuver it with minimal effort.

Despite her awful dilemma, Kate was transfixed by what she saw, her skin tingling with an odd sense of anticipation. The expressions on their faces told her that this was no ordinary delivery. Everett was more smug than usual, almost gleeful, while Walter appeared anxious and uncomfortable, repeatedly scanning the room as if he expected someone to burst in on them unannounced. At one point, they even had a heated exchange as Everett opened the door to the preparation room and turned on more lights, but Kate could not hear what they were arguing about. Walter broke off the exchange and turned back to the cargo, steering it into the preparation room where the lights were intensely bright. Just before the door closed behind them, she caught a glimpse of the word WIEN, stamped on one side of the box in bold, capital letters.

Kate rolled her back against the door and put a hand on her chest to try and slow her breathing. She had to calm down and think – quickly. The preparation room door had a window as well, which meant she'd have to risk being seen in order to get out of the basement.

Walter and Everett would likely be focused on getting their merchandise uncrated, however, buying her at least enough time to slip by undetected, but only if she moved now. Kate took a deep breath and eased out of the file room, staying low and quietly closing the door behind her. She darted along the wall and turned the corner, pressing herself as flat as she could for a look back, but she saw no movement through the narrow window.

As Kate started for the stairs, she paused and looked back a second time, pulled by her growing curiosity. "Bad idea," she mouthed silently, cautioning herself against the quick peek she was entertaining.

This was likely her only chance to see what was in

the crate, to confirm her suspicions about the chair. She didn't know how or even if it was related to the deception of Lark Hill, but it would mean one thing unequivocally; Everett was playing in a much bigger league than she ever imagined.

Finally, yielding to her impulse, Kate walked back to the preparation room door, having decided to play dumb. If they caught her peeking, she would simply say she'd heard them come in and was curious who they'd gone to pick up. It was feeble but better than nothing.

She looked directly in the window, half-expecting to startle her father and grandfather in the middle of pulling a priceless antique out of a crate, but instead, she saw nothing. Other than the usual complement of equipment, work tables, and supplies, the room was empty; no Walter, no Everett, and no crate. She scanned the room from side to side, more confused than ever until she spotted the door to the cooler. It had to be. They'd taken it in there to open it in private, to avoid just such an unwelcome surprise. Slick, she thought, wondering what to do next.

Quickly, she looked again at her cell phone and considered dialing Ben's number, but she thought better of it. She couldn't afford a distraction right now.

She would wait, she decided. She'd just stand there and wait until they came back out. It couldn't be long. The cooler was designed to be just above freezing to help preserve bodies when the work became backlogged and fell behind. Refrigeration routinely bought them forty-eight hours before embalming began, with little or no evidence of decay.

The cooler was not a hospitable place for the

living, however, and neither Walter nor Everett were wearing a coat. She guessed they would last no more than five minutes before coming out. But five minutes slipped by with no sign of movement and as she checked her watch again, five had become ten. They would be freezing to death by now, she thought. She was growing anxious again as several more minutes passed, with the cooler door remaining fixed in place.

Kate heard a hissing noise behind her and spun around. Ben was there, wide-eyed, at the bottom of the ramp, looking through the still-open basement door. "Kate! What are you doing?" he whispered. "Let's go!"

She held a finger to her lips and motioned for him to come into the basement. He waved a hand and motioned emphatically for her to come outside. One last check of her watch told her that sixteen minutes had passed since they went inside. Sixteen minutes in a freezer.

She wanted more than ever to wait it out but conceded and headed for the door.

"Where have you been?" she demanded as they jogged to Ben's rover, which he'd parked near the front. "What happened to a head's up?"

"The officer that nearly arrested me wasn't exactly in the mood to let me call my girlfriend."

"The police pulled you over?" Kate asked.

"No, worse. They found me skulking in the shadows in my car like some kind of deviant. I think they guy was wondering the whole time where I'd hidden the hooker. Anyway, I saw the hearse drive by, and I couldn't do a damn thing about it until he finally let me go. Are you alright?"

"I'm fine, but that was close. I was hiding in the

file room with the lights off when they wheeled this big box in on a dolly."

Ben threw the stick into reverse and backed the Rover out of the parking spot. "Big box? You mean a casket?"

"No, it wasn't a casket at all. It was a wooden crate with the word WIEN stamped on the side of it. W, i, e, n, whatever the hell that means."

"Vienna," Ben mused.

"What?"

"We learned that in first-year German, well, for me, only-year German. We call it Vienna in the U.S., they call it Wien. That crate is from Austria."

"Well, here's the creepy part," Kate continued. "They took the crate into the cooler in the embalming room and didn't come out the entire time I was standing by the door, peeking in. Sixteen minutes, Ben! It's thirty-five degrees in there, and they were wearing suits."

"Are you sure they took it in there? You saw them?"

"Well no, *technically*, I didn't see them take it in there, but the room was empty. I could see every inch of it. It was like they took it in there and vanished. That's the only place they could have gone with it."

"There's no other door to that room?"

Kate shook her head. "The door you saw me standing in front of is the only way out."

"It doesn't make any sense. If it wasn't a body, why would they be taking it in the cooler?"

She put her hand on her stomach, where the slightly hollow, faintly nauseous feeling had returned. "Ben, I think I may have been wrong. I think it could have been that chair, throne, whatever it was – from the picture. It would have been exactly the right size."

"Didn't you say it was worth millions?"

"If it's all real then yes, definitely."

"What if it's a reproduction, an authentic looking fake? We're talking about people who faked an entire cemetery. One chair shouldn't be a problem, even a really expensive one."

"It doesn't fit," Kate said. "Something I found in Everett's office makes me doubt it. You remember the name on the folder, Bachman, well I found the guy's business card. He's a fine art and antique dealer in, guess where."

Ben furrowed his brow. "New York?"

"Bingo."

"Did you find anything else?" Ben asked. "In the files?"

"I ran out of time, thanks to you and the hooker," Kate smirked. "But I found this." She pulled the paper out of her pocketbook and unfolded it. It may be nothing, but it just didn't make sense to me. It's an invoice for Halon 1301. Do you know what that is?"

"Sure, it's a gas they used to use in bank vaults and museums to extinguish fires. They made it illegal a few years ago because it was contributing to the greenhouse effect in the atmosphere."

"That's the stuff. Well, there's no Halon fire system anywhere on our property, but this shows where Everett bought a boatload of it."

"What if he bought it for someone else?"

"I found this in the Maintenance Log for the house and grounds, along with every kind of home improvement you could name, track lighting, plumbing, burglar alarms, the works. It wouldn't be there if they weren't having it installed, or maybe refilled."

Ben looked out into the murky darkness of the woods, just beyond the reach of the headlights, as they wound through another curve in the road. "It does all fit. You don't use Halon unless you've got something very valuable to protect. And if they just bought a million-dollar chair, they're going to need..."

Kate put her hand on his arm. "Ben, you don't understand. This receipt is from 1965."

For the second time in a week, Lieutenant Wallace sat with Marcus Leplaine, the director of Digital Edge Technologies in a meeting room; only this one was equipped with flat-panel video displays and a high-end sound system, all controlled by a remote, built into the table top.

A representative for the company had notified him early that morning that their findings were complete, and asked that he drive down for a face-to-face. Wallace had called Hughes, who had urged him to leave right away. "I need those results on my desk before lunchtime," he'd said, and to Wallace's puzzlement, had added, "Make sure they give us everything back, the tape, the data, and the reports, all copies. Do you understand? Bring it all with you when you come to my office."

Leplaine pushed Wallace's copy of the report across the table and studied the first page of his own copy. "I'll start with the tape, the physical description our analysts were able to derive. Please keep in mind Captain, that these characteristics come with a margin of error, depending on the variable in question. The subject is a Caucasian male, height five feet, eleven inches, plus or minus one inch. The variance here could result from physical distortion of the tape or reflected environmental light." Leplaine pushed a button on the table, and a graphic appeared on the screen behind him. It was a diagram of the conversation between Margaret Bayer Green and the second suspect, showing their relative heights and the position of the security camera that took the video. He explained briefly how the height calculations were derived and pushed another button. Arrows appeared to illustrate how reflected light could make the angle of declination appear greater or smaller.

"The hair color, we believe is a coarse, medium brown. In reality, it could range in hue from oak to a brown-red brick." He pulled two color squares from a folder and held them up. "Quite a bit of variation here I'm afraid, but still impressive from a black and white video, don't you agree?"

Wallace nodded. "Definitely."

"The subject is approximately thirty-four years old, plus or minus two years, one hundred seventy to one hundred eighty pounds, and in good to excellent physical condition."

Leplaine continued, describing the likely facial structure of the subject, but only in vague terms. When Wallace asked about providing information to a sketch-artist, he indicated there was simply not enough to go on. "And unfortunately," he said. "We were not able to discern any identifying marks, moles, tattoos, that sort of thing."

"What about names?" Wallace asked, eager to hear more.

"With females eliminated from the target group, we've narrowed it down to six; four ninety percent or higher, two lesser probability, between seventy-five and ninety percent. If you'll turn to page three."

On page three Wallace found a reduced, color coded diagram of the main hall in the Civic Center. Leplaine briefly went over the chart and the colors used to show the status of each guest as accounted for, present but not seated, or absent from the main hall. When he'd gone over the breakdown of fees for their services he asked if Wallace had any questions.

"No, I believe you covered everything Mr. Leplaine. You've done excellent work. There is one thing, though."

"Yes?"

"Because of the sensitive nature of this case, I've been directed to collect everything from you today relating to this job, and asked that you destroy or erase any copies you may have, electronic or otherwise." Wallace pushed a sheet of paper across the table to Leplaine, who seemed confused and somewhat taken aback. "This is a waiver stating that all such information has been released to me and that you've complied with the destruction order in full."

"This is highly unusual, Mr. Wallace. Our firm has operated under the strictest security standards for twenty-two years. The data we collect is retained in an encrypted form, for future work that may be requested by the client. We are often asked for follow-up analysis and audio-visual support during court proceedings. We will be unable to provide any such services under this arrangement."

Wallace reached across the table and tapped his finger on the paper. "Be that as it may, Mr. Leplaine, we need your cooperation. This is coming from the top."

As he drove up Interstate seventy-seven, Lieutenant Wallace studied a single sheet of paper from the box of materials Leplaine had begrudgingly turned over to him. It had six names on it, a line separating the top four from the bottom two. Their elusive subject was one of these people, and he felt certain they would know which one within the next twenty-four hours. The idea gave him a thrill of anticipation he hadn't felt since his days as a detective, but this time, along with it, he felt something else; a sense of dread. On the surface, this case seemed like any other case, a straightforward investigation, but over the last week, he'd begun to smell something rotten underneath, and whatever it turned out to be, he'd likely be stepping in it.

Chief Hughes was pacing in his office, dragging on a cigarette when Wallace arrived. "What took so goddamn long?" he demanded.

Wallace didn't like the chief's tone. It was a bad sign. "The director was complying with your request, sir. It's not something they're normally asked to do."

"Well, let's have it. What did they give us? You can skip the technical bullshit, just cut to the chase."

Wallace passed the chief two pages; one with the summary of the subject's physical description, one with the list of six names. "This is the bottom line, Chief, what our guy looks like, and six possible hits. Pretty damned good if you ask me. We get a couple of guys on this, and we'll have our man inside of twenty-four hours."

Chief Hughes held the pages side by side for a moment as if comparing them. "What about copies?"

"All in the box, sir, along with the tapes and the rest of it. They burned our data onto CDs before they wiped the files."

"Everything's in here, all of it?"

"Yes, sir. So, if it's alright with you," Wallace said, trying again to push his point. "I'll go ahead and call in Phelps and Blanton to..."

"Negative Captain," Hughes said, looking up from the papers. "You've done an outstanding job, but I'll take it from here."

The chief's statement seemed to hang in the air between them as Wallace gaped. "Excuse me, sir? I'm not sure I understand."

"I'll be directing this case going forward, and you'll resume your other work. Is there something unclear about that, Captain?"

Wallace could feel the redness creeping up his neck and into his cheeks. "May I ask why sir? You put me in charge of this investigation, and if my performance has been inadequate, I would appreciate..."

"Your performance is not at issue. It's been exemplary, for what that's worth. Now, I have to go to a meeting, so if you'll excuse me."

As Wallace got up to leave, Hughes added, "And Terry, it's important that this is not discussed outside of this office. Refer them to me if you have to. Is that clear?"

"Yes sir," Wallace grunted, as he turned and stalked out.

He'd been blindsided before, but never so blatantly as this, and never by Hughes. He was so distracted that he nearly knocked a young sergeant down on the way into his office, where he slammed the door behind him. Everyone in the precinct common area turned and stared in his direction, but quickly averted their eyes when he glared at them with a deadlier than usual scowl.

He sat in his chair and rubbed his temples, trying to assimilate what had just happened. The chief never handled a case personally – never. It flew in the face of his personal directives. Hell, it probably violated department policy, if not in letter, certainly in intent.

And why now? If he wanted to take over the case, why wait until they were in the home stretch, hours from their big break. For a moment he considered that Hughes might be making a publicity play, a grab for glory in a high-profile case, but quickly dismissed the idea. Hughes was full of himself at times, but publicly, he'd always given credit where credit was due – to the department. This was something else, something that made Hughes uncharacteristically edgy and curt.

In desperate need of fresh air, Lieutenant Wallace picked up his jacket and headed down the street to Murphy's, where he could get a vegetable plate and some real coffee. It was a local favorite, and luckily for him, one of the few places that still served food cooked the way he'd always had it growing up.

A line was already forming in front of the register, made up mostly of regulars, faces he'd seen nearly every day there. Some of them were cops, but most were local merchants and business people from Stanton's humble downtown district.

He ordered his usual and was reaching for change in his pocket when his hand closed on a folded piece of paper. A moment later he remembered; Leplaine had given him another copy of the list. He'd been so dazed by the stunt Hughes had pulled that he'd forgotten he even had it.

The woman at the register cleared her throat, and Wallace realized he was holding up the line. "Sorry," he mumbled, giving her a larger bill instead and heading off to a table in the far corner. Instinctively, he chose the seat facing out, so he could see anyone approaching his table.

Hughes had demanded every copy, but Wallace had no intention of turning this one over, especially after the way he'd been unceremoniously shoved aside. There was a reason Hughes wanted every shred of evidence about this mystery-guy, and he wanted to know what it was. When he was seated, he carefully pulled out the paper and looked again at the list of names. Above the horizontal line in the center of the page were four names: Charles Teague, Andy Greer, Ben Tuttle, and Martin Calhoun. Below the line; Wendell Stack and Dean Parks. None of the names looked familiar, but that was no surprise. These people weren't typical of the clientele in his line of work. All except one, he thought, running a finger down the list.

When he was halfway through his banana pudding, Wallace's cell phone rang. It was Sergeant Pearl, with news that made his blood boil. Barely ten minutes earlier, Hughes had called Pearl directly, disregarding the chain of command completely, and ordered him to discontinue interviewing witnesses in the Civic Center shooting until further notice.

"Jesus," Wallace growled as he abandoned the last

few bites of his lunch and strode back outside. "Has Hughes lost his damn mind?"

"Sorry, he's out for the rest of the afternoon," Janet Venetti said in a conciliatory tone. Janet was Chief Hughes' secretary of eight years and was, for all practical purposes, one of the gang. She could see that Lieutenant Wallace was furious, but all she could do was shrug. "He's in Raleigh for some meeting, that's all I know."

Wallace returned to his office and tried to dig into the mountain of paperwork on his desk, but his mind wouldn't focus. He found that all he could do was mull over Hughes' inexplicable behavior, trying to find some shred of logic in it, some angle on the case that would justify what he'd done, but every turn led him to another dead end. Finally, he gave up pretending to work and resigned himself to waiting. "The son-of-a-bitch has got to come back sometime," Wallace muttered to himself.

That morning, Kate arrived at work with a mission; she was determined to get to the cooler in the preparation room and have a look, even a quick glance, just to satisfy her curiosity. She'd only seen the interior a few times but was certain there was not enough room to store a crate that large for any length of time. And what about Charles and Mick, the other employees who worked there preparing remains? Did they know? How could they not, if every time they went into the cooler to pull out another body, they had to step around a refrigerator-sized crate marked Wien. She'd already devised a plan, and although it was weak, it might buy her a few minutes, just long enough, she hoped.

The day was particularly busy, with two morning funerals and one in the afternoon. And there were more bodies to prepare than usual; a tragic head-on collision the day before, at the intersection of Forrest and Dayton, had left three people dead, including the old man who'd run the red light. This was in addition to four pick-ups they'd made over the last three days. They would have all hands on deck today, and preparation room would be hopping.

Around nine, just as Walter was corralling the other staff for a quick meeting, Kate slipped downstairs and headed for the double doors. Through the window, she saw Mick and another man at the far table, while Charles worked at the near one. The woman on Mick's table made Kate wince; her nose and one eye socket had been crushed, and they were carefully reconstructing them with mortuary wax and fillers, a process which took hours, sometimes even days. Over Mick's shoulder, she saw the door to the cooler.

Kate took a deep breath, smiled, and poked her head in the door. "Hey guys, mind if I stop in for a minute or two?" The smell in the room hit her, and she cleared her throat to keep from coughing.

They all seemed surprised to see her, but Mick motioned her inside with a gloved hand. "Hi Kate, come on in. But you're going to need to keep the stiff-jokes to a minimum. This batch doesn't have such a good sense of humor. Not like the last batch anyway, Chuck had 'em rolling off the table, didn't you Chuck?"

Charles grunted and shook his head. "I can see why Walter put the trainee with you. It makes perfect sense."

Mick turned to the young man working beside

him, who seemed decidedly uncomfortable. "Kate this is Andy Brennan, our intern." Kate stepped inside as Mick continued. "Andy, this is Kate Greason, Walter's daughter. She's down here to take you upstairs to see Everett for your performance review."

The young man's eyes grew wide with fear, and she could see his mouth fall open, even under his surgical mask. "I thought...that wasn't supposed to be..." he stammered.

Mick slapped him on the back. "I'm just screwing with you." He picked up something that looked like a putty knife and went back to work. "So Kate, what brings you to our little corner of the world?"

"I was curious. What's mortuary school like?"

They both looked up again, even more startled by her question, but it was Charles who spoke first. "Where did that come from? I thought you made up your mind a long time ago to stay out of the family business."

Kate made her way around the side of the room, glancing casually around at the equipment, her eyes finally coming to rest on the disfigured woman's face. She willed herself to look at it without flinching. "I don't know; it's always been interesting to me. I guess I just didn't like the pressure from Walter. You know how he can be."

Mick snorted. "No, we wouldn't know anything about it, would be Chuck?"

"Nope," he replied, pulling a syringe and a length of plastic hose from a drawer in the rolling cart beside him.

"Well, as I'm sure Andy here can attest, mortuary school is no picnic," Mick said, returning to her question. "Long hours, a lot of repetition, a lot of stiffs, I mean, cadavers. I don't have to tell you that there's a hell of a lot more to it than most people think. You have to wear a lot of hats in this business; embalmer, makeup artist, dentist, sculptor, you name it."

As he talked, Kate glanced behind her at the cooler door, a mere two feet away.

"And don't forget the soft skills," added Charles, with a heavy note of sarcasm. "Marketing, psychotherapy, grief-counseling, all that good stuff."

"You have to specialize by your second year," Andy said.

"Ah, it speaks," Mick said. "Yes, you do, and Chuck and I specialized in reconstruction. We do it all, but this is where our real talent lies. Take Francis here. When their car crashed, the impact drove the glass bottle she was holding into her face. Now, with only these as a go-by," he said, holding up a pair of photographs of an attractive, middle aged blonde, "we have to rebuild a nose and part of an eye socket."

"And do it well enough that the family won't know the difference," Charles added. "It's quite a challenge, sometimes."

Kate shook her head. "I'd be afraid I'd botch it." She turned and stepped to the cooler door, trying to peer in through the tiny window, but it was frosted over. "How many do you have in the waiting room?"

"It's full up," Mick snorted. "But it's a wonderful thing, they never complain about the wait."

Kate cleared her throat again, hoping she'd adjust to the odor before she became nauseous. "Mind if I take a quick peek?"

"Help yourself, but don't stay long. It's colder than you think."

As Kate pulled the long handle, she recalled working at the campus fast food restaurant in college and going to the walk-in cooler for more frozen burger patties. The thought made her shudder as she stepped into a wave of icy air and looked quickly around her. To her dismay, there was no crate in sight. On either side of her, within arm's reach, long black zippered bags rested on racks of stainless steel shelves. Thank God they're in bags, she thought, as she scanned the rest of the room. The center aisle was no more than three feet wide and was clear to the back wall, where the control panel for the cooler was mounted on a tall steel plate. The few feet of clearance at the bottom of each row of shelves was barely enough for the boxes of chemicals and supplies that were stacked there. "Damn," she whispered, and as she turned, she heard a loud clunking sound. The door had latched behind her.

Kate's heart was racing as she stepped to the door and tried the release bar. All walk-in coolers had them for just such occasions, but for some reason, this one didn't work. She tried again, her hands tingling against the cold metal, but the door didn't budge.

She knocked on the door with one fist. "Hey, a little help here!" Her voice sounded muffled and insignificant under the hum of the fan motor. She shoved hard on the door and yelled again. This time, the door swung open and she stumbled out into the preparation room, catching herself on the door frame.

Mick and Charles were grinning and Andy the intern was looking at his shoes. "Everything okay?" Mick asked.

Kate grunted and headed for the double doors.

"Nice guys. Yeah, everything's fine. Thanks for the chat."

"Sorry about the door," Mick called after her. "It sticks."

Back upstairs, even as Kate scrambled to answer incoming calls and questions from people arriving for a service, she tried to make the pieces fit. If the guys in the basement had known something, they would have been more guarded about her presence there and her interest in the cooler. The only possible conclusion was that they knew nothing about the crate or its contents, which meant that Walter and Everett had moved it again after she left the file room, but where?

With Ben delayed by a furnace repair, Kate took her lunchtime walk to Lark Hill alone, glad for a few moments of solitude to catch her breath and think. She'd found it increasingly difficult to focus on her work since she and Ben had embarked on their search and today was worse than usual.

A breeze stirred the trees in the old cemetery, sending brightly colored leaves drifting down around her as she walked. Normally it would have made her smile, but a week of high-anxiety had taken its toll. She was too tired, too burned out to revel in the usual simple pleasures.

Instead, she found herself studying the cemetery again, only now, she focused on the pathways, wondering if there was some rhyme or reason to their layout. Again she recalled having seen the aerial view of the graveyard, a long time ago when she was a child. This time, however, the memory came clearer, with a context – a setting. She'd bumped her head on something when she'd picked it up to look at it. Kate stopped walking and closed her eyes as more details came flooding back to her; wooden boards overhead, ceiling rafters; that's what she'd bumped her head on. Then she remembered.

"It was in our freaking attic," she said, whirling around and hurrying back down the path.

"It was in a box, with some old family pictures," she told Ben when she'd managed to get him on the phone. "I'm sure of it. I don't remember what it was doing there, but that's why it looked so familiar. Ben, it's the same picture we saw in the library."

"Do you remember where in the attic? Can you still get up there?"

"Yeah, if the stuff hasn't been moved around. I just hope it's still there. Maybe Gram knows something about it. I'll ask her when I get the chance."

"I'm still stuck with the furnace guy," Ben grumbled. "He's probably waiting for me to get off the phone so he can give me the bad news, so I'd better go. But call me and let me know what you find."

When she went back inside, Kate asked Cindy, the other woman who worked in the office, to cover for her while she went upstairs for a few minutes. They frequently traded off, and Kate knew she'd be returning the favor soon enough.

The vast attic above the private residence was crammed nearly to capacity with decades of cast off, unwanted items and just plain junk that her family had been too preoccupied to sell and too greedy to give away. The labyrinth of dusty piles was accessible by way of a narrow path that wound among the mounds and stacks.

As Kate made her way through it, under the light from two dim bulbs, she tried to bring the memory back of holding the photograph and bumping her head. She remembered standing beside the window in a tiny gable, at the lowest point of the roof. She remembered a black antique sewing machine to her right, the manual kind, with a cast iron foot pedal. She remembered a steamer trunk full of dresses and a pair of wooden skis.

Even in the dim light, Kate soon spotted the tips of the skis and was able to navigate to the right spot. Beside the sewing machine, she found the boxes of family albums and framed portraits unmoved.

She knelt beside an open-topped box and began flipping through a stack of miscellaneous pictures, some framed, others mounted on cardboard. As she looked at the old black and white photos of her distant relatives, she felt no warmth of kinship, no familiarity in their stoic faces. "Who *are* these people?" Kate whispered. They might as well be strangers, she thought, and in some way, she wished they were.

Halfway through the stack, she found the picture she was looking for, the one that didn't belong. It was the same black and white aerial photo she remembered, with one exception. The image was only a portion of the one they'd seen at the library; an enlargement cropped to show only the Lark Hill portion of the cemetery in grainy close-up.

She pulled the picture out carefully, so as not to damage its flimsy wooden frame, which looked as though it could come apart at any moment. "This is it," she said to no one. "I wonder what it's doing here." She turned the

171

frame over, but there was nothing written on the back; no date, no note.

Certain that no one would miss the picture, Kate carried in out of the attic and down to her car, before returning to the office to find Cindy visibly irritated. Walter had stopped by and angrily ordered her to research all purchases made to one of their vendors over the last three years. She was deep in stacks of purchase orders while trying to answer phone calls in between. Kate dived in, and the two of them remained swamped for most of the afternoon.

At three-thirty, in the Stanton police station, Lieutenant Wallace was reviewing performance appraisals for his staff when Sergeant Vargrave, one of the younger officers in the department, appeared in his doorway. "Hey Captain, the chief's on TV with the governor. They're doing a press conference of some kind in Raleigh. Thought you might want to catch it."

Wallace jumped up from his chair and followed Vargrave into the break room, where several people had gathered in front of the TV. The banner at the bottom had a News 3 logo and read "Live From Raleigh, NC." Wallace's eyes narrowed, and a scowl creased his face as he watched the group of three men standing in front of a bank of microphones on the top of the Capitol steps. Governor Chase was in the center, flanked by Chief Hughes and Everett Greason.

The Governor spoke first. "I'd like to begin today by thanking the good people of North Carolina for their thoughts and prayers during what has been a most trying ordeal for me, my family, and especially my close friend,

Everett Greason." The governor patted Everett on the back. "I would also like to express my deepest appreciation to Chief Willard Hughes of the Stanton police department, without whose expert oversight, we would not have been able to close the investigation into the last week's tragic events."

A disgruntled murmur rippled through the police station break room and several people called for quiet.

The Governor was speaking again. "I've asked Chief Hughes to appear with me today to clear up any confusion resulting from recent misinformation in the press. Chief Hughes?"

Hughes stepped to the microphone and began. "After a thorough investigation, including exhaustive interviews of those present at the Civic Center at the time of the shooting, we have concluded that Margaret Bayer Greene acted alone." Reporters hurled a flurry of questions, but Hughes ignored them and pressed on. "Contrary to recent reports in the press, there is no evidence that Mrs. Greene was aided by an accomplice or that she was part of a group or a conspiracy of any kind. Mrs. Greene's actions were the tragic result of her diminished mental capacity, combined with an adverse reaction to experimental and currently illegal drugs, which she obtained from an unknown source." Hughes continued to ignore the reporters. "For their hard work and dedication, I'd like to commend the men and women in Stanton's police force. There's no finer group of law enforcement professionals in this state, or anywhere for that matter."

"What kind of bullshit is that?" someone barked.

More swears and grunts of disgust followed in the

break room, among the officers watching the TV. Wallace felt like he'd been sucker-punched. He could barely believe what he had just seen; Hughes, standing in front of God and everyone, had announced with a straight face that they'd found nothing and were closing the investigation. Question after question screamed in his mind. What about the list? What about the forensics, the rest of the witnesses, and the damned second suspect? Had Hughes been planning this all along?

Several men were looking at him, trying to gauge his reaction, but he turned without a word and walked out.

Charles Teague was a banker, but not in the usual sense; he liked to think, at least, not anymore. Charles had been at the Civic Center that night, a mere two tables away from Margaret Bayer Greene when she had started shooting. He honestly believed he was going to die that night and the experience had left him a changed man, vowing to distance himself from the fat-cat reputation that so many of his colleagues rightly earned. He intended to come down from his bank-manager pedestal of late and meet his customers face to face, treat them as equals, no matter what their circumstance.

Teague pondered his new strategy as he drove home to his neighborhood, rolling it over in his mind and congratulating himself on the charity of it as he pulled his car into the garage. He did not notice the black sedan with the tinted windows, parked across the road, in the driveway of the house with the For Sale sign in the yard – he had no reason to. Charles Teague had no way of knowing that his name was the first name on a very short list.

In the driveway of 418 Vinroot Court, a bald man in a suit and dark glasses waited patiently in his car, a black Lexus with tinted windows, watching the house across the street, Charles Teague's house, and studying the paper in his hand. Steve Crenshaw had given it to him late that morning, with clear instructions that for once, didn't come with a muzzle or a leash. Crenshaw had used the phrase he relished most; "do whatever it takes."

At four fifty-two, a candy-apple red Mercedes pulled up in the Teague's driveway and a man in a shirt and tie got out; a man who matched, almost exactly, the physical description he'd been given. The man, presumably Teague, pulled a brief case and a suit jacket from the back seat, loosened his tie and walked to the front door. After pulling his keys from his pocket, he let himself in.

The driver of the Lexus eased his car across the road, cut the engine, and pulled a black bag from the seat beside him. He paused briefly to assess the image of Teague that he held in his mind; his stance, his manner, his expression. This one will not go quietly, he thought; too brash, too cocky. If the bald man knew anything, he knew people, and this one, the banker, would be indignant, maybe even defiant, at least at first. But once they got started, his tough facade would crumble; they always did. Teague would tell everything he knew and then some. By the end he would beg, this one, like a child; he was certain of it. Yes, whatever else he knew, he knew people.

He dropped his cigarette on the driveway and crushed it with his heel on the way to the door. He waited only a moment after ringing the bell before a shadow crossed the peep-hole and he knew he was being watched.

The door swung open, and a man in a t-shirt and suit pants greeted him with a skeptical expression. "Yes?"

The bald man produced a badge and held it at eye level. "I'm officer Garmen of the State Bureau of Investigation. Are you Charles Teague?"

Teague's expression morphed into worry. "Yes, has something happened? Is Melinda alright?"

"Yes, I'm sure she's fine. I need to ask you a few questions about the Greene shooting."

"Okay, but I've given full statements to two different officers from the Stanton police already. Don't you guys share information?"

"When it's necessary, but we do things a little differently. Now if we could just step inside."

Teague frowned and stepped aside. "I'm very busy. Will this take long?"

The man calling himself Garmen smiled. "That depends entirely on you, Mr. Teague."

8

When Kate arrived at Ben's house, she let herself in and hurried upstairs with the framed photo. "Hello, anyone home?" When there was no answer, she headed for the hall, but a loud thump stopped her in her tracks. From somewhere downstairs, she heard Ben swear.

Kate set the picture down and trotted to the basement where Ben was rubbing his elbow and inspecting what appeared to be a new furnace. "Well, what do you think?"

She kissed him and looked again at the furnace. "I'm almost afraid to ask. How much was it?"

He grunted. "Let's just say I won't be trading the Rover in anytime soon. And that's *with* insurance."

"Hey, I brought the picture. Come up and see." She took his hand and tugged until he followed her.

Upstairs, he ran his hand over the glass and inspected the image carefully. "You're right; this is the same photo. Someone's done a blow-up, but this is definitely from the 1945 survey."

"I told you it was the same one. And for the record, Gram knows something she's not telling. I stopped by her room with it on the way out, and she got very uncomfortable."

"What did you tell her?" Ben asked.

"I told her I'd been looking for some old family photos and found it. I just said I was curious where it came from."

"And?"

"She didn't buy it. I'm a pretty good liar, at least I can be when I need to, but she knew I was full of shit. She gave me that look. Then she played dumb, said she couldn't remember where it came from. She said she supposed one of Everett's government friends had given it to him a very long time ago."

Ben shrugged. "Maybe she really doesn't remember. We're talking sixty-two years ago."

"Ben if you could have seen her face, it looked almost like she was in pain. She couldn't change the subject fast enough. I think if I hadn't been in such a hurry to leave, she'd have gotten very busy and suggested I leave."

Ben walked across the living room and sat down in a padded armchair. "How can you get her to open up?"

Kate threw her hands up in the air. "I don't know, but there's got to be a way." She paced the room a couple of times and sat down on the coffee table in front of Ben.

"What if you called her bluff?" he asked. "What if you said something to make her think you know more than you do. Would she crack?"

"Maybe," Kate replied. "But that's risky. If she doesn't know anything, it might throw her even further off balance. She could end up going to Everett and demanding to know what the hell I'm talking about – then we'd be in it up to our necks."

"Well, let's talk about it over dinner. How does salad and lasagna sound?"

"Great. Got any wine? I could use some."

Over dinner, Kate told Ben about some of the long forgotten items she'd seen in the attic, and how old it all made her feel. Ben had just launched into a retort about women being overly fixated on age when they both heard Margaret Bayer Greene's name on TV, and he stopped, mid-sentence.

They hurried into the living room, where Ben had taken to leaving the TV on in case of breaking developments in the case. The governor was standing alongside Everett while a man in a police uniform spoke into a microphone. The banner read "3:30 P.M. Governor announces end to shooting investigation."

"Wait a minute," Ben said. "I don't get it. What is he saying?"

Kate shushed him, and they watched as Chief Hughes gave some closing remarks and the scene cut to a female reporter in an overcoat. "The governor's announcement earlier today caught many people off guard, especially with unconfirmed reports still circulating that police have leads on a possible second suspect. This afternoon, Chief Willard Hughes of the Stanton police force characterized those concerns as misinformation, but declined to comment on what leads his department had been pursuing."

Ben grinned. "It's over! Do you hear what they're saying? They're not looking for me anymore. I'm off the hook. We're off the hook."

"I don't understand why they rushed to close it,

though. What was their hurry?"

"Does it matter? God, this is great. I've been worried sick for days. You have no idea."

She kissed him and dashed back into the kitchen. "We should have a toast! Where are the wine glasses?"

"Top cupboard, over the toaster," Ben called, still watching the report. "They announced this at three thirty, how did I miss it?"

"I guess you and the furnace man were occupied in the basement, remember?"

"Oh yeah, how could I forget? I'll be walking bow-legged for a week after what that guy did to me."

Seconds later, Kate's raucous laugh turned to a shriek, amid the sound of shattering glass. Ben dashed around the corner to find her sitting on the counter with one hand over her mouth.

"Are you alright?"

She nodded silently, still staring at the pile of wood and glass on the floor at her feet. The photo, and what remained of its frame, lay among shards of glass from the picture and one of the wine glasses. "I was climbing down. I must have put my hand on the picture. I lost my balance, and the other wine glass fell. God, I've ruined the..." Kate stopped talking and blinked at the mess.

"What?" Ben asked, still worried she might have been cut.

Kate slid off the counter and squatted carefully among the scattered pieces of glass. "What's this?"

Ben saw what she was looking at. When the frame had broken, it had separated from the photo, and now, a piece of paper protruded from behind it. On the paper, they saw the edge of a roughly penciled diagram.

He knelt down beside her and watched as she gingerly pulled the photo and the paper out of the debris, brushing several splinters of glass off of them, and held the drawing up so they could both see it clearly. The diagram resembled a crudely drawn blueprint or floor plan. There were three rectangles that appeared to be rooms, with gaps in the adjoining walls to signify doors. From the largest rectangle, what looked like a ladder or steps went off to one side and ended with a single word; Singer. From the other end of the larger area, what could have been a hallway, a path, or even a road, extended nearly to the bottom of the page, ending in the word Basement.

"This was hidden behind the picture the whole time," Kate said, studying the drawing carefully. "It looks like the inside of a small house."

"Yeah it does," Ben mused. "But it's not. It can't be. See this? There are doors, here, between all the rooms but none on the outside walls. And this can't be a hallway; it's five times as long as everything else combined."

"Maybe it's part of a floor plan," Kate interjected, "maybe it's part of the inside of a larger building, like an office building. That would explain the long hallway, walkway, whatever it is."

"Maybe," Ben said, sounding less than convinced. "But what's the connection? Why did someone hide it in this particular frame?"

"Better yet, why would someone risk hiding a drawing behind a photo at all, when photo-paper isn't completely opaque. Wouldn't they have been afraid someone would see it through the picture?"

Ben's expression sharpened as he gazed back and forth between the two pages. "What if that was the idea," he said softly, sliding the paper into its original position behind the photo, being careful to orient it the way they'd found it. Through the image, they could barely make out some of the lines in the drawing. "You wouldn't see it in the frame unless you knew what you were looking for, the cardboard blocks all the back-light, but take it out of the frame..." He tipped the picture up to the light and smiled. "Voila."

The diagram was clearly visible now, its lines seemingly superimposed on the black and white photo of the cemetery. The rectangular rooms were together in the upper left corner, positioned neatly beneath the same horseshoe-shaped hill they'd surveyed together. What they'd guessed were steps, ended at one of the mausoleums at the base of the hill. What they'd taken for a hallway angled downward, past the garden and the guest-house and ended at the funeral home.

Kate ran her finger over the word Basement. "Holy shit," she whispered.

Ben tapped the photo with a fingertip. "This is why no exterior doors are marked on the floor plan; there aren't any. Kate, this is all underground! It has to be. It's the only explanation. This is some kind of bunker or vault. See how it all fits so perfectly under the hill?"

Kate walked to the sink and stared into the drain, deep in thought. "The chair they brought from New York. Remember how I said they stayed in the cooler like, twenty minutes? I said nobody could take the cold for that long. But they weren't even *in* the cooler! That hallway thing on the map comes out in our freaking basement, doesn't it? In the preparation room." She turned to Ben with a knowing smirk. "I was only in the cooler for a couple of minutes, but there was a tall steel panel on the back wall. It had dials and switches on it. I thought it was a control panel for the cooler, but it could be some kind of hidden door, couldn't it? That's it; I'll bet you a hundred bucks."

"It explains everything," Ben said, still examining the photo as he stood up. He could barely contain his excitement. "We've been beating ourselves up about the cemetery, but this is why they did it. Kate, it's ingenious. You want to build a place like this and keep it secret – forever? Put a graveyard over it! It's sacred ground for Christ's sake; nobody's ever going to touch it. They built this in 1945, along with the cemetery, the house, and everything else and it's been there ever since."

"Don't forget about the airstrip."

"That too. Easy, private access in case you need to move something in or out without anyone knowing."

Kate was feeling light-headed again. "Jesus, this is huge," she murmured, walking slowly back across the room, oblivious to the crunching of glass beneath her shoes. "What have they been doing in there for sixty years?"

"I don't know, but I'll bet you a hundred bucks this was Jimmy Smoot's big story, the one Dan Bayer mentioned in the letter. Remember, he said they were perpetrating a deception on the people of Stanton?"

"Yeah, and he also said he betrayed Andrew and Mitchell, right? Do you think Dan Bayer told Smoot about all of this in the first place? Is that how he knew?"

As her questions hung in the air, and along with them, the implications of Dan Bayer's alleged suicide, a wave of fear rippled through them, souring the excitement they felt at their discovery.

Kate's face blanched. "She knew. Gram knew about this; I know she did. That's why she looked so strange when I showed her the picture. What if she knows about all of it? Ben, I have to go back." She walked past him, into the living room.

"Where? What are you talking about?"

"Home, to the house, to see Gram. I have to know. And this time, I'm not leaving until she tells me what the hell is going on."

"What about Walter and Everett?"

"Screw them," she said, pulling her coat from the back of a chair. "I don't even care anymore if she tells them." Kate glanced into the kitchen and groaned at the sight of the mess. "God, I almost walked off and left you with that."

She started to put her coat down, but Ben stopped her. "You need to go. If you think you've got a shot, go. I'll take care of this. Just call me. I can only take so much suspense."

She kissed him and hurried for the door, mentally preparing herself for whatever she might hear, hoping she could bear the truth, once she finally knew it.

Streetlights were beginning to flicker on in the gathering twilight as Kate climbed into her car and backed out of the driveway. Ben's street was quiet, and she passed no other cars until she stopped to turn left. As she started to pull out, a black Lexus sedan approached at a crawl and turned onto the street. Dark-tinted windows made it impossible to see the occupants, but as it passed her car, it stopped, and for a chilling moment, she was sure the driver was staring at her. She quickly averted her eyes and pulled away, feeling strangely unnerved by the encounter.

When Chief Hughes returned to the police station in Stanton, he was greeted by silent stares from the officers in the common area but said nothing as he strode past Janet and into his office. Lieutenant Wallace was close behind him, turning angrily and slamming the door behind them. "What in Christ's name is going on here, Sir."

When Hughes turned around, his face was pale, and his lips were drawn in anger. "Don't come in here with that tone, Terry. I'm running this precinct, and I don't answer to you, last time I checked."

"Yes sir, that may be so," Wallace snapped. "But you answer to the same taxpayers I do, and you damn well owe them an explanation about why you pulled the rug out from under this investigation. Captain, there was another player, and you know it, we had proof."

Hughes took a step toward Wallace. "We didn't have proof. We had speculation, damn it. That old bat stopped in the lobby to talk to someone. It doesn't prove anything, neither does the letter. And if the Governor is satisfied she acted alone, then she acted alone. I'm not going to buck that."

"All due respect sir, that's bullshit!" Wallace stormed.

Hughes slammed his fist down on the desk, sending a small stack of papers tumbling onto the floor. "Back off Captain, or you'll be out of here on your ass! Can I be any clearer on that?"

The two men glared at each other in silence, Wallace considering his response, Hughes struggling with the position he now found himself in, fighting with a man he'd worked closely with and respected for years; a man he'd always considered a friend.

Hughes hung his head and rubbed his temples. "Look, Terry," he said, standing and walking toward the darkened window. "This goes so far above my pay grade it's giving me a goddamn nose bleed. I've got a career to consider here and so do you, so stop busting my balls over it."

"So you're just going to roll over, is that what you're saying?"

"Get out! Take a day off. Matter of fact, take two and think about your future. We're a team on this, or you need to find another game. I'll see you on Monday."

Twenty minutes later, Lieutenant Wallace sat in his truck, in the parking lot, looking at the box of personal items he'd thrown together after his argument with Hughes. If he still felt like quitting when Monday came, it would save him the trouble.

He was just shoving his key into the ignition when he saw Sergeant Pearl waving from the precinct door, a piece of paper in his hand. Reluctantly, Wallace rolled down his window and motioned the officer over. Pearl began talking excitedly before he reached the parking lot and Wallace had to ask him to repeat himself. "Sir, I know what the chief said about calling off the interviews, but I think you need to see this. A woman named Sherry Townsend just called. She was one of the first people we talked to. Swore at the time she was already seated in the hall when the conversation happened. Now she's calling, claiming she was just scared to get involved, swears she saw the whole conversation between our guy and the old woman."

Wallace let out a heavy breath and drummed on the steering wheel with his fist. "Look, Mike, I appreciate your letting me know, but it's over. Nobody's going to..."

"Captain, she knows the guy we're looking for – knows his *name*."

Part of Wallace wanted to send Pearl back inside, but another part, the part that had worked so hard to break this case, wasn't ready to let it go. He leaned out the window and pointed at the paper in Pearl's hand. "Fine, let's see what you've got."

An hour later, Terry Wallace finally had the name he'd been waiting for; Ben Tuttle. Sherry Townsend had been more than an acquaintance of his; she'd been his girlfriend in high school. She choked back tears when she confessed that she'd withheld the information because she hadn't wanted to get Ben in trouble. She kept insisting that he would never be involved in something like this. Wallace had known immediately that she was telling the truth. By now he'd memorized the list and Tuttle's name was third.

He debated his next move as he drove back into town, furious that now, after the god-damned press conference, even if Tuttle confessed his involvement, nothing would come of it. He would likely butt heads again with Hughes if he took Townsend's lead and ran with it, but he was past caring. For all practical purposes, his days on the Stanton police force were numbered. He might as well get a little satisfaction in the process.

Wallace called the station and asked for a workup on Tuttle; bio, vehicle records, priors, anything they could find, but he didn't expect much, and he was right. As he drove past the cinema eight, they radioed back to inform him that Tuttle was lily-white; no criminal record of any kind. DMV showed no violations, ever. The guy didn't even have any traffic tickets, for Christ's sake.

When they gave him the license plate of the Land Rover registered to Tuttle, Wallace asked that a couple of officers look out for the vehicle on their regular rounds. They were not to approach but were to notify him immediately instead. He would do the honors this time.

As he was ending the call, he heard chatter over the radio. The dispatcher was sending units to 419 Vinroot Court for a possible 10-19; homicide, and when Wallace heard the name of the victim, he nearly lost his breath. He pulled off the road into a parking lot and reached for the paper in his pocket. He had to be sure his memory wasn't playing a cruel trick, but it was there, as he knew it would be. Charles Teague – the first of six names.

As Ben carefully swept up the mess in his kitchen floor, he tried to imagine how Kate's confrontation with her grandmother might go. If she relented and told what she knew, they could be looking at the whole picture, for the first time. This could be Kate's pivotal moment, he thought, wondering again how she would hold up.

Not bothering to turn on the floodlight, he carried a dust pan full of broken glass out his deck door and down the back steps to the trash can at the head of his driveway. Just as he was reaching for the lid, he saw movement through a gap in the hedge and turned to see a man in a suit getting out of a black sedan parked across the road from his house. The man was completely bald and wore sunglasses, despite the relative darkness. He carried a black bag in one hand as he crossed the street and walked briskly up to the front steps.

Ben stood still, hoping that he would not be seen in the shadows of the hedge row. Something about this man made him uneasy. Clearly no salesman, he might have been a cop, but the shooting investigation was over, wasn't it? Yes, he'd seen the announcement with his own eyes. They were no longer looking for another suspect, so who the hell was this guy and what did he want?

Ben couldn't see the man at his front door, but he heard the doorbell ring. Very carefully, he eased the dustpan to the pavement and remained crouched, fully intending to wait it out. "Hit the road asshole," he mouthed silently. "I'm not home."

When several more seconds passed with no sign of the man returning to his car, Ben tiptoed to the corner of the hedge for a better look. He was about to peer around it when he heard a click, followed by the unmistakable creaking of his front door. A sick panic gripped him as he realized what was happening; this man, whoever he was, had just picked the damn lock and walked right in.

Ben ran into the back yard, careful to stay hidden behind the trees. From here he could partially see into the house through the sliding glass door. "Jesus, I'm being robbed!" Ben hissed. The bald man was there, walking from room to room, looking for something, scanning everything around him. The sight turned Ben's fear to anger, yet he didn't dare confront the man, and he was helpless to call the police; he'd left his cell phone in the living room.

As he debated running to a neighbor's house, Ben

watched the man walk into his kitchen and set the black bag down on the table. He reached into it and, to Ben's horror, pulled out a black pistol with a silencer on the barrel. Ben felt weak, almost dizzy from fright. This was no cop; this man was there to kill him.

On the table, next to the laptop, Ben could see his car keys, and he cursed himself for not keeping them in his pocket. He watched the man pick up a stack of papers and leaf through them, pausing to study certain pages. Ben remembered that he had never thrown away the aerial photos he and Kate had printed for their trip to Bryson City. The intruder seemed keenly interested in them, removing his glasses for a better look. A moment later, the man pulled out a cell phone and made a call, holding one of the pages in his hand as he talked as if attempting to describe it to someone. A dark thought crossed Ben's mind; what if they'd gotten too close to whatever the Greasons were hiding? What if this man worked for Kate's grandfather? His mind reeled at the possibility. "That's it," he whispered. "They're on to us."

When the man in the suit finished his call, he raised the pistol and headed to the back of the house, turning on lights as he went. For a terrible moment, Ben imagined that he'd not been out in the driveway, but hiding in the house instead – but he quickly pushed the image from his mind.

Again he eyed his keys on the table and wondered how quickly he could get in and back out with them. It seemed an insanely risky idea, but it was his only good chance to get away in the Rover and go for help. If the bald man were checking the whole house, he would head to the basement next. If Ben could be ready by the deck door, he would have a few precious seconds to grab the keys and get to the car.

There was no time to consider another option; he had to move now or be stuck trying to get away on foot. Ben crept to the base of the deck steps and eased up them, crouched low, so that his head did not rise above the top step. His heart pounded in his chest as the man appeared again in the kitchen, frighteningly close now; close enough for Ben to see the pink scar under his left eye. For a moment, Ben wondered if he had misjudged, but after a cursory look around, the man turned and headed down the stairs.

Holding his breath, Ben crept across the deck and eased the door open, praying that the floorboards wouldn't give him away. He couldn't remember being so scared as he tip-toed through the kitchen to the table, ready to bolt at the first sign of trouble. He folded the car keys into his hand and was about to duck back out the door when he heard his cell phone ringing somewhere in the living room. He hesitated for an agonizing moment, tempted to make a desperate grab for it, but loud footfalls on the basement steps sent him dashing back out the door instead and down the deck steps without looking back.

Ben's breath was coming in short gasps as he climbed into the Rover and put the key in the ignition. Would the man hear him start the car? Would he give chase? "Focus!" his mind screamed, as he cranked the engine and slammed the stick into reverse. He backed the Rover out of the driveway and sped down the street without looking back. He didn't need to; he knew they would be close behind. He had to get off the main roads, find a back way to Werner-Greason, but first, he had to get to a phone. If he and Kate had been discovered, she might well have driven straight into a trap.

Kate was getting worried by the time she turned into the driveway of Werner-Greason. She had tried Ben's number twice on the way over and had gotten no answer. Now, as she tried again, she willed him to pick up, pleading with him in her mind. She felt a wave of relief as the ringing stopped. He'd finally picked up.

"Ben! It's me! Are you alright?"

But there was no answer from the other end, only silence.

"Ben, can you hear me? It's Kate."

The phone clicked off.

A sinking feeling came over her as she tried to reassure herself. It was just bad reception, wasn't it? How could it be anything else? Still, she wondered if she shouldn't turn around and go back, try this errand in the morning. "You're being paranoid," she told herself as she pulled up in the back lot, in front of the kitchen door. "Besides, you're already here."

The kitchen was empty, as was the rest of the ground floor, as Kate passed through on her way to the stairs, the photo and the map tucked firmly under one arm. Walter would have closed everything up for the night and gone up to his apartment by now, which left Kate in a much better position to catch her grandmother alone. Anxious to hurry the meeting along and get back in touch with Ben, she climbed the steps two at a time, expecting to make the short jog to her Gram's room and surprise her. Instead, when she rounded the corner, she saw Edna hurrying down the hall toward her, looking more distraught than she had ever seen her. Black streaks of mascara ran down her cheeks, and her lips were trembling. Kate was aghast. "Gram what's..."

"Katie, I don't know what you've done, but everything's a big damn mess!" Edna croaked in a hoarse whisper. "You shouldn't be here; it's not safe. Please, just go. Get back in your car and leave before they realize you're here."

"What's happened? What do you mean?" Kate pleaded, still in shock at her grandmother's wretched condition.

"They're on a tear, an awful tear, like I haven't seen in a long time; something about you and your friend. They're in there bellowing at each other about it like wild animals."

In the momentary silence, Kate could hear raised voices from the other end of the hall, and her stomach dropped like a stone. "What are they saying? You have to tell me, it's important!"

Edna cast a nervous glance over one shoulder, in the direction of the corner offices. "There's no time, Katie. There's a lot of things I should have told you but now isn't the time. For God's sake, please go."

"No, Gram," Kate stamped. "I'm not leaving until you tell me what the hell is going on around here. I have to know." Kate pulled the photo from under her arm. "And I want the truth about this."

He grandmother looked tired, far beyond her years, as she finally relented, new tears spilling down her wrinkled face. "Katie, I lied about the photo," Edna began, wiping her eyes with the sleeve of her robe. "I'm sorry. I just couldn't bear to look at it again. A dear friend gave me that, a very, very long time ago. His name was Jimmy."

"Jimmy Smoot?" Kate asked, incredulous.

"How do you know that name?" Edna gaped. "How do you know about Jimmy?"

"Gram I know a lot more than you think. He was here writing some kind of story, and he disappeared, right?"

Edna put a hand to her mouth and shook her head. "It's been so many years. I just wanted it all to go away. I wanted you to get away from here, from all of this, and find something good for yourself, but that Bayer woman went and stirred it all up again."

"Gram, what happened to Jimmy?" Kate pleaded.

"He died," she whispered, looking away.

"How?" Kate persisted.

When her grandmother spoke, her voice was choked in a sob. "He knew. Somehow, he found out about them, about everything. He was going to publish a story, tell everyone, but he changed his mind. He didn't want to hurt me. He did it for me. But they didn't know and...they killed him."

"What?" Kate gasped, recoiling at her grandmother's words. The idea that had merely been an abstraction until now, entertained by the side of her that hated him. But to hear it said, openly, in such a way that she knew it was real, was almost more than she could fathom.

"I was so young then," Edna continued. "It was such a long time ago. Jimmy and I loved each other. He tried to tell me, warn me about what my father and Andrew were doing, but I didn't believe him. I was so stupid!"

Kate put her hand on her grandmother's arm. "It's okay, Gram."

"No, it's not okay. He begged me to come away with him. He said he was willing to give up his story, anything if I would just come with him. He..." Edna paused. "He wanted to marry me. I said no. And then they found out who he was."

Just then, from the far end of the house, they heard a door slam, and Everett's voice boomed down the hall. "Edna! Where the hell are you?"

With a frightened look back, Edna opened the door nearest Kate and motioned her inside, turning on the light and closing the door behind them. The tiny storage closet was crowded with wall-to-wall linen shelves and stacks of boxes, with barely enough room for them to stand, facing each other.

Heavy footsteps approached in the hallway and stopped just outside the closet door. Kate and Edna braced themselves; sure they would be discovered. "Edna! Are you down here? God damn it!" He continued to rant, but his voice receded as he went back the way he'd come.

"Kate, listen to me," Edna hissed. "I have to go. The day before Jimmy died he told me about a box he'd hidden under a floorboard in his bedroom, in the guest house, where he was staying. He said it had all of his notes in it, about the story. He was going to leave, and he wanted me to have it. He said he hoped I'd learn the truth and come and find him, but I didn't want to hear it."

Kate's heart was pounding. "Do you have them, the notes?"

"I'm so ashamed," she muttered. "It was all too

much for me. I never had the strength to go and get it, even to this awful day. I learned later what a terrible mistake I'd made and look at me. Just look at me now."

"I should just go out there and tell him to go to hell," Kate fumed. "Just call the police and have him arrested."

Edna grabbed Kate's wrist and her face contorted into a grimace. "No! You don't understand what he's capable of. I think...I think he may be planning on hurting your friend. And I think he's capable of hurting you too."

"Jesus," Kate said. "He's my grandfather!"

Edna smiled weakly and patted Kate's arm. "Sweetie, Everett isn't your grandfather; Jimmy is."

Kate's jaw went slack as Edna kissed her on the cheek and slipped out the door, turning one last time. "Please be careful, Katie. Do what you think is right, I never did." And she was gone, leaving Kate in the dim light of the closet with her thoughts.

Everett saw Edna round the corner and charged along the corridor to meet her. "Where have you been?" he demanded.

"I was in the kitchen, not that it's any of your goddamn business," Edna growled.

Everett glared menacingly at her as Walter emerged from the back stairwell behind him, looking badly out of breath. "Her car is in the back lot," he panted. "She's here somewhere."

"Where is she?" he snapped at Edna. "That little bitch! I'll slap that lying grin off her face when I get a hold of her."

Edna was fuming. "You leave her out of this,

Everett. She hasn't done anything."

"She's betrayed us!" Everett roared in her face. "That little whore has been sneaking around with some local yokel, trying to wreck us all, after everything we've done for her." His eyes narrowed. "You know where she is, don't you? That's where you've been. Are you part of this too?"

He balled up his hand as if to strike her, but she stood defiant, glaring up at him. "No, but I damn well should have been. And if you as much as harm one hair on her head I'll..."

"You'll what, mother," Walter sneered from behind Everett. "Have another drink? Maybe a double? Why don't you crawl back in your bottle? I like you better that way."

"Walter you're a disgrace! You should be ashamed of yourselves, both of you!" Edna barked. "You're nothing but a couple of..."

Everett's fist smashed into the side of her face, sending her careening into the wall. She collapsed in a heap on the floor at his feet and lay still, groaning softly through her bloodied lips. He stepped over her and strode down the hall. "Check the ground floor," he called over his shoulder. "Find her!"

Terry Wallace was driving down Regis in an unmarked Crown Victoria, on his way to the address where Ben Tuttle lived, when a Land Rover, matching the description of Tuttle's, emerged from a side street a few hundred yards ahead of him. As the vehicle rolled past a stop sign and accelerated quickly onto Regis, Wallace's pulse jumped, and he eased his speed up to keep pace. He checked the license plate against the DMV rundown they had given him earlier on Ben Tuttle and got a hit.

Wallace cursed Hughes and the lousy timing of it all. The apparent futility of his effort and that of his department enraged him as he watched the tail lights of the Rover. If they had identified Tuttle even a day earlier, Hughes would not have been able to close the case, and more importantly, Charles Teague might still be alive.

Teague's murder had finally convinced Wallace that this case was rotten – from the head down. Everything about it reeked; the snap-diagnosis of Margaret Bayer Greene's state of mind, Hughes' obsession with keeping the list of names from the video analysis secret, even within the department, and worst of all, the prearranged farce of a press conference to close the investigation as quickly as possible. He had begun to question everything about the case, including the demise of the old woman herself; wounded yes, but the doctors had given her a reasonable chance of survival. It was decidedly convenient that she expired so quickly that night, before regaining consciousness; before she had a chance to clarify what she said to Everett Greason at the podium, just before she opened fire.

All of it pointed to a much darker scenario, one in which some of the state's most powerful people were pursuing a private, violent agenda – one involving Ben Tuttle and the mysterious envelope. Whatever the Greene woman had given him was apparently of such importance that they were willing to stop at nothing to get it.

As the Rover's brake lights came on and Wallace watched it pull into a gas station, he made up his mind. He knew what he had to do. There would be consequences, yes, but Ben Tuttle was his only chance to prove that this case was about something much more important than Margaret Greene. He wasn't going to sit by and let Hughes take it from him.

All Ben could think about as he whipped into the gas station parking lot was Kate. He jumped out and grabbed the pay phone, furious at himself for not being more careful, for not seeing something like this coming. He'd never be able to live with himself if something happened to her.

The phone was dead. He swore and slammed it down, spinning around both ways to look for another one anywhere close by, but there was nothing. He barely noticed the burgundy Crown Victoria pulling into the parking lot until the driver got out and pointed a pistol at him.

"Stanton police! Turn around and put your hands behind your head!"

Ben gasped and raised his hands. "I. . .you don't understand," he stammered.

"Turn around, now!" the officer barked, tightening his grip on the pistol.

Several people at the gas pumps backed off, and one woman ran inside as Ben turned and laced his fingers over the back of his head, his mind racing, trying desperately to think of a way out. He would have to tell them the truth now, incriminating or not, and beg for their help. It was the only way.

"Walk slowly back toward me," the officer ordered. "Stop! That's far enough. Now spread your feet apart."

Ben heard footsteps behind him, and a rough hand patted him down for weapons, running quickly up and down his sides and both legs.

"What's this about? What did I do?" Ben demanded.

"Put your hands behind your back."

Ben fought the urge to bolt and run as the officer slipped a thick plastic band around his wrists and pulled it tight. "What did I do?" he repeated.

"Are you Benjamin Christopher Tuttle?"

"Yes, I am."

The officer turned him around and holstered his weapon. "We have an outstanding warrant for your arrest."

"For what?"

Without answering, he pulled Ben by the arm and led him around to the open passenger door of the Victoria. "Have a seat."

The screeching of tires startled them both, and they looked up to see a jet black, military-issue hummer, stopped in the road just beyond the pay phone, its engine racing. The officer tensed, and Ben's stomach lurched.

"That's them!" Ben said. "That's the assholes that are after us! You didn't give me a chance to explain."

"Wait here. Don't move," the officer said, taking a step away from Ben, toward the front of the car, his hand resting again on his nine millimeter H and K. With a deep roar, the Hummer sped off, accelerating through a solid red light before disappearing over the crest of a hill.

"Jesus," Ben groaned, as he climbed into the passenger seat. "That's not even the same guy who broke into my house. That guy was driving a Lexus, and he had a gun, with a silencer on it. That's what I'm trying to tell you. They're after Kate and me. She may be in danger; they may have her for all I know. I've got to find her, please! I need your help."

"What are you talking about? Who broke into your house? Just slow down," the officer said as he climbed into the driver's seat.

The plastic band dug into Ben's wrists as he twisted in his seat to face the officer. "I don't have time to slow down. If this is about the shooting, I had nothing to do with it, I swear to God! Please don't arrest me; I have to find Kate."

Wallace tried to keep a clear head. "I'm not charging you with anything," he said. "At least, not yet, but I want some answers. You've got some very powerful people after you, and I want to know why; I want to know what you and Margaret Greene talked about that night at the Civic Center and I want to know what she gave you. And don't try to fuck with me on this. From where I'm sitting, I may be the only friend you've got."

"Fine, but if you're not going to charge me, take these damn things off," Ben said, swiveling sideways to display his bound wrists. "I'm not exactly the criminal type. I've never even gotten a ticket, for Christ's sake."

"I know," Wallace muttered, as he reached to cut the tie. Ben started to talk, but Wallace's cell phone cut him off. It was officer Payne, a close personal friend of Wallace's since childhood, who now worked as a dispatcher. "Terry, it's Bob. I called to give you a heads up, but we never had this conversation, got it?"

"Yeah," Wallace grunted.

"I don't know what you're into with Hughes, but

he's pissed. He just had me roll two units to pick you up! They're headed to your twenty right now."

Wallace's eyes narrowed. "How the hell did you know my twenty, Bob? I haven't called in."

"I didn't. Hughes told me. Don't ask me how he knew. I can't talk, but that's the deal. Good luck." He clicked off.

Wallace scowled as he remembered the Hummer. "What the fuck is going on here?"

"It's Everett Greason," Ben said, rushing now to talk. "He's got some kind of con going up there at Werner-Greason Funeral Home. It's too complicated to explain, but you've got to believe me, it's something big. That's what the letter was about. It was from Dan Bayer, Margaret's father. He worked for Greason and Werner at the end of World War Two."

"Jesus, give me minute here. Bayer is the guy who killed himself in the fifties, right?"

"But he didn't!" Ben said. "He says in the letter that he betrayed them, he told their secret to some reporter from Denver who went missing not long after. Bayer knew they were coming for him. He knew they were going to kill him for it, and they did. They just made it *look* like a suicide. That's why she did it; that's why she tried to shoot him. She wanted all this time to prove that Everett Greason was a fraud, but she couldn't find the evidence. She gave me the letter to give to Kate, Everett's granddaughter."

Wallace rubbed his forehead with one hand. "Are we talking about the same Everett Greason – the guy getting the *Lifetime Service Award?*"

"I know how it sounds, but we've nearly got it all

figured out. They know we're close! That's why they're after us."

"Who's we? Who are you working with on this?"

"Kate Greason, Everett's granddaughter. She's my, my girlfriend, I guess. I mean, since the shooting."

Wallace grimaced. "Okay, go on."

"This is the crazy part; the old part of the cemetery up on the hill is a fake. The headstones were all put there at the same time, the year they built the place. It's a cover, for some kind of underground bunker. We've even got a map."

A blue light startled them both, and Wallace tensed. An unmarked car had pulled in behind them and was flashing its strobe.

"Where did this guy come from?" Wallace said as he rolled his window down and held his badge out in plain view. "Bob didn't say anything about an unmarked."

Ben counted several seconds, but the driver of the other car didn't move.

"I don't like this," Wallace confessed. "This guy didn't have time to drive all the way from the station. Something's wrong here. Put your belt on, now."

Ben obliged, his senses now hyper-alert at the rising sense of danger. Wallace stared intently into his side-view mirror, and as the man behind them climbed from his car, Wallace eased the stick into Drive. Ben held his breath.

With lightning speed, Wallace slammed the gas pedal to the floor, throwing Ben backward in the seat. Tires screeched on the pavement as they sped over the curb and slammed hard onto the road. Ben heard two loud pops behind them and felt a sting on the side of his face.

"Get down!" Wallace barked, shoving Ben low in the seat.

They careened through a curve and sped down a side street, and as Ben looked up, he saw a ragged-edged bullet hole in the front windshield.

"That's no cop!" Wallace shouted as he grabbed the radio. "Base this Wallace!"

As they neared a side road, the black Hummer appeared, as if out of nowhere, roaring toward them at breakneck speed. For a split second, Ben saw the front of the Hummer, framed neatly in Wallace's window, then, a mind shattering crash sent him tumbling into darkness.

He awoke seconds later to a strange silence, the smell of burning oil – and pain. One eye was clouded with blood, and when he opened the other, he saw chaos; twisted metal and broken glass where seconds before, a car interior had been. The driver's side had been crushed inward. Ben tried to breathe as he saw Wallace, slumped sideways against his chest belt, his head lolled forward, dripping blood onto his shirt and the white fabric of the deflated airbag in his lap. The steering wheel had been driven down, against Wallace's lap and his legs disappeared under the wreckage of the dash.

Ben heard a car door slam and someone approaching. He tried to move, but his muscles wouldn't respond. His mind was spinning, his vision blurred. He struggled against the confusion amid a rising panic.

Got to get out, he thought, fumbling for the door handle. It was jerked open instead, and cold air rushed in, followed by a fist. Another stab of pain as his head was snapped sideways, his jaw nearly broken. Ben screamed.

A blade was cutting the seat belt, and he was jerked from the twisted remains, ears ringing, barely conscious now. He saw pale, expressionless faces and hands holding a black cloth bag. He tried to cry out, but they stuffed it over his head as the world went dark.

9

When the sounds of Everett's and Walter's footsteps had receded, Kate cracked the door and peered out to find the hallway deserted again. Still reeling from her grandmother's confession, she wiped a trickle of sweat from her forehead and crossed the hall, to the top of the main staircase. There she paused, listening for any sound of movement from below, but there was only silence.

The latest revelation had cemented her resolve to discover the full extent of her family's corruption, yet she had never been more afraid. Her mind floundered, grasping for something safe to cling to as the fabric of her reality continued to unravel at every turn. Her trust was gone, replaced by creeping doubt; everyone and everything that had been her life was suspect; all except Ben.

And even as she leaned against the door frame, struggling to regain her equilibrium, thoughts of him only spurred her anxiety. Unable to reach him after several tries, she found it increasingly hard to fend off the idea that some harm had come to him, that they had done something to him. But she had to believe he was alright, had to will her mind to keep going, to focus on the information at hand, the break her Gram had given her; the hiding place of Jimmy Smoot's notes.

A cough somewhere below, and footsteps in the ground floor hall broke Kate from her trance. She hurried down the hall in the opposite direction, toward the old wing, which housed the former apartments of Mitchell Werner and his family. Near the end, a narrow set of stairs led down to the North hallway on the ground floor, emerging beside a coat closet near the side exit. It would bring her out farther away from the guest house, but she didn't care. She had to get outside where she could breathe, where she could hide, and where if nothing else, she could flee if she had to. The house felt like little more than a death-trap to her now.

After descending the steps, Kate reached the side door without incident, frequently stopping to listen. She winced at the creaking of the outer door on its hinges, but the sound brought no one running. The hallway was still clear as she stepped outside, into the welcoming night air and closed the door behind her. But as she turned to step down to the walkway, a glow to her left caught her eye, and she heard the sound of an engine. Headlights danced over the crest of the hill and Kate dived for the only cover she could see; a row of bushes that lined the driveway, scarcely fifteen feet from her.

She had barely hit the ground when a large, loud vehicle sped up the driveway, flooding everything around her with the beams from its headlights and choking her in a cloud of noxious exhaust. Through the bushes, she saw the unmistakable profile of a Humvee, an imposing vehicle by any standard, which, from her position prostrate on the ground, appeared utterly massive. The vehicle slowed as it rumbled by her, turning the corner out of sight, into the back parking lot of the house.

When Kate realized she hadn't been seen, the momentary wave of terror subsided, and she raised herself to a crouch, brushing loose grass and dirt from the front of her clothes. Staying low, she moved to the corner where she could see the back parking lot. The Hummer had pulled up in front of the basement doors, and its occupants were piling out. There were three of them, one in a suit and two in black fatigues, and all carried guns.

Kate's breath faltered as they opened the rear hatch and lifted someone out; a man with a black bag over his head. His hands were bound, and he swayed on his feet as they held him on either side. Even before she recognized his shoes, Kate knew it was Ben. She covered her mouth with her hand and choked back a sob, tears streaming down her face, barely able to suppress the impulse to scream his name and run to him, to confront his captors and demand that they let him go. But the futility of it screamed back at her. She wouldn't be helping Ben; she would only be handing them what they wanted.

The basement doors opened, and Walter emerged, followed closely by Everett. Walter appeared on edge, his head turning from side to side, scanning the parking lot and surrounding trees. And with barely a word between them, the men in fatigues handed Ben over to Kate's father and Everett, turned, and climbed back into their vehicle. Kate was trembling now, as she lingered for a final look, watching as they ushered Ben through the basement doors. And as she ducked back down in her hiding place behind the shrubs, she wondered if she would ever see him alive again. Lying face down on the ground, Kate put her head in her arms and cried, glad at once that her sobs would not be heard over the roar of the vehicle's engine as it passed by.

Kate had never felt so utterly alone, so consumed with despair, and yet, she knew she was the only chance Ben had. Without the absolute proof that Jimmy Smoot's notes contained, her claims would be dismissed as the ravings of a woman who had lost her grip on reality. Like Margaret Bayer Greene, she would be cast as pathetically impaired and emotionally unstable. They would point to the failure of her marriage and the counselor she'd seen as proof, along with whatever other anecdotal evidence they contrived. And the more adamant she became, the more she railed, the less credible she would appear. After all, there was a history of instability among the Greason women, at least according to Everett. "After all," he would say, benevolent and sad. "Look at her grandmother."

Kate picked herself up and hurried for the shadows of the Bradford pear trees that lined the far side of the driveway, grateful for whatever small measure of safety the darkness provided. She turned again, her breath rapid and shallow, and checked the house for any sign that she had been spotted, but there was no movement. Everett and Walter would be occupied with Ben, but Carl Lentz was almost certainly combing the house at Everett's request, looking for her. Worse still, Carl had a small army of workers at his disposal. If he wanted to, he could call in a half-dozen of them to help with the search. Fortunately for her, Everett would likely be too concerned about secrecy to ever allow that. Carl was clearly their partner in whatever seedy dealings they were engaged in, but she doubted his crew had any knowledge of what was hidden beneath their feet every day when they worked the grounds in Lark Hill.

As Kate moved from shadow to shadow, skirting behind the free-standing garage in the northwest corner of the back lot, she felt as though she were trapped in a hellish sort of nightmare that she couldn't rouse herself from. Only this was no dream; it was all too horribly real. As she ducked through the hedge and sprinted through the garden, she tried not to think of what they might do to Ben, but her fears overcame her will and the awful images that ensued brought tears of rage to her eyes.

The garden path brought her to within thirty yards of the guest house, and as she looked at the light in the upstairs window, doubt struck her like a hand across the face. What had she been thinking? How was she supposed to get in there without knowing if he was home? And how was she supposed to find a loose floorboard in his bedroom? No time, she thought, scolding herself as she glanced at her watch. She had to try, plan or no, for Ben's sake.

Approaching the back of the house at a crouch, Kate gently tested each of the downstairs windows but found them locked. She debated going around and trying those on the front of the house, but she would be too exposed, in plain sight of the kitchen windows. Instead, she rounded the corner and studied the rusting fuel oil tank that sat against one side of the screened in porch. The tank stood five feet high, enough to put her within reach of the porch roof, which was somewhat level. If she could get onto the roof, she would go in through the upstairs bathroom window, whether it was unlocked or not.

She picked up a rock and put it in her pocket, licked her lips, and began the climb, being careful not to slip on the flaking metal surface. She cringed several times as her knees bumped the tank, sending a low rumble echoing across the yard. If Carl was inside, she hoped he would mistake the sound for thunder.

Once on top, she pulled herself up onto the roof and lay flat, breathing hard and rubbing the abrasions she had gotten on one leg. Countless crickets filled the night air around her with their chorus as she looked out over the sea of ghostly white grave markers spreading out into the darkness. Rising, she walked slowly across the shingles, on tip-toes, up the slope of the roof until her face was level with the bathroom window. There was a tiny gap in the closed curtains, and through it, she saw the open bathroom door and directly across the hall, Lentz's bedroom. His bed was made, and the armchair was empty. Kate let out a long breath. She had been correct; Carl, it seemed, wasn't home.

On the second try, the bathroom window loosed its grip and slid upward. Kate reached inside and took hold of the antique radiator that sat beneath the window sill, using it to pull herself in, head-first. The silence was deafening as she stood up and waited, poised to scramble back out the window at the first sign of trouble.

After a moment, she tiptoed out of the bathroom and across the hall, into Carl's bedroom, where the air smelled stale, like old cigarettes. The room was sparsely furnished, in accordance with Carl's taste, with only a bed, a nightstand, a vanity, and an armchair. Mercifully, the richly stained hardwood floor was largely bare, save a narrow rug by the side of the bed and a pair of dirty coveralls just inside the door. Kate ducked down to keep her shadow from falling on the closed blinds and giving her presence away.

At first glance, none of the boards appeared loose or ill-fitted. She had no idea where to begin, nor did she have anything to test them with, save her shoe, for stamping. She had seen a movie once in which a detective located a murder weapon by stamping on floorboards until he heard a hollow sound, yet here, under her present circumstances, it seemed absurd. "That's definitely out," she whispered, shaking her head, thinking hard for some alternative.

The notes, if they existed at all, would give her enough leverage to secure Ben's release; she was sure of it. But she had to hurry. She needed something sharp, anything, a knife or a letter opener. The house had a small kitchen, but it, like the office, was downstairs, where she would almost certainly be caught if Lentz returned. Still, it was her only option.

Kate crept out into the hall and peered down the stairs, into the darkness. She took a deep breath and walked down them, holding nervously to the hand-rail. The ground floor was dark, save the faint glow from a security light on a pole, at the front corner of the house. She hurried down the hall to the back of the house, where the tiny kitchen overlooked the near edge of the cemetery – a notion which, even now, struck her as odd.

She found a knife rack on the counter, beside the stove, and chose the one with the sturdiest blade before turning to leave. As she stepped into the hallway, she heard a thump, followed by the click of a metal latch, and her nerves went taught. She froze on the spot, squinting through the murky light, constricted by fear as she watched the front door swing slowly inward.

The pain in Ben's head came in waves as he tried to walk upright beside the men who held him. He was badly disoriented, stumbling in perpetual darkness, trying to grasp what was happening to him. His arms were tightly bound behind him again. He had been riding in a vehicle, a loud vehicle, the Hummer, he guessed, lying on his side, rocking wildly on a rutted metal floorboard.

Still numb from the crash, he had not spoken when they pulled him out and made him stand, and now there were new voices, one of them strangely familiar. His mind clung to the sound of it, replaying its intonation until finally, it registered; the voice was Walter Greason's. The other would undoubtedly be Everett.

He was certain now that he had been delivered to Werner-Greason, ironically, the place he'd most wanted to go, only not like this. As they led him inside, away from the chilled night air, onto a carpeted floor, he wondered what had happened to Kate. Had they been waiting for her, ready to spring the moment she arrived? Was she here somewhere, bound and blindfolded, held against her will by her own family? The absurdity of it tore at him still.

And too, there was the chance, however slim, that she had caught on and slipped away before they could grab her. Maybe she was hiding somewhere, wondering about him, asking herself the same questions. She would have tried to call him, he was certain, but his phone was sitting uselessly in his living room. It was a mistake that would haunt him until he knew she was safe.

Another door swung open, and Ben was ushered into a room that had an unpleasant, chemical smell. The floor was hard, perhaps concrete or tile and their footsteps caused a faintly tinny echo. From everything Kate had told him, this had to be the preparation room, which meant there was little doubt where they were taking him. Ben only wished they would remove his hood so he could at least see the chamber that he and Kate had been searching so intently for.

A clunking noise in front of him, a latch of some kind, and he was pushed forward, into a blast of cold air. Here their footsteps were muted, their voices muffled. They were in the cooler. It is exactly what Kate said, he thought, smiling slightly. The entrance was in the cooler. Damn, she was good.

A hand gripped his arm and jerked him to a stop, while he heard the clicking of buttons being pushed. Another door opened, and they led him through. This time, he did not need to guess the size of the room. They were in a passage so narrow that they had to walk single file.

"Is Carl watching Edna?" a voice behind him asked. It was Walter's voice.

"No need," Everett said from the front. "We won't be hearing any more out of her. I think she got the point, loud and clear. She's probably off somewhere licking her wounds. Carl's checking the rest of the house."

"Do we need to get someone to help him? She could be anywhere."

Ben's ears pricked at this, sure Walter was referring to Kate.

"Out of the question," Everett snapped. "Carl can

handle it. He's locked the gate so she can't drive out. There's nowhere else for her to go. Besides, when she finds out we have him..." An open hand struck Ben across the face, sending another stab of pain through his temple. He groaned softly as Everett continued. "She'll come running; you mark my words. That little bitch is spineless."

Ben gritted his teeth under the cover of the hood, wishing he could choke the old bastard with his bare hands, but he bit his tongue instead; he didn't want them to curtail their conversation because he was listening.

Walter's hand pushed him hard between the shoulder blades, nearly pitching him forward. "Move, we haven't got all night."

Ben realized he had slowed to a shuffle and picked up the pace. He detected a turn, or at least a curve in their path, followed by another straight stretch. At last, they emerged into an open space that could only be the chamber he and Kate had seen drawn on the map, which meant they were underground, directly beneath the U-shaped mound in Lark Hill.

"Put him in there," Everett said.

"Are you sure?" Walter asked.

"Where else?" Everett shot back. "And tie him to the chair."

Ben's pain had eased considerably and the fog in his mind was clearing; the emotional numbness was beginning to give way to a sickening fear. He thought of dying here in this hole, a black hood over his head, without ever getting to see Kate or his family again, and his knees buckled. Ben pitched sideways into a heavy, waist high object and doubled over. His arm lay on top of something cold and smooth. "Jesus, get him off of that!" Everett

215

barked. "That's why I don't want him in here!"

Hands on either arm jerked Ben hard and threw him backward onto the floor where his full weight landed squarely on his bound hands. He lay on his side curled up and groaning, one wrist nearly broken from the impact. One of them grabbed his feet and started to drag him when something in him snapped. "Get off me!" he screamed, pulling his feet free. "I can walk. Just give me a chance to stand up for fuck's sake!"

There was silence as Ben rose, albeit unsteadily this time. A hand took his arm and pulled him to one side. He walked maybe ten steps and was pushed into a high backed wooden chair. When he was thoroughly bound, the hood was jerked from his head, and his eyes closed reflexively against the blinding light of the room.

Ben blinked and squinted. Everett's face was the first thing he saw, weathered and hard, glaring contemptuously at him. Walter was beside him, looking far more snake-like, with a narrow, almost reptilian jaw, black-framed glasses resting on his hawkish nose and a narrow mustache perched on his upper lip. It occurred to Ben for the first time that the two men looked nothing alike, to be father and son.

They were in a small room; an office of sorts with a desk and a filing cabinet, but no door. Behind Everett, through the doorway, Ben saw what, at first glance, looked like a flea-market. There were assorted pieces of furniture, cabinets with small drawers, lamps, candelabras, tapestries, and dozens of paintings on the walls. Only this was no junk collection; light reflecting off of the yellow metal that adorned nearly everything gave the space a warm, other-worldly glow. Ben had seen objects made of gold before but never like this, at least, never outside of a museum.

"What's in there doesn't concern you," Everett growled, turning Ben's head to face forward. "What's in here damn well should. I want to know who you really are and who you're working for, and I want to know now."

"Give me your word first that you'll leave Kate alone," Ben demanded, surprised by his own words.

Everett's face twisted into a menacing scowl and he grabbed Ben's throat, choking off his air supply. "Don't fuck with me you little shit, or I'll kill you where you sit. You're not the one calling the shots here, got it?"

Ben nodded, unable to speak. Everett released his grip, paced to the desk and turned, crossing his arms expectantly. "Talk"

Ben tried desperately to think. Should he tell them the truth? Maybe if he did, they would let him live. But how could they? He already knew too much. No, he decided, they would kill him anyway, as soon as they had what they needed. He had nothing to lose by stalling. It might buy him time to think of something else. He would have to bluff like in poker, only this time, the stakes were much higher. This time he was playing for his life.

Ben wet his parched lips with his tongue and tried his best to feign confidence. "I know everything about your operation, Mr. Greason. So do the people I work for. We've seen the blueprints. We know about your operation and about how you built Lark Hill as a cover." The shock that registered on their faces emboldened him, and he pushed on with an almost cocky edge. "We know about the airstrip, the out of town pick-ups in a hearse, the whole story. And just for the record, we know what really happened to Jimmy Smoot and Dan Bayer. And if anything happens to me, you can tack another life sentence onto what you've already got coming."

Ben's words hung in the silence of the room as Everett glared at him. Walter looked wildly between them, having obviously taken the bait. "Everett? What the hell is he saying? How do they know all that? I told you we..."

"Shut up!" Everett snapped, stopping Walter mid-sentence. But his eyes never left Ben, and after a moment, one corner of his mouth drew up in a kind of crooked smile. "Nice try, Mr. Tuttle."

"Everett, how could..."

But Everett cut Walter off again. "Can't you see he's bluffing? The people he says he works for don't exist, and, correct me if I'm wrong, Mr. Tuttle, but I'm guessing half of what you just told me was speculation, based on some weekend detective work and the help of my ungrateful whore of a granddaughter."

Ben's heart sank, but he struggled to maintain his veneer of bravado, unsure how to keep the ruse alive. "Fine," he shrugged, grasping now for anything. "Think what you want, but Dan Bayer sold your father and Mitchell Werner down the river. He gave his daughter and Jimmy Smoot copies of everything he did for your family. He sent her a letter telling her everything before he was murdered. Oh yeah, we know about that too; made to look like a suicide, only nobody ever found a note. That's because Margaret Greene had it the whole time, along with all the other evidence. She hired me, my firm, I mean," Ben stammered, "to fill in the missing pieces and turn all this over to the authorities."

The smile on Everett's face was gone, and his jaw worked back and forth in a slow, grinding motion. Walter stood nearby, gaping.

Ben continued, struggling to keep the momentum going. "You knew exactly why Mrs. Green tried to kill you, didn't you? Mentally unstable made a better story I guess. She had arranged a meeting with me that night to give me the final payment and the rest of the documents. We have them all now Mr. Greason; we're just checking the facts before we go to the feds."

"And what about Kate? Where does she play into all of this?" Everett snarled. "I suppose you're going to tell me she's secretly working for this mysterious firm as well?"

Ben tried to think fast. He had to choose his words carefully or risk endangering Kate more than she already was. "We used her to get to you, I'm afraid," he said slowly, forcing a sarcastic smile. "Mrs. Greene told me she could be easily fooled, so I played the boyfriend. She thinks we're in love, even now. It was unfortunate but necessary."

Everett was livid. He muttered something to himself as he turned and stalked out, with Walter on his heel. They launched into a heated debate in the outer room, and because there was no door on the tiny office, Ben was able to pick out some of what they said despite their attempts to keep their voices low.

"Yes, it's necessary," Everett said. "Tell Ramie to have the plane and crew on standby. We can't afford to take the chance."

There was more inaudible conversation before Walter's voice rose again. "Jesus Everett! We can't just pick up and leave. That was never part of the deal."

"That was always part of the deal, whether you wanted to admit it or not. You've benefited from this arrangement your whole life, but you never wanted to get your hands dirty. Well take a good look, because they're already dirty; as dirty as mine."

Walter was not convinced. "What if this son-of-bitch is lying?"

Everett looked away in the direction of the passage. "Go and get me a hammer and a bone saw from the prep room. We'll cut pieces off of him until we get the whole story and then we'll cremate what's left of him."

Everett glanced sideways at Ben, locking eyes with him. "And I can assure you he'll go in there very much alive."

As the old man's words sunk in and the gravity of Ben's situation hit him like a fist, he suddenly felt like he would faint. Walter's lips were moving now, but Ben could no longer hear him over the thundering of his own heart in his ears.

With no time to think, Kate ducked back into the kitchen of the guest house, clutching the knife to her chest and holding her breath. The front door closed again, quietly, and she heard shuffling on the floor, followed by the creaking of a step.

He knows I'm in here, she thought, trembling with fright at the prospect of being discovered. What would she do if he tried to hurt her? There was the knife, but she was repulsed by the idea of stabbing another person, especially someone she had known her whole life.

If she fled, she would never get the notes. Ben's only chance for rescue would be gone, and she couldn't let that happen, no matter what the cost.

Forcing herself to move, Kate eased back into the

hallway in time to see legs ascending the steps. They appeared to be bare, and for a moment, she thought her eyes must be playing tricks in the dim light. But it was true; they weren't Carl's legs at all. As the light of recognition went on in her mind, Kate raced to the foot of the steps. "Gram!" she hissed.

Edna let out a squawk and whirled around, grabbing at the hand rail for support. She put a hand to her heart as she squinted and leaned forward, peering down to the foot of the steps. "Kate! I was hoping I'd find you here. Come up here, quickly!" Edna was wearing her robe and slippers, looking as though she'd come down from her room for a midnight snack and had gotten lost.

Kate was elated and hurried up the stairs. "Gram what are you doing here? I thought you were..." But as she got closer, Kate recoiled at the deep purple on the side of her grandmother's face and the still open cut on her lip. "Oh my God, Gram, what happened?"

"It doesn't matter, Katie. I'm all right. Put that knife down before you stab someone."

In the moment, Kate had forgotten she was brandishing a large butcher's knife. "I got it to pry up floorboards."

Edna smelled strongly of alcohol but shook her head firmly. "You don't need it. Follow me." And without another word, she turned and disappeared around the corner. Kate didn't understand until they were in Carl's room. Without hesitating, Edna went straight to the far corner of the room, behind the armchair, and knelt down, running her fingers along the groove between two boards. She looked up at Kate and motioned her over. "It's here."

"I thought you said you'd never..."

"I said I'd never read them," Edna replied. "But I almost did, once, not long after it all happened. I came here when Carl was away and found this board and the box under it, I...just couldn't. I'd been through so much. But when I saw what you and your friend had gotten yourselves into, well, it's just got to stop. I can't watch anyone else get hurt, you of all people. You didn't ask for any of this, and you deserve better."

"Better than what?" Kate pleaded, a knot rising in her throat at her grandmother's shame.

"Better than us," she murmured, as her fingers found a hold and she pulled up one end of the floorboard, revealing a dark compartment beneath. Craning her neck, Kate saw the top of a metal box, no wider than a shoe box, through the opening.

Edna reached in and carefully retrieved it, turning it sideways so it would fit through the gap. She brushed a layer of dust from the top of the box and set it at Kate's feet. "You open it, Katie, please. But be quick."

Kate knelt down and took a deep breath before pulling gingerly at the latch. It flipped open, and she lifted the lid. Edna turned away and struggled to her feet.

"Gram?"

"I don't want to see it. Just...look and tell me."

The box was crammed full. Several spiral notebooks were bent over a disorganized wad of papers of all sizes. Some of the larger pieces had been rolled or folded many times to fit in the modest box. Kate pulled out the first notebook and bent it flat. It's once red cardboard binding was dingy and torn, but she found the pages intact and eagerly began flipping through them, skimming the writing she found there. "This is his writing," she whispered. "Jimmy Smoot's writing. It's a bunch of notes about our family and the business. Property sales, contractor notes. He's even got the name of the man that surveyed the property. It's all jumbled up."

She kept turning pages. "He's got a family tree diagram, sort of. It shows all the family at the time; you, Aunt Jean, Great Uncle Rufus, all of them."

Edna's hands were balled up over her mouth as she paced at the back of the room. "Go on," she urged.

"Mitchell and Andrew are at the top, but there's nothing more above them except question marks. It stops there."

As Kate turned the next page, a folded paper fell out onto the floor, and she carefully opened it, rotating it to one side to get a better look at the diagram in contained. It closely resembled the map she and Ben had found; only this one more closely resembled a blueprint. It was a map of the bunker, drawn in precise detail, and it had markings for electrical fixtures and vents, with notes about climate control. And this version had something else the other one didn't; a set of steps at the back of the chamber, leading to a drawing of a mausoleum. The word "Sinclair" was written on the tiny mausoleum icon, beside the words, "hidden entrance."

"This wasn't on the other one," Kate said animatedly. "I'm keeping it." As she tore it from the notebook, Edna let out a gasp.

"They've got Ben, Gram! This could be a way to get to him. There's no way I'm getting in through the prep room."

"You're right, I just. Never mind. What else is there?"

The next set of pages contained notes about the war. "It looks like he was collecting information about two men, officers in the war; one named Jerry Marconi and the other Heinrich Mueller. Mueller's name has "Nazi" written beside it. It's underlined a bunch of times like Smoot was mad."

Edna let out a low groan and, to Kate's surprise, pulled a small flask from her robe pocket and took a deep swig.

"Gram!"

"Awe screw it Katie, you know what I am. Just ignore it. I'm going to need a lot more of this before you're finished and you may too."

Kate turned her eyes back to the paper. "It's got dates of enlistment, ranks, units, but the word discharge has been scratched out, and "deceased" is written in its place, beside another question mark." Kate's eyes narrowed, and she ran her finger to the bottom of the page. "Gram this is talking about the Nazis and all the stuff they stole from the Jews before the camps; gold, jewelry, art." Her voice fell almost to a whisper as she read aloud, the tightness growing in her chest. "Where stored? Mueller and Marconi made a deal for transport. Mueller ran interference with SS, Marconi with Allied command. Authorizations forged. Another question mark. Transported by..." She paused and looked away in the direction of Lark Hill and the iron fence with its menacing Keep Out sign. "By air," she said. Finally, there was a roughly scratched note that made the hair on Kate's neck stand on end. "No record of Mueller and Marconi after the war. No record of Werner and Greason before the war."

Edna was watching Kate now, tears running down

her face. Kate tried to speak, but the words caught in her throat. "Graham, for God's sake," she finally managed. "Is this all true? Were Andrew and Mitchell…?" She was crying now, overcome with rage and sadness. "Not even their real names? They were someone else, Nazi criminals, douchebag parasites? And this is what they're hiding down there?" Kate's upper lip curled in disgust at the thought of it.

Edna nodded and turned away again. "I didn't know Katie, I swear, not until I was nearly grown, none of the women in the family knew. After Jimmy and I…after I got pregnant, Everett went on a tear. One day Jimmy was there, trying to tell me all of this, trying to convince me to come away with him, and the next day he was gone. I never saw him again." She sniffled and wiped her nose on her robe.

Kate thought again of Ben and knew what she had to do. She picked up the box. "This is the proof. It's everything we need. If they know we have it, they'll have to let Ben go."

Edna took a faltering step toward Kate. "Katie, please be careful, for God's sake. There's nothing they wouldn't do to keep this filthy secret, including harming you."

Kate stood up and put a hand on Edna's arm.

"Gram, I love him," Kate said. "I'm sorry, but I have to try."

Kate could tell by the look in her grandmother's eyes that she knew it would be futile to try and convince her otherwise.

"If you find them, try and talk to Walter. You may have a chance. There's still some part of Walter that's

225

human. Stay away from Everett. He's a monster."

"Okay, Gram. Now please go back to your room. You shouldn't even be here. You need to get some ice on your cheek." Kate said. "And call the police. Now that we have something solid, we can show them."

Edna looked even more dejected. "They already know, Katie. I think they've been involved all along. That police chief and your..." she paused "I mean, Everett have been friends for years. I hate to say it, but I think we're on our own."

Kate was stunned. "Jesus, I should have guessed. How could I have been this blind?"

Edna's eyes fell on the box again, and she reached out a trembling hand. "Please Katie, let me keep it. We have to keep it safe," she said. "And it's all I have left of Jimmy."

For a moment Kate hesitated. She knew Edna was right. Once Everett and Walter knew of the existence of the box and its contents they would want it at all cost. She carefully handed it to her grandmother. "Take this back to the house and hide it, Gram. Hide it where nobody can find it."

From across the cemetery, they heard the unmistakable whine of a yard cart moving at high speed.

"Hurry, we've got to go," Edna said, her voice dropping to a hoarse whisper. "Carl and his baboons are out looking for you. I just hope they don't think to look here."

Kate kissed her grandmother on the cheek and turned to leave, but as she reached the door, she stopped and looked back. "Gram, you know if this gets out everyone will know that you and Jimmy..." She hesitated, trying to choose her words but she never got to finish.

A strange look of resolution came over Edna's face. "Screw it." She spat as she reached with her right hand and pulled the large diamond wedding ring from her left hand. Without hesitation, she stepped to the open window and threw it out. "I'm ashamed I'm a Greason, and I don't give a tinker's damn anymore who knows it. Now go, Katie!"

10

Terry Wallace felt pain in the darkness; a throbbing pain in his head and mouth. There was noise all around; voices, some urgent, others laughing. A woman groaned quietly. Phones were ringing, and there was a beeping noise, clacking of plastic, and the sound of a rolling cart. He felt a hand gently move his left arm. He opened his eyes and squinted against the light.

A young woman's face was hovering to his left. She had cropped blond hair and wore scrubs with a stethoscope draped around her neck. From his few unfortunate injuries in the past ten years, he recognized the inside of a treatment bay in the Hawthorne Memorial emergency room.

"Well hello," the woman said, smiling faintly. "It's good to see you awake. You've been in a car crash, and you're in the hospital. We're taking good care of you. I'm Cindy Easton an ER doctor here at Hawthorne."

She produced a pen light from her pocket and began shining it in his eyes, one at a time.

"Can you tell me your name?" she asked.

He tried to speak, but only air came out. He

cleared his throat. "Terry," he managed. "Terry Wallace, Lieutenant with the police department."

"Very good, Terry, and can you tell me what day it is?"

But Lieutenant Wallace didn't hear the question. The fog was rapidly lifting from his mind and the events of the last few hours rushed back to him, along with a surge of panic. In the few minutes he had with Ben Tuttle before all hell broke loose, the frightened young man had levelled explosive allegations about Everett Greason and their family business; allegations of a decades-long criminal cover-up that not only rang true, but confirmed Wallace's own worst suspicions that the governor's office and his own department were complicit. It was the only explanation for his boss's bizarre behavior and a strong motive for silencing anyone who might have been given information by Margaret Bayer Greene; information damning to Greason and others involved.

"Ben Tuttle, where is he?" Wallace asked, louder than he meant to. "What happened to him?"

"Terry, Lieutenant, I need you to relax," the doctor began. "You've been in a…"

Despite the pain, Wallace forced himself up to a sitting position and brushed off the doctor's hand as she reached for his shoulder. "I need you to listen to me, doctor. There's been a murder, and other people are in danger. Where is Ben Tuttle, the man in the car with me?"

The smile on the young doctor's face had evaporated. "I'm sorry, who?"

"He was in the passenger seat when the hummer broad-sided us," Wallace said. "What happened to him?"

"Lieutenant, I'm not sure who you're talking

about. You were the only patient transported from the scene of the crash. I was by the scanner at the time they picked you up, and there was nobody else. Now I need you to settle down, please, for your own safety. You've had a mild concussion and a few lacerations on your face. Our first priority…"

"Shit!" Wallace hissed. "They've got him."

From the corner of his eye, he saw the doctor press a nurse-call button and reach for a syringe on the cart beside his bed. He knew he had to act fast.

"Wait," he said, putting a hand firmly on the doctor's arm. "You seem like a nice person, and I'm sure you're good at your job, but understand I'm good at my job too and we're both in the business of saving lives, so please cut me a little bit of slack here. I don't have time to explain, but I have to get my phone and get out of here."

A male nurse appeared from around the cloth curtain and looked immediately concerned. "Is everything alright here?"

"Please," Wallace said to the doctor, almost under his breath.

After hesitating for what seemed to Wallace like an eternity, the doctor turned to the nurse and said "Thanks, but we're okay here. I'll call if we need you."

"You sure, doctor? I'll be glad to help."

"No really. We're good."

The nurse reluctantly turned and left.

"Thank you," Wallace said, releasing the doctor's arm. "You won't regret it."

Her hand moved away from the cart with the syringe. "Somehow I doubt that, Lieutenant Wallace. I don't like this, and it's against my better judgment, but none of your injuries are life threatening. I can't keep you here against your will."

She pulled a business card from the pocket of her coat and handed it to him. "Do what you have to do but call my office by tomorrow for a follow-up. We need to make sure those cuts don't get infected."

She opened a drawer under his bed. "Your clothes and your phone are here, but I'll need to update the officers in the waiting room and let them know you'll be checking yourself out against medical advice. A nurse will come by to get that IV out and give you some release forms to sign."

"What officers?" Wallace asked, the hair standing up on the back of his neck.

"They came in just after the ambulance. They insisted we inform them of any change in your status. We even got a call from The Chief of Police asking about you." The smile returned, and she turned to leave. "Nice to know your co-workers are so concerned about you, eh?"

Wallace knew that Hughes had no intention of letting him walk out of the ER. He would have minutes to make a move. Once the doctor had disappeared around the curtain, he struggled to his feet and pulled the curtain closed with his free arm, then gritted his teeth and ripped the tape from his other arm and pulled out the IV needle, jamming some gauze and tape on the wound to stop the bleeding. His head throbbed like it would explode as he hurriedly dressed and grabbed his cell phone, wallet, and keys. As he prepared to slip out from behind the curtain, he caught a glimpse of himself in a mirror. The battered and swollen face looking back at him was barely recognizable. "Jesus," he muttered, quickly running his fingers through his hair and trying to smooth it down.

Wallace stepped out from behind the curtain and turned the opposite direction from the way he had seen the ER doctor go, gambling that she had been heading to the waiting room. He carried a piece of paper he had picked up from the cart and lowered his head as if he were reading it, trying to walk normally. At the end of the expansive room, he went through a set of double doors and turned down a side hallway beneath a radiology sign, scanning for another exit. After a few more turns and a close call with a nurse who asked if he was lost, Wallace followed an exit sign only to end up in front of an alarm door.

"Shit!" he hissed through bared teeth. He knew the alarm would bring them right to him, but there was no other way. The doctor had probably already discovered him missing.

Just then he heard a woman's voice behind him. "You can't go out that way. You'll need to go out through the waiting room. Are you checking out?"

Thinking quickly, he pulled his cell phone from his pocket and put it to his ear. He turned to see a portly lab tech standing in the hall with a clip board.

Wallace pointed to the phone. "Sorry, I'm just making a quick call."

The tech frowned. "Please keep it short. You're not supposed to use those in this area."

Wallace feigned a whispered conversation and waited until the woman was gone. As he was reaching for the door, the intercom crackled and he heard his name. "Patient Terry Wallace, please report to the ER nurse's station. Terry Wallace, please report immediately to the ER nurse's station. We need to process your paperwork."

"Paperwork my ass," Wallace snorted and stepped through the door. The wailing of the alarm sounded impossibly loud, driving a wedge into his already throbbing head. He cringed and hurried along a covered walkway, down some steps, and across the back parking lot, grateful that the night would offer some cover. As he stepped through a hedge row, he looked back to see several faces in the now open doorway, but nobody had followed him.

It was nearly seven thirty in the evening, and Chief Hughes had been pacing in his office for the last twenty minutes, his stomach in knots, waiting for word on Lieutenant Wallace and a callback from Steve Crenshaw. Hughes was a career officer who did not panic easily, but when he had learned that two of the six people on the list he had turned over to Crenshaw had been found dead in the last twenty-four hours, he had nearly come unhinged. He knew that Greason and Crenshaw were hell-bent on containing something, no doubt old dirt from Greason's past, and they were willing to pay Hughes handsomely for his cooperation and pull the necessary strings to get him a significant promotion. He also knew they played dirty, very dirty, but they had assured him the most they would do was rough a few people up. Now two people were dead, their prime suspect was missing, and Wallace had disobeyed a direct stand-down order and had nearly been killed in a highly suspicious hit and run that had Crenshaw's stink all over it. Hughes had left an urgent voicemail for Crenshaw, demanding an explanation, terrified that what should have been a little heavy-handed detective work had suddenly cast him as an accessory to murder. Never mind his career, this could send him to prison.

Just then Hughes' phone rang, and he snatched the handset. It was Sergeant Duggins from Hawthorne. "Hughes," he snapped. "What's the update on Wallace?"

"Sorry to report sir, but Wallace is gone. It appears he…"

"Gone?" Hughes shouted into the phone. "The guy was nearly killed in a car crash! An hour ago he was unconscious for Christ's sake, and now you're telling me he's gone?"

"It appears someone tipped him off and he went out a back exit, through a security door," Duggins replied, his voice noticeably shaky. "We've got two units out looking for him, sir. We'll find him."

"Well you better, and find him fast, or I'll come down there and personally rip you a new asshole. Have you got that?" Hughes slammed the phone down before Duggins could reply.

Lieutenant Wallace got away from the hospital as quickly as he could, using side streets and staying out of sight behind businesses and tree lines, checking frequently behind him as he went. His head was spinning as he stopped by a vacant office building and sat on a stack of wooden pallets to try and catch his breath. A safety light overhead bathed the whole area in a garish fluorescent glow. He had to find Ben Tuttle, but he had no car, no weapon, and no leads. He knew they had him, but he wasn't fully sure who "they" were or where they might have taken him. Unless Wallace took a cab to the Werner-

Greason Funeral Home, knocked on the front door, and politely asked them to produce Ben Tuttle, he was at a dead-end. Then he remembered something Ben had said when they were in Wallace's car. He said he was working with Everett's granddaughter, Kate Greason; that she was his girlfriend. He took out his cell phone and risked a call to Bob Payne. He silently gave thanks when his friend answered.

"Terry? Is that you?" Payne asked in a near whisper. "Christ, are you okay?"

"Yeah, it's me. I'm a little worse for wear, but I'm okay. I need a favor."

"Shit, Terry, I've got to be careful. I've never seen Hughes like this. He's practically out of his mind about something." Payne's voice dropped even lower. "He's ordered all of us to report any contact with you."

"Sorry, Bob, I wouldn't ask if it wasn't life and death. You know that. I just need a cell phone number for Kate Greason, Everett Greason's granddaughter. And I need it yesterday."

"Let me think a second," Payne said. "We should have that in her deposition record. Give me five minutes, and I'll text you."

"Thanks, Bob, I'm sorry to put you in a bad spot. I owe you, big time."

Payne was silent for a moment. "Listen, Terry, it's nothing personal, but after this, I really can't talk to you anymore. I'll lose my job and maybe worse if I get caught."

Wallace felt a stab of guilt but knew he had no other choice. "I understand, Bob. I won't call again. But I meant what I said, I owe you."

While he waited, Wallace left his hiding place and

moved a block down the street to a nearby park, scanning his surroundings as he went. Twice he saw a blue light pass by several blocks away, but fortunately, neither of the cars had come in his direction, at least not yet. There would be more cover in the park and fewer street lights.

He passed a young couple walking hand in hand coming out of the park and mumbled a quick hello in response to their greeting, but kept his head down. A moment later he felt his phone vibrate. True to his word, Bob had located Kate Greason's cell number. He replied a quick "Thx" and called the number from the shadows of an immense Magnolia tree.

The phone rang several times and went to voicemail. "Hi, this is Kate. I can't get the phone right now but leave me a message."

Her voice sounded kind and authentic, and Wallace wondered what kind of person she was and whether she had any idea what she was mixed up in.

"Kate, my name is Terry Wallace. I'm a lieutenant with the Stanton PD. You don't know me but I know Ben, and I'm trying to help him. He may be in danger and it's urgent you call me back as soon as possible."

As he ended the call, he caught sight of what looked like two flashlights scanning the grass and the trees on the far side of the park.

"Damn," he said.

He called Kate's number again. "Pick up, Kate. Please pick up," he whispered into the phone.

11

The cool night air felt good on Kate's face as she ran from the back door to the corner of the house, pausing in the deep shadows to let her eyes adjust to the darkness. She scanned the yard and the cemetery as far as she could see but there was no sign of Lentz. Apart from the far off barking of a dog, the night was quiet again. The maintenance shed stood at the back of the yard, and Kate knew it was her only chance of finding something to cut through the chain padlocked across the outer door of the Sinclair mausoleum. Despite her best efforts, the image of Ben as a prisoner, suffering at the hands of Everett and Walter, loomed briefly in her mind and she fought back the awful fear it elicited.

Kate jumped as her cell phone vibrated, catching her off guard. She snatched it from her pocket, desperately hoping it was Ben calling to tell her he'd escaped and was somewhere safe, but this was a number she didn't recognize. It was a Stanton area code but a completely unfamiliar number. For a brief moment, she considered answering but thought better of it and stuffed the phone back in her pocket instead, letting the call go to voicemail.

"Focus," she told herself in a whisper before sprinting the twenty yards to the shed. Mercifully, the door was unlocked, and once inside she scanned the endless array of tools hanging on the walls. Kate spotted what she was looking for in the back, behind the riding lawn mowers; a heavy chain cutter. She had to stand on a crate to reach it and had just pulled it off the wall when her cell phone vibrated again. She checked it quickly and was again disappointed not to see Ben's name. It was the same number as before, and something told her it was not a junk call. "Telemarketers don't usually call back," she said to herself, continuing to stare at the number.

On impulse, she answered the call, careful to keep her voice down. She was in no mood for niceties. "This is Kate. Who's calling?"

"Kate Greason? Thank God I got you." The caller sounded anxious and spoke very softly. "This is Lieutenant Terry Wallace of the Stanton Police Department."

Kate's tensed. She recalled Ben's theory that the police may somehow be involved in Everett's scheme, so she immediately suspected a trap. She hurried to the shed door and peered out but saw no one.

"You don't know me," he continued, "but I need to find out what happened to Ben Tuttle. I think he is in danger. We were together before the car crash, and he told me about you and about what Everett is…"

"What car crash? What are you talking about?"

"It's complicated," Wallace said, watching the searchers and their flashlights crisscrossing the park, "and I don't have time to explain. I didn't believe Ben was innocent, but I do now. I think they may have him and his life is in danger."

Kate answered before she could stop herself and immediately felt tears welling up. "They do have him, and I'm trying to get to him before they...before something bad happens to him." Something about the man's voice, or perhaps her desperation made her decide to trust him. "Can you help us, please?"

The question stung Wallace because he knew there was little or nothing he could do in time to save Ben if they were intent on killing him.

"I don't know. I'll try. Where are you and where is Ben?" Wallace asked, unwilling yet to give her any details about his current state of affairs.

"I'm at the funeral home, at Werner-Greason, behind the guest house in the maintenance shed. They've got Ben in the underground vault or whatever it is that's underneath the old cemetery."

"Ben said something about a fake cemetery, Lark Hill I think he called it."

"Yes, that's it. There's a hidden entrance in the basement of the house, but there's an older entrance through one of the mausoleums in Lark Hill. That's where I'm going."

"Kate these people are dangerous, very dangerous. They're guaranteed to be armed, and I believe they've murdered people to keep whatever this is from getting out." Wallace hesitated. "What are you going to do?"

His question brought the gravity of her predicament into sharp focus. She suddenly realized that she'd been so intent on getting to Ben that she had no real plan for what to do when she got there.

"I'm going to tell them I've got proof about what they've done; the vault, the gold, and art they've been stealing for all these years, the fake cemetery, bogus identities, all of it. It's enough to burn them, and I'm going to make them let Ben go."

"Jesus," Wallace whispered. Ben Tuttle had been telling the truth. As Wallace struggled to get his mind around what he was hearing and the implications for a wider conspiracy, an idea struck him.

"What do you have?" he asked. "What proof are you talking about?"

"It's a journal and notes from a guy named Jimmy Smoot. He was a reporter from Denver who was doing a story on all of this when he disappeared in the 50s. He had maps, shipping logs, names, dates, everything."

As Kate spoke it dawned on Wallace that their fates were tied very closely together and that both hinged on the proof Kate had found.

"Do you have the documents with you?" he asked.

Kate thought about her Gram and had a sudden sinking feeling. "No, I don't have them. My Grandmother took them to hide them from Everett and Walter. She's gone back to the house."

Wallace heard a dog barking and peered out again through the thick branches of the magnolia. The police had brought a canine unit to the park, and he knew he was out of time.

"Kate, I've got to go. I only have a few seconds, but I need you to do something. Text me your Grandmother's number and let her know I'll be calling her. And I need her to trust me. Can you do that?"

Kate knew it would be a hard sell for Edna. "I'll try. I'll send you her number, but what about the police?

Aren't you going to send someone?"

"I'm sorry Kate, but I can't," Wallace said as slipped from his hiding place and hurried down a wooded path that led out the back of the park. "I think it's highly likely the police chief is on your grandfather's payroll."

In the darkness of the maintenance shed, still reeling from Lieutenant Wallace's final words, Kate hurriedly did as she had promised and was just finishing the call with her Gram when she heard one of the yard carts heading her way. She ducked behind a riding mower and listened. It stopped a short distance from the shed. Peering out through a small window Kate saw Carl Lentz walking carefully up the steps of the guest house; a pistol gripped tightly in one hand.

Her jaw went slack at the idea that Carl, a man she had known her whole life, would be capable of hurting her at all, much less shooting her.

"Damn," she whispered. "What kind of power does Everett have over these people?"

From her vantage point, she could clearly see that the John Deere yard cart parked in the grass beside the guest house and her eyes were drawn to the reflection of the keys still dangling from the ignition switch. The idea of stealing the cart right out from under Carl's nose was outrageous and very dangerous, yet she knew it would get her to Lark Hill much faster than on foot. And if someone discovered her, it would give her a fighting chance to get away.

She exhaled slowly, trying to cement her resolve as she watched Lentz's silhouette move through the downstairs. As soon as the upstairs lights came on, she made her move, holding the chain cutter under one arm and sprinting to the cart. She had driven carts many times over the years and almost reflexively slipped behind the wheel after carefully putting the chain cutter in the bed.

Knowing she would have barely a few seconds to get out of pistol range once the engine started, Kate turned the key and jammed the accelerator to the floor. The cart lurched forward, spinning briefly in the grass before speeding across the side yard and through the back. Kate left the cart lights off and headed for the paved path that led to the outer edge of the new cemetery, straining to see the way by the sparse security lights in the cemetery and a sliver of waning moon left in the night sky. Moments later she heard a short series of pops, like firecrackers in the distance and all doubt about Carl's intentions vanished.

Kate knew the cemetery like the back of her hand and took the shortest route to Lark Hill, despite the fact that it took her temporarily out in the open. As she sped along with the wind in her face, she glanced at the lights of the main house in the distance and wondered whether Lieutenant Wallace had reached her Gram. She slowed the cart as Lark Hill loomed ahead with its ancient twisted trees, rolling hills, and tightly curved paths. It was much darker here, and there were no security lights, so Kate switched on the headlights of the cart. She made her way through several hairpin turns on the way to the row of mausoleums which sat near the back of the old cemetery, in a bend at the base of a hill. The cart headlights played across the sea of headstones that surrounded her, stones of all shapes and sizes with decaying words and creeping mold and moss. She had to remind herself yet again that it was all a lie, an elaborately constructed prop designed to keep visitors from ever questioning what was beneath their feet.

"Joke's on us. No body's home," Kate said aloud, smirking darkly at the pun.

The Sinclair mausoleum was second from the end, a freestanding structure like the others; it was built to look like a Greco-Roman style temple in miniature, with half columns in relief, detailed molding and a faux tiled roof that was crowned with a small statue of a partially nude woman draped in cloth. Kate left the cart idling and got off in front of the narrow double metal doors in the center of the small building. The doors were heavily rusted and had a large chain wrapped and padlocked around the wrought iron handles. She pulled the chain cutter from cart bed and walked to the mausoleum, which looked other-worldly bathed in the white light from the head lamps. She considered herself athletic, but the chain was thick, and Kate struggled with the cutter, trying to apply enough pressure while not banging the metal door. She was afraid the noise would carry to whatever chamber was below and tip them off to her presence.

Kate was so focused on getting through the chain that she did not hear the smaller electric golf cart approaching through the cemetery behind her. What little sound it made was drowned out by the whir of the gas engine on the Deere. Carl Lentz watched Kate closely as he pulled the cart behind a large family stone twenty yards back and stepped out. The pistol was tucked into his waistband, and he carried a baseball bat he had retrieved from the shed when he grabbed the cart. If he could get close enough, he would not need to risk using the pistol. He kept low and moved quickly.

With Walter gone to the prep room, Everett was alone now with Ben. The older Greason paced in silence just outside the small office, his mind working furiously as he weighed his options. He glanced repeatedly at Ben with a mix of contempt and something akin to fear. When his phone rang, he stepped away from Ben's line of sight and answered. It was Crenshaw.

"Everett, what the hell is going on there? We've got someone at the front gate, but nobody's tried to leave. Have you taken care of Tuttle?"

"Tuttle's not a threat anymore, at least not directly. We've got him locked down, but he's spouting a story about working for some firm that the Bayer woman hired to investigate me and the business. And some of the information he's got is pretty goddamn accurate and it's making me nervous."

"Everett, he's bluffing," Crenshaw said.

"How can you be certain? And how do you explain what he knows?"

"We've run the full background on this guy. He's a tech wiener for a software startup in Stanton, nothing more. No other employment and no connections to the government or the press. We've been through his house and his wallet. I'm telling you, anything he knows he got from your granddaughter and from poking around in the library. We know the Bayer woman passed him something, but if it was anything with teeth, she would have come at you with it years ago. This guy is an amateur who just got lucky." There was a pause before Crenshaw continued. "Everett, I don't have to tell you how urgent it is that we bury this thing…tonight. There can't be any loose ends."

Crenshaw had intentionally not mentioned Kate by name, but his meaning was clear.

"We'll take care of it," Everett said darkly. "All of it. But I'm going to get the truth out of this little shit before we do. What about that cop, Wallace?" Everett asked, remembering what they had told him when they brought Ben in. "What was he doing in the car with Tuttle?

"I'm not sure, but Hughes has been on it. From what he's told me, Wallace had gone off the reservation after the investigation was closed; most likely trying to be the hero cop and bring in the bad guy, but we couldn't take that chance. He went AWOL from the hospital after the accident, but they tracked him down a few blocks away just outside a park. Hughes knew the deal and took care of it. Seems one of his rookie officers thought Wallace had a gun and took him out. It was dark, you know, unfortunate accident."

"Good. That's good," Everett said quietly. "Did he talk to anyone?"

"We don't think so. We can't find his cell phone, but we're getting the records from the phone company just to be sure."

In the darkness of the Lark Hill cemetery, as Kate stood before the Sinclair mausoleum door, bathed in the glare of the yard cart's headlights and fighting with the chain cutter, she was unaware that Carl Lentz was now only a few steps behind her. With a loud groan, she gave a final push, straining both arms to the breaking point, and heard a loud click as the chain snapped and fell apart. As her arms dropped, still holding the cutter, she saw a second silhouette rise on the mausoleum door beside hers, and without stopping to think, she spun wildly around, swinging the heavy metal tool with all her might. She was blinded by the bright light but felt the end of the cutter connect with something and heard a distinct crack and a grunt just as something hard smashed a glancing blow to her head. Kate staggered back against the stone mausoleum and nearly fell. Putting her hand to her head, she felt a small patch of blood.

Kate blocked the light with one hand and walked several feet, ready to swing the chain cutter again. She saw Carl lying face down, motionless on the ground, half on the path and half in the grass. A baseball bat lay several feet from him, and she saw a deep gash on his right temple. His shirt was raised in the back and she could also clearly see the handle of a pistol sticking out of his waistband.

"You son of a bitch," she said, her voice shaking.

She knew she had been lucky, because he had opted for the baseball bat rather than the pistol, and because she had swung first; otherwise she would likely be dead or dying. She quickly checked his pulse and determined that she had not killed him, although at that moment she did not particularly care one way or the other.

She was not a fan of firearms, but Kate took his pistol never-the-less. Desperate times called for desperate measures. She went back and removed the chain from the rusting metal doors before pulling them open. They creaked on their hinges but swung freely back to reveal a small stone room with an oblong granite sarcophagus in the center. Kate quickly scanned the interior, looking for something resembling a door but she saw nothing besides the raised stone panels adorning the walls on all sides.

"It's got to be here somewhere," she muttered, entering the room and making her way around the sarcophagus for a closer look at the walls, but still nothing. She considered the sarcophagus itself and tried pushing the granite cover stone, but it would not budge. Remembering a trick, she had seen in the movies, and on TV she tried drumming her fist on the rectangular stone panels on the walls. Most of them felt and sounded like solid stone except one; the middle panel on the west wall made a hollow noise when she struck it. She ran her fingers around the outside edge looking for a latch, and when she reached the bottom, she found one. She pushed it sideways, and the panel popped loose and swung slightly open.

"Got it!" she said, feeling amazed and terrified at the same time. Behind the faux stone panel, there was a more modern looking metal door with a recessed handle and to Kate's dismay, a card-key lock. She swore under her breath and tried to think, and then she remembered Lentz. Clearly he was in Everett's inner circle of trusted associates. If anyone would have a card key, Lentz would. Kate hurried back to the motionless figure, and despite her fear that he would awaken, she pulled his wallet out of his back pocket. She had just opened it to look for a key when the yard cart engine sputtered and died. The lights dimmed but remained on.

"Shit," she hissed, "out of gas." She knew she would only have a few minutes more of light, if that, while the battery ran down. She abandoned searching for the card and carried the whole wallet into the mausoleum and placed it against the card reader. To her surprise, the light turned green, and she heard a click. She pulled the metal door open and saw a set of steps leading down into the darkness.

"Here goes," she said, and stepped through the door, closing it behind her.

Ben could do nothing but wait. Sweat rolled down his forehead and torso, soaking the already blood-stained shirt he was wearing. Thoughts of what agony awaited him under the skilled hands of Everett sat like a hot brick in his stomach. His flimsy story had raised doubts in their minds but would not hold up under any level of scrutiny and certainly not under torture. He wondered again about Kate, praying that she was somewhere with Edna, out of harm's way.

With Everett out of sight, Ben quickly scanned the room and noticed a raised panel on the back wall with green LEDs beneath a small bank of black and white monitors, apparently for a vintage video surveillance system. It was difficult at first to make out the images, but the first one looked like the preparation room. The next was a view of a narrow corridor; most likely the one they had passed through when they led him in. The LED under this image turn red briefly, then back to green and a chill rippled through Ben as Walter appeared on the screen and passed by, holding something shiny and metallic in one hand. They must show the status of security doors, Ben thought. Green was closed, red was open. The third screen showed a small, brightly lit room with a long rectangular box in the center. He could not make out what he was seeing until he remembered the crudely drawn map he and Kate had found in his condo, hidden behind the photograph of Lark Hill. There had been a second entrance marked on the map, apart from the primary entrance through the funeral home.

It's the inside of a mausoleum, Ben thought. The map was right. And as he watched, a woman stepped into the picture. Her back was to the camera, and oddly she appeared to be beating her fist on the mausoleum walls. Ben's heart sank as the woman turned and he instantly recognized Kate.

" Kate," he whispered to the monitor. "No, Kate."

Walter and Everett were just finishing their conversation and stepped through the office door. Ben quickly averted his eyes from the monitors and prayed they wouldn't turn around. Everett now carried a small curved stainless steel saw in one hand and a shiny ball-peen hammer in the other, however, it was what Walter carried that made Ben's stomach lurch; he had a large roll of clear plastic tucked under one arm.

"Put that plastic down under him," Everett said. "I'm not about to leave a mess in here."

Walter obliged, casting repeated wary glances at the implements in Everett's hands. As Walter spread the plastic out around and underneath the chair, Ben was sitting on he noticed that Walter's hands were shaking and there were beads of sweat on his forehead.

"Jesus," Ben erupted, unable to contain his fear any longer. "I've told you everything I know. The people at my firm know I'm here and if I don't call in in the next few minutes…"

"Bullshit!" Everett bellowed, and without warning he swung the hammer down hard on the top of Ben's left hand, smashing the bones against the wooden chair arm it was tied to. Ben screamed and arched his back as Walter recoiled and turned away.

"There is no firm you little cockroach," Everett growled. "And you're going to admit it before I'm through taking you apart. You're going to admit everything. I've worked my whole life to build this business, do you hear me? My whole God-damned life and built half this town in the process and I'll be damned if I'm going to let a clueless nobody waltz in here and trash it all. You have no idea what I'll do to protect this family and this business Mr. Tuttle, but you're about to find out."

"Please," Ben pleaded through clenched teeth. "Please don't do this. I won't tell anyone."

Ben could barely see through the curtain of pain, but he was able to see the LED beneath the third surveillance monitor change briefly from green to red, and he knew that Kate had found the way in. She had passed the point of no return, and he had no way to warn her about what she was walking into.

As Everett continued to glare at Ben, he laid the hammer on the desk and stepped to Ben's other side with the curved saw in one hand, kneeling beside him. He looked up at Ben and smiled a sinister smile. "I'm going to take off your right foot now, at the ankle. And it's going to hurt. When I'm finished, you'll tell me exactly how you know what you know."

As Everett grabbed Ben's ankle, he reflexively jerked it away as a whimper escaped his lips.

"Walter, hold him," Everett ordered.

"Everett no," Walter said, looking ghostly pale. "I'm not doing this. Kill this kid and get it over with but not like this, for Christ's sake!"

Everett stood up and took a menacing step towards Walter, but stopped when they all heard a hissing, crackling noise followed by a woman's voice. "Everett, I know you're there. You listen to me!" It was Edna's voice, coming from somewhere in the main vault.

"What the hell?" Walter said as he and Everett exchanged glances and then turned toward the source of the sound. There was a small intercom unit mounted on the wall by the main entrance. "Where is that coming from?"

"She's in my office," Everett gaped in disbelief. "She's in my damn office, and she's found the intercom." Since the business had been established, it had been one of Everett's strictest rules that nobody enters his private office for any reason. He kept it locked, and only he and Walter had keys. He had threatened Edna with violence if she ever set foot in it and he had never seen her try, until now.

Kate carefully and quietly made her way down the narrow steps in the darkness and crept along a short passage, nearly overcome now by the fear that she might be too late, that they might have already done something terrible to Ben. She pulled out the pistol and realized her hands were trembling badly. *How has it come to this?* She thought, barely able to believe their awful predicament.

"Focus," she told herself again as she reached the end of the passage and knelt down, hearing voices coming from the lighted room around the corner. They were in heated conversation, and she instantly recognized Walter and Everett. Her heart was pounding as she peered around the corner, squinting against the light. She was at the back of a long rectangular room crowded with crates, decorative objects, furniture, and artwork. At the far end of the room, she could see Walter and Everett standing behind glass in a smaller room beside a seated figure. It was Ben. There was blood on his face and shirt, and he looked terrible, but his eyes were alert, and he was scanning the room as if looking for something.

Just then she heard another familiar voice coming from what sounded like a school intercom and her breath caught in her chest. "Gram, oh, my god," she whispered as if her grandmother could hear her. "What are you doing?"

"You've gone too far this time," Edna's voice barked. "I've had enough! We've all had enough. You've made liars and criminals out of all of us and ruined this family for three generations and for what, more goddamn money?"

Kate could not see where her Gram's voice was coming from, but Walter and Everett had stepped out of the smaller room and were both looking at a spot on the far wall that was blocked from her view by a large crate. She listened closely for the familiar slur in Edna's speech, but her words were clear and her sentences fully coherent; for the first time, she could remember, her Gram sounded stone sober.

"What in the name of Christ do you think you're doing, Edna?" Everett said in the direction of the wall, his voice echoing through the underground chamber. "Get the hell out of my office and get out now!" he ordered, "Or so help me God I'll make you sorry you ever lived."

"I'm doing what should have been done twenty years ago, putting a stop to all of this. Damn the consequences! And if you want to talk about sorry, the

252

only two things I'll ever be sorry about are letting you talk me into marrying you, and not telling the authorities twenty years ago what the mighty Everett Greason really is; a big fat fraud!"

As Kate's jaw dropped open, she saw Everett's face turn deep red with rage, and his fists clenched into balls by his sides. "How dare you!" he bellowed. "The only things I've ever done, I've done for this family. And if it weren't for me everyone in town would have known you were a whore, spreading your legs for that weasel Smoot. He didn't give a shit about anything except bringing down this family. After he got what was coming to him, you crawled into a bottle, and I've been making excuses for you ever since; my pathetic excuse for a wife."

Walter put his hand on Everett's arm. "Everett, let it go. We don't have time for this."

Kate was stunned by the rage and utter contempt in Everett's voice, barely recognizing the man, but she quickly realized the distraction might give her the few seconds she needed to alert Ben. While Everett and Walter had their backs turned, she stood up and leaned far enough out from behind the wall, so she was clearly in Ben's line of sight.

Ben had been nervously glancing into the main room of the vault, half hoping, half dreading to see a glimpse of Kate. He couldn't bear the thought of her witnessing his torture, much less the thought of her being caught and harmed. He was certain that Everett was beyond any mercy that family ties would otherwise provide. As he peered into the shadows at the far end of the main storage room, he caught a glimpse of something moving, and he realized it was Kate. She was mostly concealed in the darkness beyond the open doorway and but he could see her face and she was waving one hand. Ben's eyes widened when they met hers, and he reflexively shook his head, silently mouthing the word "No."

Edna's voice was shaking now, and she showed no signs of backing down. "The gall you've got talking about Jimmy. He was a good, decent man; a better man than you'll ever be, and you murdered him in cold blood!" She choked back a sob. "You never told Walter, did you? You never told him who Jimmy really was?"

"Shut your mouth, you drunken bitch!" Everett barked at the wall.

"That's right, Walter," she continued. "He lied to you all these years just like he lied to everyone else. You're not a Greason at all!"

Walter looked questioningly at Everett. "What the hell is she talking about?

Everett was shaking all over now, pacing from side to side. "She's lying, can't you see that? They're all lying, trying to turn us against each other. But they've got nothing, no proof."

"Ha," Edna snorted, "That's where you're wrong. I'm holding all the proof you want right here in my hand. It was under your feet all these years in the floorboards of the guest house."

Kate cringed as she listened, helpless to stop her grandmother's seemingly suicidal rant. Worst of all, Edna was about to do the one thing they had agreed could not happen; she was about to tell Everett about the notes and where they were.

Despite the deep throbbing pain radiating from

Ben's hand up his arm, he was hanging on Edna's every word, stunned by the bizarre turn of events.

"Jimmy was good at his job," she continued, "the best. And he had it all, every scrap of evidence about who Andrew and Mitchell really were; about the Nazis and the shipments from all those towns in Europe; Lichtenstein, Wiesbaden, and Vienna; it's all here. He's got purchase receipts for half of everything in that sham of a cemetery, and oh," she paused, "in case you're wondering, he's got the actual blueprints for your goddamn vault. And the real icing on the cake; I'm looking at a list of names of soldiers they desecrated by hiding blood gold in their coffins, then re-routing their remains to Stanton. How many soldiers have the men in this family stolen and burned over the years, just thrown them away like garbage?"

Something in Everett appeared to snap, and as Edna continued to speak, he turned and picked up a pistol from the small table outside the office. He shoved it in Walter's hand and pointed to Ben. "You finish this, now! And get Carl on the phone. We're going to find Kate and make this go away, and I mean tonight." He looked back at the intercom. "I'm going to go do what I should have done years ago; shut that bitch up, permanently."

With that, Everett strode out of the room and Ben watched him on the monitors hurrying down the passageway to the main house. He passed quickly through the cooler and into the prep room where he picked up something that resembled a meat cleaver from one of the prep tables. *What is she doing?* Ben asked himself, thinking of Kate's grandmother, certain that if she were still in Everett's office when he arrived, she would meet a very bad end.

12

At the Stanton police station, Chief Willard Hughes shut the door of the small interrogation room and closed the blinds, ignoring the concerned stares of the officers out in the hallway. He turned to the man beside him. "Take that jacket off your head and sit your ass down. You better tell me every damn thing you know and tell it fast." The man complied, sitting down hard in a one of the wooden chairs at the small square table and pulling the windbreaker off his head.

Terry Wallace looked worse than Hughes had ever seen him; worse than most people who weren't in a morgue. One eye was nearly swollen shut, and there were deep bruises across his cheeks and nose. A gash on his cheek had small butterfly bandages over it, and a dried trail of blood led down his cheek and along his chin.

"Why didn't you kill me?" Wallace asked, never breaking eye contact with Hughes. "I know that's what they…"

Hughes cut him off. "Because I'm not doing it, that's why." He hung his head and ran his hand through his hair. "I'm in a world of shit right now, and I don't know what the fuck is going on, but I'm not wasting one my best men without a damn good reason, I don't care who that asshole Crenshaw works for."

"What did you tell him?" Wallace asked.

"I told him you're dead; said it was an accident. One of the officers thought you had a gun and shot you. I threatened the team if anyone said a word, but they'll find out. We don't have long, so spill it. Very powerful people want you dead, and I need to know why."

Wallace stood up. "I know you don't have any reason to trust me, but we don't have time for explanations. Greason and his goons have kidnapped Ben Tuttle, and they're going to kill him if they haven't already. Kate Greason, Everett's granddaughter, is working with Ben, and she may be next. Before the crash, Ben told me about a huge criminal cover-up by the Greason family that's been going on for decades."

The strange expression on his boss's face told him that Hughes was not hearing anything new. Briefly, Hughes seemed to be wrestling with some internal anguish, but his expression quickly faded to one of dark resignation. "I knew it would come it this. I fucking knew it."

Wallace saw his chance, gambling that his assumptions about Hughes were correct. "You're a good man, Will. You're better than this. I don't know what you're into here, and I don't care, but you've got a chance to make some of it right. Innocent people are dying. Please help me stop this before it gets any worse. Please."

Hughes silently clenched his jaw as he looked for a long moment at Wallace, considering his words. At last, he pulled his keys from his pocket and gave a weak half smile. "What the fuck," he said. "At this point, I'm screwed either way. Let's go."

As they left the interrogation room, a small group of officers who were gathered around the nearest desk looked up with anxious expressions.

Hughes pointed at one of them. "Dean, roll three units to Werner-Greason and tell them to wait for me at the BP station. I'll be there in ten."

Officer Blanton nodded and started toward dispatch. "Yes, sir. What's the call?"

"Possible 103 in progress," he called over his shoulder as he headed for the side door with Wallace close behind him.

"Homicide?" Blanton called back.

"Yeah," Hughes replied. "And tell them to gear up. These people are armed and extremely dangerous."

A voice called from the far end of the room. "Chief, I've got a Steve Crenshaw on the line for you. He says it's urgent. I think 'God damn urgent' were his exact words." It was Vicky, the night dispatcher.

"I'll bet it is," Hughes muttered as he opened the door. "Tell him. Ah, hell, tell him whatever you want!" He shouted as he and Wallace stepped out into the cool night air and hurried to his unmarked cruiser.

In the vault beneath Lark Hill, Walter wiped the sweat from his forehead with a handkerchief and gaped at the now closed door to the main passage, as if Everett would reappear and give him some further orders, but the door remained closed. He glanced nervously at the pistol in his hand and at Ben, who sat watching his every move.

"He's coming for me, isn't he?" Edna's voice

crackled again from the aging speaker. "Walter if you're there, you have to hear this. Jimmy was only doing his job. He was trying to do the right thing. He was a good man, and I loved him."

"Shut up!" Walter growled. "Why are you telling me this?"

"Because you have a right to know," she replied. "You have a right to know where you came from and what lies you've been told all these years. You have a right…" her voice caught in her throat, "to know who your real father was. Walter, it was Jimmy Smoot. He's your real father and Everett had him killed to shut him up."

A small groan escaped Walter's lips, and without warning he turned and fired the pistol several times at the intercom speaker, shattering it and silencing Edna's voice. The shots were painfully loud, echoing in the underground chamber and sending concrete chips flying through the room.

"You did this!" Walter snapped and turned to Ben. "You poisoned her! You poisoned Katie too." He pointed the pistol at Ben. "It's a lie. Say it!"

"No!" Kate screamed from the back of the room as she lunged from her hiding place and pointed her own pistol at Walter. "It's not a lie."

Walter jumped and spun around, waving the pistol in Kate's general direction.

"They're telling the truth," Kate said, fighting the nearly uncontrollable shaking in her arms and legs, "we've got the proof, about everything. I've seen it. I know the whole story. "

"Kate put the gun down" Walter ordered, "You don't…"

She ignored him "Turns out, everything I've ever known in this house since I was a little girl is a lie; all of it, the smiles and the parties and the politics; being paraded around in my Sunday best for the bigwigs; it was all bullshit. You were all just liars and thieves," her voice cracked "and now I find out you're murderers?" Kate choked back a sob. "Jesus! What kind of monsters *are* you?"

Walter's face had gone pale, and his mouth hung slightly open, but the pistol was still raised. "Damn, it Kate, you don't understand. You have no idea what we've done for this family; what we've built. I offered you everything, but you walked away; turned your back on our business."

Ben was drenched in sweat now, straining with his good hand to get free of the cord that tied him to the chair, his eyes never leaving Kate.

"Well, I'm not like you!" Kate screamed. "And I never want to be like you." She looked at Ben. "Let him go. None of this is his fault. I dragged him into it."

"No, Kate!" Ben shouted.

Walter licked his lips and took a step closer to Kate. "You know I can't do that, Kate. You know damned well I can't do that. You and your friend here have put us all in a very bad position."

Ben had been watching Kate and Walter and had not noticed the movement on the video monitor in the mausoleum. He had not seen the figure of Carl Lentz, blood smeared down one side of his face, stopping briefly in front of the hidden door before opening it and stepping through it. The security light had turned red, but only for a moment.

Now, as Walter spoke, Ben saw the silhouette of a man appear from the shadows at the back of the room, behind Kate, something raised high above his head.

"Kate, look out; behind you!" Ben screamed.

As the figure swung the object down, a deafening gunshot sounded in the chamber. Kate screamed, and Ben heard another shot. He watched the figure behind Kate pitch forward, as if in slow motion, and fall to the floor, knocking her off her feet and onto her hands and knees. The pistol she was holding clattered across the floor in the direction of the office. Walter groaned loudly and staggered backward, clutching his left side.

"Kate!" Ben screamed again.

"Oh no," Kate cried as she struggled to her feet and staggered toward Ben, glancing back at the motionless figure of Lentz lying face down behind her in a growing pool of blood. "I thought Walter was shooting at me. I think I hit him."

Walter's shoulders sagged as he leaned precariously against the wall in the office, directly in front of Ben. He continued to moan through clenched teeth as his eyes flickered between Ben and Kate, the pistol still clutched in one hand. Blood soaked the front of his shirt and ran down the front of his pants.

"Walter, please!" Kate pleaded as she reached the office door. "Put the gun down and stop this. You need a doctor."

Walter raised the gun again and pointed it at Kate. "No," he grunted. "No doctor." His hand weaved unsteadily, and his eyelids were beginning to droop. "Katie, you can save all this. You can have it all, don't you understand?" He spat red onto the floor. "You'll never have to want for anything again, never."

Ben's heart pounded in his chest as he watched helplessly, unable to free himself from the chair.

Kate realized now that Walter had killed Lentz, rather than let him hurt her, so she gambled that he would not be able to bring himself to shoot her now and walked slowly towards him as she spoke. "This is your world, Walter, not mine. It's wrong, what you're doing; what you've done. I just want to have a normal life. Now, please put the gun down. Enough people have been hurt. Please."

Kate was now only a few feet from Walter and Ben held his breath as she slowly reached out her hands and gently took the pistol from him. "Thank you." She said, barely above a whisper. "We can help you if you'll let us."

Walter shook his head. "No, Katie. You can't help me; it's done." He turned to look at Ben. "And you can't help him either, but you can save yourself and take what's rightfully yours."

Without warning Walter reached for the control panel and flipped open a clear plastic guard, covering a large red button. To Ben's horror, he made out the word Halon beneath the button just before Walter pressed it.

"Kate, get out!" Ben screamed as a loud hissing echoed through the vault and white halon gas streamed into the room from all directions.

Everett's face was contorted with rage, and he growled obscenities as he climbed the back stairs to the second floor, a meat cleaver clutched tightly in one hand. Without stopping to catch his breath, he stormed down the long hallway and rounded the corner, his eyes narrowing as he reached the double doors to his office. They stood open, and he could see past the desk and credenza to the door on the back wall. It was the door to his private office; the place where he kept his most guarded secrets and allowed no one in. The thought of *her* violating his sanctuary was almost more than he could bear.

"Edna!" he bellowed, as he kicked a chair out of the way and grabbed the handle of the door. He twisted hard, but she had locked it from the inside.

"Open this goddamn door!" He hammered the heavy oak door with his fist. "You have no right to be in there! No right!"

He leaned against the door, waiting for her defiant reply, but none came. He put his ear to the polished surface and listened. There was no sound except a faint whirring and clicking noise, and after a stunned moment, Everett realized it was a printer or a fax machine. The blood drained from his face, and his eyes bulged as he grasped what was happening.

"Edna!" he screamed again, slapping his hand on the door. "Stop whatever it is you're doing in there." He stepped back and kicked the door as hard as he could, but he knew the effort was futile; the door along with the entire back wall of the office had been designed specifically to guard against forced entry during a potential break-in.

Remembering the 12-gauge shotgun he kept in the wardrobe on the east wall, Everett hurried across the office and jerked open both wardrobe doors. The shotgun was propped in the back corner, and he swept aside the coats and picked it up, along with a box of shells. For a dark moment, the grimace on his face turned to a half smile as he loaded the shotgun and walked back to the inner office door. "You ungrateful bitch," he growled, raising the gun to point at the door handle. "I'm going to cut you in half."

The shot sent Everett staggering backward and wood splinters flying in all directions as a grapefruit sized hole appeared in the door. Edna screamed, and as Everett peered through the hole, he saw her standing beside the fax machine, gaping at him, ragged papers clutched in both hands. He chambered another round and stepped back for a second shot.

Just outside the locked front gate at the entrance to Werner-Greason, two men in trench coats paced beside a black Chevrolet Suburban. Both of them smoked, and the tips of their cigarettes glowed and bobbed in the darkness as they walked. Each man carried a Glock 9mm pistol in one hand and wore a Walther MP5 submachine gun in a shoulder holster beneath his coat. The men tensed and dropped their cigarettes as several pairs of headlights appeared suddenly through the trees of the long driveway and rounded the bend, bathing them in light. Both men raised their pistols, bracing for action until they realized that the cars were Stanton police cruisers.

As all three cars came to a stop and the door of the lead car opened, one of the men lowered his weapon and walked toward the driver, whose face was not visible. "Thanks, guys, but we've got this under control," the man said. "Tell Chief Hughes we appreciate the gesture."

"No need. You're talking to him," Hughes said as he raised his pistol and shined a flashlight on the man in the coat. "I need you drop your weapons and do it now."

As he talked, other car doors opened, and more officers stepped out, weapons drawn.

The man chuckled but did not drop his pistol. "Hughes? What the fuck? Have you lost your fucking mind showing up here with a bunch of bubble-tops? What is this?"

"I'm going to ask you one more time to drop your weapons and turn around with your hands on the back of your head," Hughes barked. "I'm not bullshitting here."

Two officers with their pistols raised were now walking slowly towards the second man by the Suburban, who had not lowered his weapon. "Drop it now!" one of them ordered. The man reluctantly complied, placing his pistol on the ground at his feet and turning with his hands cupped on the back of his head. The two officers rushed forward and wrestled him to the ground while the other man's eyes never left Hughes.

"You'll burn for this," he hissed. "You're as dirty as they come and you know it. We'll hang Wallace's corpse around your neck, and you'll burn."

"That'll be a little hard to do," Wallace said, stepping from the passenger door of the cruiser into the flashlight beam, "what with me up walking around and all."

The man's mouth gaped for a moment, and his face suddenly changed to an icy rage. Without warning, he raised his weapon and spun toward Wallace. Hughes did not hesitate. A shot rang out, and a spray of blood exploded from the back of the man's head as his lifeless body dropped to the pavement of the Werner-Greason driveway.

"Damn it, Terry," Hughes said, "I told you to stay

in the car." He glared at Wallace but tempered it with a knowing look. Wallace's surprise appearance had achieved the desired dramatic effect. "Harkin and Lake, check him, police this up and get a team out here. Allred put your cutters on this chain and get the gates open. Stop gawking and get your ass in gear! I mean now!"

Ben knew that they had less than a minute before the deadly gas filled the underground vault, sucking out all oxygen that a fire would need to burn and suffocating them in the process.

"Run, Kate! You've got to go, now!" he screamed, as his eyes began to burn.

"No!" Kate screamed back over the hissing of the gas jets. "I'm not leaving you. We're getting out of this, both of us." She knelt beside him, glancing at Walter who had crumpled to the floor and lay motionless, his eyes half open. She tore at the ropes on Ben's wrists and managed to free his wounded hand, even as she felt her lungs beginning to strain for air.

Ben cried out in pain as he forced himself to use his broken hand to help Kate with the other ropes. "Take a breath, Kate. Take a deep breath and hold it," he yelled.

They both inhaled as deeply as they could and frantically untied the last of the ropes in eerie silence, barely able to see now through the thick halon fog. Ben jumped from the chair and grabbed Kate's hand with his good hand, pulling her to the door of the main passageway. He wrenched the handle but the door was locked, and in that sickening instant he remembered that halon systems were designed to automatically seal the exits shut.

Kate fought back her fear and pulled Ben through the main room toward the back passage and the hidden exit. Their hands extended in front of them feeling blindly in the fog and their lungs burned from lack of air as they stumbled over unseen objects, twice knocking crates to the floor. As they reached the back passage, Ben felt Kate's hand clench his in a crushing grip and saw her eyes go wide as she exhaled and tried to breathe, but the halon had done its job well, and no air remained.

Ben grabbed Kate around the waist and ran, knowing he had seconds to get her out. Her body began to jerk reflexively from lack of oxygen, and he knew she was suffocating. His lungs were on fire, but he scooped Kate up in his arms and staggered the last twenty feet to the narrow steps and then half dragged, half carried her up to the small door. Praying that the door was not controlled by the halon system he threw his weight against it and to his amazement it burst open, even as his lungs forced him to exhale. He fell forward into the darkness of the mausoleum, banging his shoulder hard against the large granite sarcophagus as he fell. Kate tumbled to the ground beside him. He gasped great gulps of air as he struggled to his knees. She was not moving, and by the dim moonlight, he could tell her lips had turned a frightening shade of blue-grey. Without hesitation, Ben put his mouth to hers and pushed several deep breaths into her lungs, but she did not respond.

"Breath, Kate. Please breathe," he pleaded, caressing her matted hair and patting her cheek. He gave her several more breaths, despite the terror that gripped him. Ben was crying now, tears streaming down his face.

"Breath, damn it!" he shouted and slapped Kate's

cheek hard, knocking her head to one side.

As he hung his head, convinced he was too late, Kate gave a wracking cough and took a deep gasping breath, followed by several more.

"It's okay, Kate," Ben said, smiling weakly with relief. "You're okay. We're out. You saved us."

Kate's eyes darted wildly around, and she tried to sit up, cringing from the pain in her cheek. "Where are we?"

"Mausoleum, I think," Ben said, "we just made it."

"What about Walter," she asked, glancing into the darkened passage beside them.

Ben shook his head slowly but did not reply. His meaning was clear.

Kate pulled Ben to her and kissed him. "I love you," she said. "I thought I'd never have the chance to tell you. I love you so much."

Ben wiped his cheek with his good hand. "I love you too," he replied.

Kate's smile suddenly vanished. "Oh no," she said. "Edna. We've got to get to Edna. Everett will kill her if he gets the chance. I'm sure of it. Help me up."

Kate led the way out of the mausoleum and by the moonlight they were able to find the electric yard cart Carl Lentz had left parked behind a large family grave marker. The key was still in it, and Ben sat behind Kate, holding onto her waist with his good arm. She drove them as fast as the cart would go and as they left the cloying darkness of Lark Hill and sped along a well-lit paved path through the new cemetery, Kate watched the yellow glow in the upstairs windows of the main house. She began to shiver, partly from the cold night air and partly from the growing fear that they might be too late to save the one person in her family she truly cared about.

"Stay away from me, Everett!" Edna screamed. "You stay away!"

Ignoring her, Everett shoved his arm through the ragged hole in the door to his private office and fumbled for the lock. He quickly had the door open and stepped inside, continuing to glare at Edna, who had moved away from the fax machine and now stood shaking behind the mahogany desk. A small whimper escaped her lips as she eyed the cleaver and the shotgun he carried.

"You worthless whore," Everett growled, moving slowly towards her and looking wildly around the room at anything she might have touched. "What have you done? You broke into my private office where you have no business and rummaged around until you found what, some old shipping manifests, some inventory sheets and appraisals; my ledger perhaps?" He raised the cleaver and swung hard, burying the blade in the top of the wooden desk. Edna flinched, and her hands flew to her mouth.

"It proves nothing! I've dealt in fine antiquities as an ancillary business for the last half century. Everyone knows this."

"Not everyone, I'm afraid, Mr. Greason." Everett jumped and whirled to his left at the sound of a voice he did not recognize. It came from the conference phone on the small meeting table by the book shelves. Only then did he notice the bright green light on the phone, indicating a call in progress.

"My name is Jerry Barker. I'm with the U.S. State

Department in Washington," the caller continued.

A look of disbelief passed over Everett's face as he glanced at Edna, then back at the phone.

"Joining us on the call is Special Agent in Charge Bill Nance of the FBI's Charlotte North Carolina office. We've both been contacted by local law enforcement in Stanton about your suspected involvement in the illegal trafficking of antiquities and cultural property from Europe."

The cleaver slipped from Everett's hand and fell the floor with a clatter. He steadied himself on the edge of the desk, looking suddenly frailer than Edna had ever seen him. His mouth hung open, and he said nothing as the man on the phone continued. "Mrs. Greason has provided us with various documents supporting these claims, and we've obtained a federal search warrant for the premises of Werner-Greason."

In the distance, they both heard sirens approaching, and Everett took a faltering step backward and sat down hard in an armchair by the desk, the shotgun across his lap. Edna's hands were balled into fists that covered her mouth as she eyed him warily from the corner.

"These are federal crimes, Mr. Greason, and under UNESCO you are subject to a fifty thousand dollar fine and up to eighteen months in prison for each cultural object illegally in your possession."

As Kate and Ben sped through the semi-darkness of the new cemetery toward the main house they heard the faint but unmistakable pop of a gunshot. Kate's heart leaped to her throat. "Shit!" she groaned as she wrenched the throttle wide open. The cart lurched forward with a burst of speed, nearly throwing Ben off the back, but he managed to hold onto her waist. They bounced wildly in their seats as Kate steered the cart off the path and across the grass, directly for the side entrance. She stared at the light in the upstairs window, hoping to catch a glimpse of a silhouette but there was nothing.

As she slid the cart sideways to a stop in the grass beside a hedge row, Ben grabbed her shoulder and pointed in the direction of the front gate. "Kate, look!"

The distant tree line was lit up by a sea of blue strobe lights. "Thank God, the cops are here," Kate said. "Hurry, please hurry."

Just then they heard another gunshot echo in the distance, only this time it came from the direction of the gate. They exchanged worried glances and climbed off the cart.

"I don't know what the hell is happening down there, but we can't wait for them," Kate said, grabbing Ben's hand and heading quickly through the hedge and up a short set of steps. She tried the door, but it was locked. "Damn. There's a key under that flower pot," she said, pointing to a large clay pot by the walk. Ben pushed the pot over with one foot and retrieved the key. Moments later they stood, hearts pounding, in the corridor that led from the viewing rooms to the downstairs kitchen.

"Maybe we should wait for the police," Ben whispered. He's got a gun, and we've got nothing."

"We can't afford to wait," Kate replied. "She might already be dead."

Ben saw the fear in her eyes and knew that she would not wait. "Jesus," he said, shaking his head. "Okay, let's go."

They cut through the kitchen to reach the back steps, which would bring them to the second floor closest to Everett's office. They had just started up when they heard sirens approaching the house. Kate turned to Ben. "Go and meet them," she whispered. "I'm going up."

"No," Ben objected. "You can't go alone."

"Please," she pleaded. "You've got to show them the way. There's no time."

Without waiting for a reply, she kissed him and turned to climb the remaining stairs.

"Be careful, Kate," Ben said as he reluctantly turned and headed back down the stairs. As the sirens grew to a crescendo, he made his way to the back entrance beside the parking lot where he had first met Everett. He saw police cars arriving in the lot and stepped out of the side door, into the beams of their headlights as the sirens stopped.

He held his good hand over his eyes to shield them from the light, and a voice yelled "Freeze! Stop and put your hands behind your head!"

"Wait!" Ben shouted. "I'm Ben Tuttle. Everett Greason's the one you want. He's upstairs, and he's got a gun."

"Tuttle?" a familiar voice called from beside the second car. "Is that you?" It was Wallace.

"Lieutenant Wallace?" Ben said, squinting. "Yeah, it's me. Please hurry. Kate and her grandmother are upstairs with Everett."

"Edna's up there with them?" Wallace asked, moving quickly to the steps, his pistol drawn.

"You know her?" Ben said.

"It's a long story," Wallace replied. "Lead the

272

way."

Kate crept quickly down the carpeted upstairs hallway toward Everett's office, glancing nervously in all directions for any sign of trouble as she went. She caught a glimpse of herself in the full-length mirror beside the guest bathroom as she passed and barely recognized the woman staring back at her; wild-eyes and torn, mud stained clothes; matted hair with blood spatters on her face and hands. "Jesus," she whispered but did not stop.

As she approached the open doors to Everett's office, she heard a crash and a strange gurgling noise as if someone was choking. The air smelled like sulfur, and she sprinted across the office to the door of the study, horrified at the gaping hole where the lock should have been. At a glance, she saw the shattered remains of the conference phone scattered around the floor of the study and Edna lying halfway across the desk. Everett was hunched over her; his hands locked firmly around her throat. Edna's eyes bulged in their sockets as she tore futilely at his arms and hands, the gurgling coming from her gaping mouth.

Everett's back was to Kate, and without slowing she grabbed a bronze book end from the nearest shelf and sprinted up behind him, raising the heavy object above her head as she went. She brought it down hard, striking Everett's head a glancing blow. His body went limp and collapsed across the desk, partially pinning Edna beneath him.

"Gram!" Kate screamed as she tugged at Everett's arm, rolling his motionless body off of her grandmother. He fell to the office floor with a loud thud and Kate heard a sharp crack as one of his arms snapped.

Edna held her throat and gasped for breath.

"It's okay now, Gram. It's over. You'll be okay," Kate said, holding Edna's shoulders and patting her face. "I'm here. The police are on their way."

The fear had not left Edna's eyes, however, and she struggled to prop herself up so she could be sure Everett was no longer a threat. He lay face down on the office floor a few feet away from the now empty shotgun, a small trickle of blood visible on the side of his face. Everett had used his last round of ammunition to blow the phone to bits in a fit of rage and had thrown the gun down, coming after Edna with his bare hands.

"Is he dead?" Edna gasped, her face cringing from the pain in her throat.

"I don't know, Gram," Kate said, suddenly sick to her stomach at the thought that she may have killed him.

At that moment they heard heavy footsteps coming down the hall at a run and Ben appeared in the doorway with several police officers close behind him, pistols drawn. They fanned out, scanning the room for any threat as Ben ran to Kate's side.

"Kate, Edna, are you both okay? What happened?"

"He went after Gram," she said between deep breaths, sure now that she was going to be sick. "He was about to kill her," she managed before she turned away from him and wretched behind the desk.

A police radio crackled as one of the officers kicked the shotgun away from Everett and knelt beside him, checking his pulse and calling for an ambulance. To Kate's relief, she heard the officer tell the dispatcher that

Everett was alive.

Terry Wallace appeared beside them with another officer who attended to Edna and helped her stand up. "Mrs. Greason, Kate, I'm Lieutenant Wallace, Stanton Police. Are you both alright?"

Kate nodded but still appeared unsteady, one hand covering her mouth.

Edna was pointing at Everett with a shaky hand. "That bastard was," she began but started to cry instead.

Wallace put his hand on her shoulder. "It's alright Mrs. Greason. He can't hurt you now. You're safe."

"Don't call me that," Edna managed, wiping her eyes. "I'm not a Greason, and I don't ever want to be called that again. Call me Edna, please."

"Okay, Edna," Wallace said with a faint smile. "An ambulance will be here in a few minutes, but I need you to tell me what happened."

She took Kate's hand and kissed it. "Katie saved my bacon, that's what happened. He was choking the life out me, but she came out of nowhere and cracked him a good one with that book end." Edna managed a smile. "Good for you, Katie. Good for you."

Ben squeezed Kate's other hand.

"What happened before he attacked you?" Wallace asked

"Well, I called the people, like you said; that Barker fellow in Washington and the other one down in Charlotte, the FBI man. Oh, I can't think now."

"Nance" Wallace added.

"Yes, Bill Nance. I told them you had asked me to call and they were very helpful. They gave me a fax number and asked me a lot of questions." She turned to look at Everett with something like pity. "Heaven help me, I told them everything; the whole dirty story from front to back. I faxed them as much as I could from Jimmy's notes and Everett's files. I'm afraid I've scattered them everywhere."

Ben and Kate exchanged glances and looked down at the floor. Kate recognized the yellowed pages and the handwritten notes lying at their feet immediately. "I'll be damned," Kate whispered under her breath. "You go, Gram."

"I was just faxing his private contact list when " her voice trailed off.

There was another flurry of activity as the paramedics arrived with gurneys for Everett and Edna.

"The Nance fellow had said to put them on speaker phone and leave the call open, so I did," Edna added. "You should have seen the look on Everett's face when that man spoke up and said who they were. At first, I thought Everett was going to faint, but he just snapped instead; shot the phone with that shotgun and came after me."

Wallace and Hughes were taking notes as the paramedics carefully loaded Everett onto the first gurney.

Edna's expression darkened as she remembered the vault and Walter. "Katie, what happened in the vault? How did you get your young man out?"

Kate's eyes brimmed again, and she looked down at the floor. "It was bad, Gram. It was really bad. I'm sorry. They were torturing Ben. Walter had a gun, and it all happened so fast…"

Ben interrupted her. "He tried to kill us. He turned on the Halon system while we were all in the vault.

Kate and I managed to get out, barely."

"Ben saved me. He pulled me out and got me breathing again, but Walter didn't make it." Kate said. "I'm so sorry, Gram."

Edna hung her head and put a hand over her mouth.

"Where did all this happen?" Wallace asked. "Can you show me?"

Ben nodded and looked at Kate. "Will you be alright?"

"I'll be okay, but you need to get them to look at your hand. I'm no doctor, but I'm pretty sure you're going to need a cast."

He continued to cradle his broken left hand near his chest. "When there's time." He said. "I'll get it looked at when we get back." He turned to the officers. "Come on. I'll show you the way."

Despite her objections, Wallace insisted that Edna be transported to the hospital and properly examined. He assigned two officers to her for protection with explicit instructions that they not leave her unattended. Kate remained behind and recounted for Chief Hughes and another officer all that had happened over the last several weeks, beginning with the mysterious letter from Margaret Bayer Greene and ending with the tragic and surreal events of the last twelve hours.

Hughes had sealed off the area around the front gate of Werner-Greason and ordered that a mobile command center be set up in the front parking lot. More police and emergency vehicles continued to arrive by the minute, including units from neighboring Warren County who had offered their assistance at Hughes' request. And although the initial media frenzy over the shooting at the convention center had recently died down, he knew they were in for a firestorm the likes of which the police and the town of Stanton had never seen.

As Kate answered questions from a detective who had arrived late, Hughes stepped out into the hallway and looked at his phone. There were sixteen missed calls from Crenshaw, four from his wife, and two from numbers he immediately recognized as press.

"Shit" he whispered. "I'm so fucked."

With a heavy sigh, he called Porter County District Attorney Meredith Freeman's home number, knowing he would wake her and dreading the conversation. A moment later she answered, mumbling a terse "this has better be important."

"Meredith, it's Will Hughes. I'm sorry to wake you, but we've got a developing situation at the Werner-Greason estate. The Greason family is involved, and there are multiple fatalities."

"What? Everett Greason's family?" she asked, her voice rising.

"I'll fill you in when I can, but there's something else. I need you to call the DA in Raleigh right now. Wake him up if you have to but let him know that I'm going to have Steve Crenshaw taken into custody and charged with conspiracy to commit murder, and that's just to start."

There was a pregnant pause on the other end of the line. "Steve Crenshaw, the Governor's Chief of Staff? Are you out of your mind? What evidence do you have?"

Hughes cringed and pinched the bridge of his nose, forcing himself to say the words. "I have personal knowledge of his crimes. What I mean to say is," he hesitated. "I know because I'm involved."

"Jesus, Will. What are you telling me?"

He started to answer, but she cut him off. "Never mind, you're going to meet me at my office in 30 minutes and tell me just exactly what the hell is going on. And you better be ready to give me everything you've got on Crenshaw and explain how the hell you're involved. If I'm going after a sitting Governor's right-hand man, I'm going to be damn sure this is something with teeth. And if you've crossed a line here, so help me God!" She did not finish the sentence or wait for a response but slammed the phone down.

13

For the next month, the area around the Werner-Greason property resembled the aftermath of a nuclear accident. Local and state police were positioned at regular intervals around the front and rear of the property and the entire 36 acres immediately surrounding the house and cemetery was cordoned off with yellow tape. When the story of the Greason's decades-long smuggling operation had broken, barely 24 hours after the confrontation in Everett's office, the national media had descended like locusts on Stanton, where they had formed a growing sea of trucks and camera crews that extended several hundred yards from the front gate. The broadcast antennas from the trucks resembled a grove of metallic trees rising thirty feet over the Bradford Pears that lined the quarter-mile driveway. A steady stream of law enforcement and state and federal government vehicles came and went regularly through the carefully guarded entrance and on two occasions, a group of five armored Brinks trucks flanked by State Highway Patrol and unmarked black Suburban SUVs had entered the estate and left several hours later.

The international scale of the Werner-Greason operation and its apparent origin with the Nazis in World

War II had sent shockwaves through the international community and left state government and law enforcement officials scrambling to explain how it could have happened on their watch. With his chief of staff in federal custody, charged with multiple felonies and heavily implicated in the explosive scandal, Governor Michael Chase took the brunt of the heat. He tried in vain to deflect the blame and plead ignorance, but when photos appeared on CNN of open coffins with gold, jewels, and artwork mingled with the bones of American soldiers from the battlefields of Europe, Chase's hand was forced. He held a press conference the following day and announced that it would be in the best interest of the state and the investigation if he stepped down as governor. Cell phone records and financial documents in Greason's private study were pointing to an elaborate web of financial influence that extended all the way to Washington, and several legislators there including Paul Richards had already begun to publicly distance themselves from Greason.

Stanton Police Chief Willard Hughes confessed to bribery, conspiracy to defraud the federal government, and obstruction of justice, but agreed to cooperate with the investigation in exchange for a lighter sentence. He was stripped of his position on the force and was summarily replaced by Terry Wallace, who was promoted to Chief and awarded the Medal of Valor for his heroic efforts to expose the truth and save lives in the Greason case, despite great personal risk.

Autopsies of Walter Greason and Carl Lentz had been ordered by the district attorney before their bodies were finally turned over to their respective families for burial. Lentz had died from a gunshot wound and even though Walter had also sustained a gunshot wound the official cause of death was asphyxiation from exposure to Halon gas. Everett sustained a cracked skull and a severe concussion, slipping in and out of consciousness for a week before recovering sufficiently to be formally arrested and charged. Ben's left hand had required extensive surgery to wire the shattered bones back together, and he and Kate had been interviewed repeatedly for nearly a week by the FBI, but no charges had been brought against them, and they both had eventually been released. Edna had been treated for abrasions and a bruised larynx but had been released from the hospital within twenty-four hours only to learn that the entire Werner-Greason house and grounds had been declared a crime scene and she would have to stay somewhere else until further notice. Because Edna had alerted the authorities and cooperated so fully with them, she was granted immunity from prosecution but was instructed to remain in the area for the immediate future. "Where the hell else do you think I'd go?" she had quipped to the FBI liaison officer.

Kate, Edna, and Ben all endured a relentless onslaught by the media, who crowded them, shouted questions, and shoved cameras in their faces every time they appeared in public. Paparazzi were camped out on Ben's street and in the parking lot of Kate's condo, where Edna had taken up temporary residence. Despite Kate's best efforts to keep her grandmother sober, Edna quickly returned to her old ways, even offering a reporter an exclusive if he would bring her a bottle of vodka. The photo on the front page of the local paper the next day showed a close-up of Edna wearing a bathrobe and a defiant scowl and giving the photographer the middle finger.

"She's back," Kate sighed as she put the paper down on the coffee table and leaned back on the sofa.

Ben sat beside her, shaking his head. "I see now where you get it," he said.

"Get what?"

"Your strong personality," he finished, leaning into the word strong. "The apple doesn't fall so far from the twisted tree."

Kate instinctively reached for his good hand. "Under the circumstances, I'll take that as a compliment."

Ben's smile faded. "How is she?"

"Not so good, I think," Kate replied. "I don't see how all of this hasn't killed her. God knows it's nearly killed us." She kissed his hand. "I'm so sorry about your work."

Ben shook his head and sighed. "Don't worry about it, seriously. I hated that fucking job anyway; bunch of cowards. I'll find something else; IT people always do."

Kate propped her feet up on the coffee table and stared at the purple polish on her toenails. "I have to get out of here," she said, "I don't mean take a break, I mean permanently. There's no way I can stay here, and I wouldn't want to know even if I could."

Ben felt a knot forming in his throat. "You mean, just pick up and go?"

She nodded. "Yeah, pretty much."

"What will you do about the business?" he asked. "Apparently you're fifty percent owner now, and there's nobody left to run it."

Kate snorted, "You're kidding, right? Even if I wanted to run it, which I wouldn't do for any amount of money, there won't be a business to run. Nobody in Stanton will ever go within a mile of that place again. Hampton's operation across town has apparently hired six new hands including three from Werner-Greason, and they're already taking all the funeral business. I bet they're dancing in the aisles over there about the demise of 'The Coffin King.' Nope, I'd say the old family business is toast. Besides, the feds will probably sell the place off piece by piece to cover the fines and back taxes."

"Where do you think you'll go?" Ben asked.

"Ah, that depends," she replied, a faint smile creasing the corners of her mouth. "Remember when all this started I told you there wasn't much of an upside to getting involved? Well maybe, seeing as how you're recently unemployed and still single and all, you might consider going with me? I mean, that could be an upside."

Ben held up the cast encasing his left hand and examined it. "See this? This is what being involved with you has gotten me. Now, why would I want to come back for more?"

She broke into a wide grin and leaned into him. "Cause, I know you. Clearly you have a thing for cute but somewhat dysfunctional mortuary chicks. It's nothing to be ashamed of. You should just give in to it."

He couldn't suppress a laugh. "Yeah, you do know me pretty well, don't you? That's actually the best offer I've had in years."

They kissed for a long moment, and Kate suddenly pulled back. "Hey, listen, if you're having second thoughts, there's always Roger. I've got him on speed dial and…"

He cut her off with a second kiss. "Want to go look at a map?"

"Let's do it," she replied.

EPILOGUE

High in the western North Carolina mountains, the sun was sinking low in the afternoon sky as Sarah, the office manager for the Kory Center began to sort the mail. She glanced out the window at the city lights in the valley far below them and knew by the gathering gray clouds on the horizon that it would be raining by nightfall. The post bag contained one large manila envelope and the usual smattering of letters from family members of the residents there; letters that came despite the fact that many of their charges could no longer read and some could no longer understand. Perhaps the families knew this or suspected, but the letters were a way of assuaging the guilt that so often accompanied the internment of the aging in a facility, even one as spectacularly opulent as the Kory Center. The thick manila envelope was addressed to Andrew Greely, one of their oldest and wealthiest residents. It had no return address, save a handwritten name, Edna Smoot.

Like most of the Kory Center residents, Mr. Greely was not registered under his real name. When billionaire Bill Kory had established the center, he had done it to fill a very specialized niche, to supply services that other facilities could or would not; perhaps the most import of these was utter anonymity. By design, even the line management of the center did not know the backgrounds of its residents, nor their real names in most cases. Medical records were scrubbed and new ones created during the very elaborate and highly confidential intake process. Kory had designed the center to contain everything necessary to ensure that residents did not ever need to leave. In addition to the finest dining hall, library, and exercise room that money could buy, it was outfitted with cutting edge medical facilities, including a fully equipped operating room, a pharmacy, physical therapy wing, and a world class spa. A helicopter pad on the roof allowed specialists and surgeons to be flown in for emergency procedures. When describing the center's mission to his most trusted confidants, Kory was known to quip, "For the right price we make people vanish, but we certainly do it in style!"

Sarah studied the thick manila envelope for a long moment before dropping it into the mail bag and heading out on her afternoon rounds. Mr. Greely had one of their high-end suites, the highest in fact, on the corner of the third floor. The living room had a breathtaking view of the Smokey Mountains that extended east across Pisgah National Forest and the small town of Maggie Valley miles below. Yet despite his apparent status in life, she could not remember delivering a single letter or package to him in the seven years she had been office manager there.

She did not find the old man in his room, however. His motorized wheelchair allowed him to travel around the facility at will, and despite his extended age and severely declining health, he frequently traveled to the sun porch on the south side of the building where he sat for hours, sometimes sleeping, other times staring into the distance with a troubled look on his face, as if reliving some dark time from his past.

Today, the old man was awake, the lone occupant of the sun porch, he sat near the long row of windows, staring out at nothing in particular, his hands clasped in the center of the tray on his chair.

"Good afternoon, Mr. Greely!" Sarah called cheerfully; raising her voice so he would be able to hear her. She knew from long experience that he would not acknowledge her presence in any way other than to stare at her with his narrow and disapproving eyes. She tried not to take it personally since it was all too common in the geriatric population, but there was something about Greely that had bothered her more than most over the years.

"There's a package for you. It just came in this afternoon." She held up the envelope, and he cocked his head to one side, squinting at it. He smiled his oddly crooked smile and pointed a bony finger at the name on it.

"Oh, I'm sorry, I wasn't thinking," she said. "It's from someone named Edna Smoot."

The smile vanished, and a look of bewilderment fell across the old man's face as he pointed again at the name and grunted "Who?" A battle with throat cancer had left him barely able to speak, and he rarely tried, mostly grunted and growled.

"It says, Edna Smoot."

Greely's expression morphed into a dark scowl, and he tapped the tray on his chair with a fingertip.

"Would you like me to open it for you?" Sarah asked, feeling uneasy now about his reaction to the package.

He rapped the tray forcefully with his knuckles but said nothing.

"Okay, I'll just set it here," she said as she put the envelope on Greely's tray and turned to leave. "You have a good night, Mr. Greely."

"Greely," the old man snarled. "Bullshit!"

Sarah did not respond, but hurried down the hall, glancing back long enough to see Greely tearing at the envelope with both hands.

An hour later, while starting his evening rounds, the Kory Center night manager found Mr. Greely slumped over in his chair, motionless with no pulse. The old man's eyes and mouth were stretched wide and frozen there as if he were a wax figure of someone gasping for breath. The manager did not call a code, however, as Greely had a DNR, like most of their residents. Instead, he called the director, as protocol demanded, to let him know that he would have Greely taken to the basement morgue and processed there according to the instructions in the contract.

When the night manager ended the call, he noticed the newspapers for the first time. There were two of them, side by side on the old man's tray. The first was the Raleigh News and Observer, with a headline that read "GREASON SCANDAL WIDENS – NAZI TIES CONFIRMED." The second was an issue of The Denver Examiner that sported the headline "MYSTERY OF MISSING DENVER REPORTER SOLVED" with the subtitle "North Carolina Mortuary Tycoon Implicated In Disappearance."

His curiosity piqued, the night manager picked up

the Denver paper and carried it to a nearby bench, where he sat down and began to read. Outside, as the last light of evening faded to darkness, the rain finally began.

ABOUT THE AUTHOR

Jeff McEntire is a native of North Carolina. He is an artist and an author. Jeff lives with his wife Jen in Durham, North Carolina.